GRACE AND XAVIER

A Twentieth-Century Marriage

By

Helen V. Flanagan

Copyright © Helen V. Flanagan 2020
This book is sold subject to the condition that it shall not, by way of trade or otherwise, be lent, resold, hired out, or otherwise circulated without the publisher's prior consent in any form of binding or cover other than that in which it is published and without a similar condition including this condition being imposed on the subsequent publisher.
The moral right of Helen V. Flanagan has been asserted.
ISBN-13: 9798662700048

This is a work of fiction. Names, characters, businesses, organizations, places, events and incidents either are the product of the author's imagination or are used fictitiously. Any resemblance to actual persons, living or dead, events, or locales is entirely coincidental.

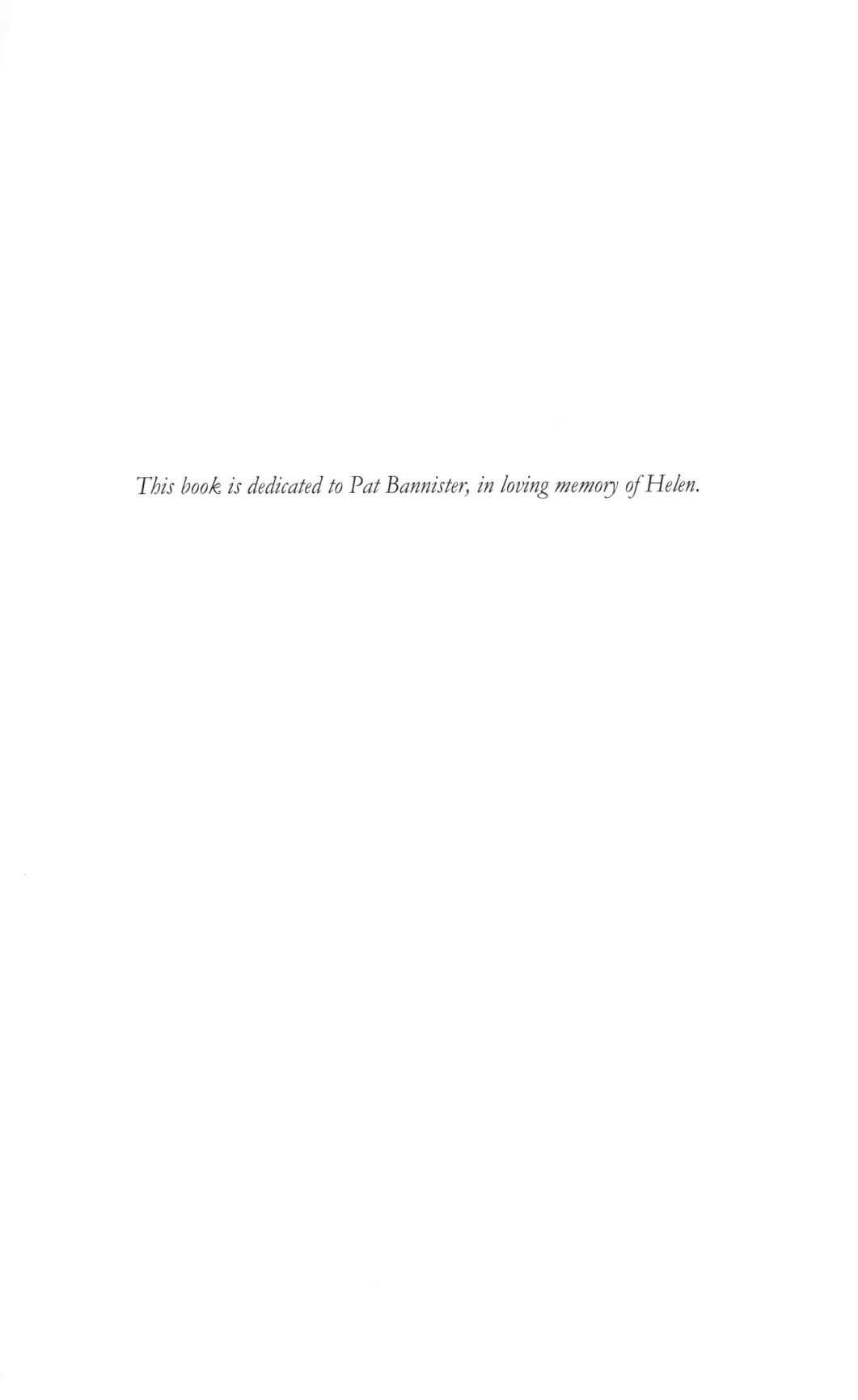

This book is dedicated to Pat Bannister, in loving memory of Helen.

CONTENTS

FOREWORD	i
1	1
2	14
3	32
4	46
5	64
6	75
7	89
8	102
9	117
10	134
11	147
12	164
13	177
14	186
15	200
16	211
17	225
18	243
19	259
20	275
ABOUT THE AUTHOR	290

FOREWORD

My half-sister Helen Veronica Flanagan was born in May 1945 (the day after VE Day) in Belfast, where our father was in a reserved occupation as an aeronautical engineer for the Ministry of Defence. He had worked there throughout the war, but he was born in Hull and lived in Hopwood Street, the youngest son of Patrick Flanagan. Patrick had been a founder member of the local Labour Party and was a leader of the first Bricklayers' Union; by the time he died, in 1923, he was a Justice of the Peace and a member of Hull's City Council. In Helen's story the patriarchal character, "Red" Jack Brennan, is firmly based on Patrick Flanagan, our grandfather.

The Catholic Church, Hull and the East Riding, and the lives of our paternal relatives inform this novel, which is set in the first half of the twentieth century. Although the characters and plot are fictional, the events described here are part of our family mythology: we were the Flanagans and the Devines, however, and not the Brennans and the Quinns.

Helen died towards the end of 2006. Her dearest friend, Pat, has asked me to edit her novel and prepare it for publication. It was a privilege to complete this work just before what would have been Helen's 75th birthday. It is dedicated to Pat Bannister, in loving memory of Helen.

Anne Everest

June, 2020

1

1923-1929

Oh, they were lookers when they were younger, my brothers. Better than Barrymore, better than Valentino – and not celluloid shadows, but breathing flesh with real bone, blood, and skin. Hopwood Street knew as its own the five Brennan brothers: Pat, Mick, Declan, Vinnie, and Sean. Every one of them had his father's dark hair, blue eyes, and broad shoulders. They were bright, able boys too, so quick that the masters at St Charles' Boys' School rarely had to raise a strap to a Brennan. And charming. My mother, Nora Brennan, agreed with her neighbours: she was blessed in her sons.

I adored and envied them.

Declan fought my battles and Vinnie helped me with my homework, and my big brother Pat was bigger than anyone else's big brother. My childhood was safe in the protection of my rare brothers. As the youngest child, I was proud of them. And then, when I was ten, I discovered that I was not like them.

That was the year when Declan brought home his Italian girlfriend, Josefina. With her came her Granny Ponti. This old lady used to sell roast chestnuts in the market by Holy Trinity Church. She could barely speak English. Granny Ponti squatted down in a corner of our front room. (Hunkering down, I called it, since I was collecting and applying new vocabulary in the way my brothers built up collections of conkers, marbles, and cigarette cards.) Smiling her gummy smile, she revealed a tooth that glistened with spit. It was her one tooth, and I found it hard to look away from it, harder still not to comment. As she looked around the room that time, weighing up the six of us, she said something in Italian. Only Josefina could understand her, and Declan asked her to translate the mumbled and decidedly foreign words. Unwillingly, she did so.

"She says ... she says it's a shame the boys in this family have all the looks."

I was humiliated. And amazed.

"Why don't I look like the boys?" I asked Mammy.

"You do, pet," Mammy told me. But the high forehead, strong nose, and cleft chin that sat so well on Mick, Vinnie and the others dwarfed my smaller face. And I didn't have my brothers' height, I didn't have their careless elegance, and I wasn't pretty.

"Never you mind," Daddy said. "You've more brains in your little finger than any of the boys have in his whole head."

"Daddy's right," Vinnie said. "You're the cleverest of us all, Mary Grace. None of us can hold a candle to you."

Because Daddy said it and because Vinnie agreed with him, I believed it. I clung onto that belief, working so hard at my lessons that I had soon outgrown St Patrick's Elementary School. Against everyone's expectation, including mine, my father agreed that I should take up the scholarship I had won. I wasn't the first Brennan to win such a scholarship, in fact I was the third, but I was the first to be allowed to take advantage of it. Somehow Daddy had never found the time to sign the forms for Declan and Vinnie. He was too busy with his Union work and his role as a JP, Vinnie told me when I thought to ask about it. But he was still busy when I won my scholarship, and working for the Labour Party, even though he was resisting pressure from friends and colleagues who wanted him to stand as a parliamentary candidate.

"Ramsay MacDonald will be Prime Minister before the year's out," he said. "He doesn't need me: Hull does."

Which made it even stranger that he showed interest in something as unimportant as my education. We had all grown up knowing that his family would always come second to Jack Brennan, much as he loved us. I half expected that when it came to it, he would not, after all, have time to sign the acceptance form for my assisted place at the convent. But he did and I was grateful, looking forward with passionate eagerness to the day when I would put on my navy and saxe-blue uniform and travel by trolley bus across the city to my new school.

When I finally made the journey, stiff and uncomfortable in my new clothes, I hated the school. I knew no-one. I was no-one. My father's prominence in the local Labour Party, which had made me feel proud and famous, was a matter for scorn here, not pride, and no-one else in my form class lived so near to the city centre and the docks. I had thought us rich, and so we were, compared to my classmates at St Patrick's. But now I discovered that, as a scholarship girl, I was among the poorest in my year. Money, not academic ability, had secured places at the convent for most of my contemporaries. And money – or what it bought them – was their main topic of conversation. In this area, as I soon found, I could not compete.

At first, I was intimidated. But gradually I learned to despise my peers. I would sit at my high desk at the front of the class, where the nuns had placed me in alphabetic order between Margaret Brady and Frances Calhoun. The first two fingers of my right hand were permanently stained with ink from the cracked inkwell. I would write so fast that the nib of my pen frequently crossed, and ink would sputter over the page I was working on. As a result, my work was messy, no matter how hard I tried; even the AMDG I wrote conscientiously at the top left-hand corner of each page in the margin was usually blotted and blurred. From the very first day, as the nuns explained, all our work was dedicated in this way to the greater glory of God: *Ad Maiorem Dei Gloriam* (or AMDG); it was even more important than the date and competed for pre-eminence with the prayer that was chanted at the start of each lesson.

In the main the nuns, particularly the Irish nuns, forgave me my untidiness because of my eagerness to learn, and everyone knew that Mary Grace Brennan was the cleverest girl in the class – perhaps, I dreamed, the cleverest girl in the whole school. I might not be pretty or rich, I might live in the wrong part of Hull, I might have a father who had turned his back on the one true church, but all that was not going to bother me. It was not important. At least, not for most of the time.

But there were days when I longed for a friend, for someone to talk to. And as I grew older, these days occurred more and more often. I wanted someone who was interested in the things I was interested in, someone who worked as hard as I did and did not think it strange.

At home there had always been Vinnie. My first memory is of standing by the scullery sink then inches above my head, while Vinnie, four years older and considerably taller, carefully lifted down a cup of milk for me to drink. (I remember also the cool feel of the cup in my hands and the greasy smell of the checked material that hung from the draining-board and screened the slop bucket from view.) Later, I followed Vinnie everywhere. I had no time for Sean, who was only a year my senior and would gladly have played with me. But he had none of Vinnie's mysterious glamour. There was nothing in Sean to look up to; he was no brighter than I was, no nimbler, not even as brave. It was Vinnie I wanted. Flattered and amused, Vinnie tolerated the little sister who ran after him at every opportunity. A closeness grew up between us, which no one else in the family, except perhaps our mother, understood.

When I was eight and Vinnie was twelve, we had measles together. None of the others caught it, though perhaps the older boys had had it earlier; I do not know.

Mammy made up beds for us both in the front room, and for two weeks we lay restlessly in the green light that filtered through the curtains, itching, scratching, sleeping, and talking. I told Vinnie the stories I made up in my head when I could not sleep, stories about fairies who lived in the box room and about a blue tiger who haunted the garden shed. Vinnie listened to me without mocking. In turn he told me his plans, how he was going to be an engineer and go away to sea and come back with presents for me: "presents from the farthest corners of the earth". The words buoyed me up, became a talisman against the disease that united us while it separated us from the rest of the family. Both of us were seriously ill. The rash tormented us and made us querulous; our heads ached, and we longed for daylight, which was forbidden. Mammy told us tales of children whom measles had blinded, and she frightened us so much we didn't dare to pull back the curtains. Even so, because I was with Vinnie, I was happy.

When at last we began to feel better, something undreamt of happened. Mammy came in one evening, sat down on my bed, and said she was sending us away. We were going on a holiday, to the seaside. Daddy's brother, Uncle Martin, and his wife, Auntie Eileen, had a small corner shop near the sea front in Withernsea, not far from the lighthouse. We were going to stay there for a fortnight, to recuperate – I stored the word up for future use – so that the sea air could build us up.

"All of us?" I asked. "Are we all going?"

"No," Mammy said. "Just you and Vinnie. You're the ones who have been ill. And Uncle Martin doesn't have room for us all, even if we could afford it."

Vinnie and I looked at each other in delight. Going to the seaside in term-time was treat enough, but to go together, without the rest of the brothers, was wonderful. I flung my arms, scabby from the rash, around my mother's neck.

"When do we go?" I asked. I wonder now if she was hurt by my eagerness.

We travelled by train from Paragon Station. Mammy saw us off. We did not expect our father to take time from his work to send us on our way. And he did not. We climbed onto the train demurely enough, but once it started off, I found it impossible to sit still. There was so much to see, and I rushed from one side of the compartment to the other, exclaiming at everything – the backs of terrace houses, rail-side allotments, children playing in the ten-foots. Vinnie, who had been doubly humiliated, first by having to wear a cap and then by being consigned with me to the care of the guard, sulked in the corner of the carriage for the first part of the journey. But soon the cap came off, the guard had not bothered to check on us, and Vinnie too was waving to people on bridges and cows in fields. We were both sorry when the train pulled in to Withernsea Station. We clambered out – I remember the steps down from the carriage were still too high for me to negotiate easily – and stood on the platform with our luggage, waiting for Uncle Martin to come and claim us.

Mammy had talked about sea breezes, but I had paid her words little attention. We had wind in the city; wind was wind surely? Now, though, the wind from the sea blew great brine-scented gusts of air towards me. My nostrils tingled with the newness of it, and I drew in an exaggeratedly deep breath. Vinnie nudged me.

"People are watching," he whispered. "Behave!"

Then Uncle Martin appeared, hurrying, puffing, like Daddy in appearance but also unlike, shorter and stouter and with a ruddier complexion. Even so, his legs were much longer than mine. Still weakened by two weeks in bed, I stumbled as we hurried to keep up with him. He seemed not to notice – he and Auntie Eileen had no children of their own – but he talked to us and showed us the lighthouse, and before long we had reached his shop, Brennan's Corner Stores, and made our way through sacks of sugar and salt and potatoes, and bottles of boiled sweets, to the narrow staircase at the back.

The rooms in the flat were small, though no smaller than the rooms at home, but there were only two of them. Two rooms and a tiny kitchen. The living room had Uncle Martin and Auntie Eileen's bed in it, as well as a solid rectangular table and four chairs. It was strange to see the big wooden bedstead and its shiny blue quilt pushed up against the wall, only two feet from the dining table. I said as much to Vinnie, when we were in our own room, with its two small beds and vast wardrobe and pile upon pile of cardboard boxes, the overflow from the shop below.

"Perhaps it's not always like this," Vinnie said. "Perhaps they've moved things round to fit us in."

Having to sleep in the living room struck me as such a great sacrifice that I was careful to behave as Mammy would have wanted me to behave. I made myself so helpful and obliging, and so generally unlike my normal self, that Vinnie asked me if I still felt ill. But it paid off. Uncle Martin and Auntie Eileen were so enchanted with my impeccable manners that they allowed us far more freedom than we had expected. I had only to suggest that we should like to go down to the beach, and they sent us off with sandwiches and a glass bottle of lemonade, with a marble for a stopper, to spend the day as we chose. We paddled in the scummy foam at the sea's edge; we built castles and moats and intricate waterways; we watched the great brown North Sea waves break on the sand. I collected razor shells and brown strappy seaweed to decorate our castles. Once I found a mermaid's purse left on the shingle by the receding tide. It was early in the year, April perhaps, and the beach was almost deserted. We preferred it like that, or imagined we did, for we had never been to the seaside in high season, had never been to the seaside at all except on rare day trips with St Patrick's Elementary School. No-one stopped us when we attempted to climb the crumbling path to the top of the cliff; no-one exclaimed or fussed over us when we slipped and fell; no-one told us to keep our sandals on when we explored the rock pools. If we had been close before, we became closer now, and we were intensely reluctant to return to the city, school, and home.

I managed a few tears at the station. "Perhaps, if I cry, they'll let us stay another week," I whispered to Vinnie. But it was no use. Uncle Martin patted me on the shoulder and made embarrassed noises. He bought us both bars of chocolate from the machine outside the waiting room, but he did not suggest that we should stay longer. Instead he sent his regards to our father and mother. We must come again another year: it had been a pleasure to have us, and he knew he spoke for Auntie Eileen as well. That was something, but it was not enough and, as the train travelled inland, I could feel myself shrinking. Even Vinnie seemed diminished, and neither of us cared any longer about looking out of the window at the fields and houses flashing by. Instead we sat opposite each other, sucking slowly on our Five Boys chocolate bars in order to make them last as long as possible. But they had vanished long before the train had reached its destination; and when we pulled into Paragon Station, only our sun and wind-flushed faces and renewed vigour gave any hint of where we had been.

"Did you have a wonderful time?" Mammy asked us as we stepped down from the carriage.

"It was all right," I said. She smiled and ruffled my hair. She was never fooled by my attempts at nonchalance.

At school every lesson began in the same way. You lined up your dip pen and pencil in the groove at the top of the desk next to the inkwell. Your ruler, if you had one – and you were expected to have one – was placed above them. You took out the textbooks and exercise books you needed for that lesson and placed them in a neat, graded pile on the left of the desk lid. Then you waited. When the form prefect alerted the class to the fact that the teacher was coming, you stood behind your chair in silence, looking straight in front of you. The form prefect held the door open and the nun – all the teachers were nuns – swept in, her long black skirts brushing the floor on her way to the teacher's desk, her wooden rosary clicking at her side. Before a word was said, you all made the sign of the cross in unison, and then everyone, teacher included, recited a prayer. If you were lucky and the teacher was one of the less devout nuns, Sister Joseph, say, or Sister Thaddeus, you got off with one Hail Mary. Others, like Sister Antony, insisted on a full decade of the rosary, which was all very well if you did not like the lesson and did not want to make a start on it – but usually I did. It was one of the reasons why I was unpopular with the rest of the class.

After the prayer, Sister Anthony or whichever nun it was, bade the class good morning or good afternoon and gave the signal to sit. So you sat and opened your exercise book – a new page for every new piece of work and never mind the waste of paper – and you wrote the date on the top line on the right hand side and AMDG in the margin on the left. Then, and only then, could the lesson begin.

This process gave my enemies great scope for harassment. Margaret Brady, who sat at the desk to my left, was tall and broad – "like the side of a mountain", as the caretaker once said. Sometimes she would sit on the lid of my desk until the last minute, so that when the teacher arrived I was still scrabbling to assemble my possessions in the correct way. On the worst days Margaret Brady took the books from my desk and threw them on top of the classroom cupboard, which was so tall that the only way I could get them down was by standing on the teacher's chair. (My own seat, like those of all my fellow pupils, was firmly attached to my double desk.) The teacher never caught me – Margaret Brady knew she would have far too much explaining to do if that happened – but the threat of it was enough to freeze my law-abiding soul.

Then there were the possibilities afforded by the board duster. Carefully thrown, the cloth made a huge splash of white chalk across a navy-blue gym slip; it could also be shaken out over a pile of schoolbooks or thrust under an unsuspecting nose. And if all else failed, small objects like pen nibs could be placed on the desk seat, so that when I sat I found it hard not to cry out and leap to my feet again. Eileen Calhoun, who shared my desk, sometimes warned me, but she was a quiet girl who had no desire to make life more difficult for herself. She never stood up to Margaret Brady.

I did. Not at first, partly because I was scared to do so and partly because after my first numbing days at the school her bullying was what I had come to expect. But as the term went on and the bullying continued, I began to resent it. I did not speak about it at home, I did not say anything to the nuns, but I thought about it more and more until, eventually, it seemed to me that I must either act or die of suffocation.

The chance came sooner than I expected. One afternoon I entered the classroom to find my desk lid open and Margaret Brady standing behind it. Without thinking, without hesitation, I leaned forwards and slammed the desk lid down hard. It caught Margaret Brady on the forearm, just above the right wrist. She yelled, I jumped back, astonished at myself, and Sister Anthony appeared in the doorway, all in the same moment.

"And what is going on here?"

"I was just shutting my desk lid, Sister," I lied quickly. "I didn't know Margaret had her hand in it."

If Sister Thomas disbelieved this part of my story, she did not show it. Instead she turned to Margaret Brady, who was clutching her arm and seemed on the point of tears.

"And why was your hand in Mary Grace Brennan's desk, Margaret?"

"I – I was returning a book, Sister."

"A book you'd borrowed? What sort of work?" And then, when no answer was made, Sister Anthony turned to me. "Mary Grace, what do you know about this book?"

"Nothing, Sister," I answered truthfully, not out of desire to get

Margaret into further trouble, but because I could not think of anything to say.

"So," Sister Anthony said. "You borrow a book from Mary Grace's desk without thanking her. You then put it back without asking her, and in the process, the desk lid falls on your arm. If you ask me, Mary Brady, it is no more than you deserve. You will write me a hundred lines by tomorrow morning. 'I must not interfere with other people's property.' Is that understood?"

"Yes, Sister."

"And you, Mary Grace. There is never any need to slam a desk lid as I saw you do when I came into the room. Closing it gently is quite straightforward. Make sure it doesn't happen again."

"Yes, Sister. Thank you, Sister," I said. Surely that could not be a smile I saw twitching the skin at the corners of Sister Anthony's mouth?

"Now, girls. In the name of the Father …"

"I'll pay you back for this, you see if I don't," Margaret Brady promised at the end of the lesson.

"No, you won't," I said, suddenly filled with confidence. "You are a coward and a bully and in future you are going to leave me alone. Or else."

"Or else what?"

I did not answer. For the first time, I discovered that silence can be more effective than words. I raised my head, tilting my chin upwards so that for once I was looking Margaret Brady in the eye, and I could tell by the set of my cheek muscles that my face showed the contempt I felt. Margaret looked away. I had never felt so powerful.

If things happened the way they did in the Angela Brazil novels that I pretended no longer to read, Margaret Brady and I would have become great friends. I would have found myself celebrated for my bravery. Of course, nothing like that did happen. Margaret Brady suffered no decline in popularity or power. I was no longer bullied, but neither was I included. Eileen carried on speaking to me, as did one or two others who were not influenced by the crowd, but for the most part I was left alone. My name continued to appear at the top of the class list every time we received the results of a test; the nuns continued to ask me for answers when it became clear no one else could provide them. I was not, I realised, unhappy. But the slow pace of the lessons bored and depressed me. I wanted a change. I wanted a challenge.

2

Twenty past three on a Friday afternoon in 1925, on the hottest late September day of my life. I was thirteen; there had been many hot September days. Later that evening I would accompany my mother and Sean to St Patrick's Church to celebrate the Nine First Fridays 'for a special intention'. That was all Mammy had told me, but I wondered whether it had anything to do with the strained silence with which she had greeted my father's latest fit of anger. He had come in raging at the national Labour Party's decision not to link up with the British Communist Party. The priests at St Patrick's, the nuns at the convent, the Catholic newspapers, and my Mammy had all told me that Communism was evil. I did not understand why my father (who had recently become known to his fellow dockers as Red Jack Brennan) couldn't see the truth of that evil. I decided it was better to do as Mammy had suggested, and place my trust in the Sacred Heart of Jesus, who would not allow my father to be lost, even if, as he often said to my mother's obvious distress, he had no time for bog-priests come over from the Old Country, and no time for the Holy Catholic Church.

Meanwhile, towards the end of this hot school afternoon, the convent chapel was breathless with the suffocating sweetness of beeswax. The back of the pew on which I rested my joined hands was too highly polished to be sticky – the lay sisters had seen to that – but the dark wood was slick to the touch. Even the stone floor of the chapel no longer struck cold. I forced myself to hold my head up, keep a straight back. This was a school day, after all, and the nuns were watching. I couldn't slump forward as I did on Sundays at St Patrick's, letting my bottom just rest on the ridge of the seat behind, while Father Ryan said Mass. Besides, the English priest, the Dominican who was staying at St Patrick's presbytery, was at the altar, with his elegant movements and calm English voice. Even my father was prepared to admit that Father Sebastian was an intelligent man. Usually I took pleasure in the words of the Mass when Father Sebastian officiated, as he had done several times over the last few months. But it was hot, so hot that my head swam and sweat started from my temples as I tried to concentrate on the liquid cadences of the Latin words.

Slanting light shone through the flecks of dust above the communion rail. The gilt sunburst of the monstrance dazzled me. My damp fingers were so tightly locked for prayer that I could feel the dark pulse of blood through my veins. In the front pew on the right-hand side, in the seat nearest the aisle, Maureen Rafferty, that year's head girl, rang the bell three times for the Exposition. I'll do that one day, I thought, envying the careful movement of her wrist, the silver voice of the bell. Of my brothers, only fourteen-year-old Sean still served regularly at the altar, distant and handsome in his black serge and white lace. All the boys in our family had in their turn passed beyond the rail, poured water over the priest's fingers, given the responses. I could never do that. I was a girl. Unfair, I thought, unfair, like so many other things. And then I was distracted by the lightest of weights landing suddenly, unexpectedly, on the middle knuckle of my left forefinger.

A fly? No, worse than that, unbearably worse. A fat dazed heat-drowsed wasp, its antennae moving feebly, its six terrible legs carrying it the length of my hand, catching in the tiny hairs that were upright with horror. It had reached my wrist now. I closed my eyes against the sight of the wasp, tried to close my mind against it, only to feel the slow tickle edging its way beneath the cuff of my blouse.

No. I refused to believe it. There was no wasp making its way up my forearm. The sweat that poured down my face and that soaked the back of my blouse was caused by heat, not fear. But the hair on my skin refused to accept it; I could feel the goose bumps rising and my flesh crawl with awareness of the wasp.

It stung me three times. Without provocation. Once on the fleshy part of my forearm, once on the thin skin of my elbow, and once in the tender crook of my arm.

Now tears mingled with the sweat. Slowly and with great care, I unlocked my numb and sweating fingers, opened the button of my cuff, let my arm hang out at an angle from my body over the aisle. For a moment nothing happened. Then the fat buzzing body of the wasp fell out, flew away on wings that seemed too fragile for the task. Under the cotton of my blouse, heat formed round the needles of pain, flesh and skin swelling and hardening into angry lumps. It was no use. I caught my breath in a sob.

"Is something wrong?"

The whisper came from behind me. I did not dare turn my head.

"A wasp stung me."

Hearing the girl behind me get to her feet, I glanced guiltily over my shoulder and saw Kit Morrissey – Kit Morrissey! – walking up the aisle to the front of the church, to where Mother Bernard sat alone in the staff pew.

"If you please, Mother, Mary Grace Brennan has been stung by a wasp."

Every voice in the chapel head the clear little voice. Every head turned Kit's way. On the altar Father Sebastian stopped in mid-sentence, one English eyebrow raised, then carried on with the closing prayers.

Kit Morrissey was special; everyone knew that. New to the school, she was rumoured to be impossibly clever. Her father was a doctor; she was the only child. The family lived in a detached house overlooking Pearson Park. Her school uniform was better cut than that of the other girls, and she wore it with style. In a school where every girl who was not a Mary seemed to be a Catherine, a Kathleen or a Kate, she alone was Kit. And she had a perfect Greek nose, for which I envied her most of all. But did that make her special enough? Did it excuse this unheard-of departure from acceptable behaviour? Was she, in short, going to escape Mother Bernard's wrath?

It seemed so. There was a quick exchange of words, a deferential bob of the head, and then Kit came back down the aisle towards me, her heels confident on the stone floor of the chapel. She was smiling.

"I'm to take you to Sister Clement in the school office."

Unnerved, I scrambled to my feet. The noise of our footsteps followed us down the aisle, through the heavy doors and on to the landing above the main entrance. Even with my left elbow throbbing and Kit Morrissey at my side, I could not resist touching the foot of the statue in the alcove, trailing the fingers of my right hand along the dark, polished line of the banister, noting and passing the shining full stops of the finials at the end of each shining curve.

"You'd better turn your sleeve back so Sister can see. Here, let me help you."

Swift fingers rolled back my left cuff as far as it would go. It wasn't far enough. The opening was too narrow. The thought of having to take off my blouse in front of a nun, the shame of appearing in my vest, and of having to explain why Mammy, knowing how I heated the heat, had allowed me to come to school without the regulation liberty bodice, made me reckless.

"Tear it."

"What will your mother say?"

"I'll tell her the truth. Just tear it."

There was something satisfying in the long sigh the material gave as it ripped apart between Kit's fierce little hands. The sleeve rolled back easily now, exposing the three hard red lumps that marked the site of the stings. I touched one of them tentatively with my right forefinger. It turned momentarily white and then, as I withdrew the pressure, the flush seeped back.

"Come on," Kit urged me.

The young nun who served as the school secretary was in the office. She looked up from a ledger made out in perfect copperplate, startled by this intrusion at what should be a quiet part of the day. Kit and I competed to explain.

"A wasp …"

"A huge wasp …"

"In the middle of Benediction …"

"She didn't make a sound …"

A quick, sympathetic intake of breath, and then Sister Clement was searching in the bottom drawer of Mother Bernard's desk. Triumphantly she brought out the little, locally made bag of Reckitt's Blue, carried it to the outside sink to dip it in water, tripped back, and pressed it firmly against the three stings, one after the other, the blue dye spreading over my inflamed skin in a most satisfactory way.

"There! Does that feel better, child?"

Curiously, it did. The firm pressure and the cool water soothed away the sharp core of pain, eased the throbbing.

"Now roll down your sleeve."

Kit and I exchanged glances.

"If you don't mind, Sister, I'd rather leave it up for a bit. Let the air get to it,"

"So long as you roll it down before you go home. We can't have a great girl like you out in the street in that state."

"Yes, Sister. Thank you, Sister. Can we go now?"

"**May** we go now, Mary Grace. I'm sure you **can**."

"May we go, please, Sister?"

Sister Clement nodded and, as she did so, we heard the hand-bell ringing for the end of school. Whoever was ringing it had not yet acquired the knack; perhaps she had her fingers on the metal of the bell, for it came out muted and somehow far away. We stopped off in the classroom to collect our book-bags left there before Benediction, so very long ago.

"We'll walk to the bus stop together, shall we?" suggested Kit Morrissey and, in an instant, I had forgotten all the pain and embarrassment of the afternoon.

"I'd like that," I said demurely, the voice within me anything but demure. Wait until Vinnie hears about this, it said. Wait till Vinnie hears about this!

Somehow, Kit persuaded our form teacher, Sister Anthony, to let her change places with Eileen Calhoun, so that she and I could share the double desk at the front of the room.

"It's my eyes, you see, Sister," Kit lied fluently. "My father thinks I need to wear glasses, but I have to have my eyes tested first. I can't see the board properly from where I am now. But if I could sit at the front in the middle where Eileen sits, I'd see everything. I don't want to fall behind with my work."

Sister Anthony, who began every day with the words, "Now remember, girls. Work as if everything depended upon work, and pray as if everything depended upon prayer," was impressed by Kit's unusual – and new-found – devotion to her studies. She allowed Kit to move her books to the front of the class, an operation that took longer than it should have done and held up the history lesson by a good ten minutes. It was not Kit's fault – she was eager to settle into her new place. But Eileen Calhoun was a hoarder: in addition to her textbooks and exercise books she had amassed pen nibs, pencil ends, scraps of paper covered with indecipherable notes, and, unforgivably, biscuit crumbs in her desk. Sister Anthony, who had come in to check that the desk was completely empty before Kit laid out her possessions, looked down her long nose and made a small sound of surprise and disgust. Eileen Calhoun flushed, gulped, and burst into tears. It took several minutes before she recovered sufficiently for the lesson to proceed. Since I found the way history was taught at school both boring and undemanding, I was, for once, not sorry to see time wasted.

"I wish my name was Kit," I said that evening after school as we walked to the trolley stop. "Mary Grace is so old fashioned. I wish I had parents like yours."

"They didn't choose 'Kit' if that's what you're thinking. I did."

"You did?"

"Mammy used to call me Katie, but that's a child's name. So, on my twelfth birthday," she said grandly, "I decided I didn't want to be a child any longer. I told them I was going to be called Kit from then on. And I am. You could try it."

I was uncertain.

"How? I don't want to be called Mamie, or Marie, or Maria, and everyone's called Mary."

"Well, Grace isn't bad," Kit said. "It's different. I don't know anyone else called Grace. Why don't you drop the Mary and just call yourself Grace? It sounds good: English and upper-class."

The idea was attractive. It did not stop me from objecting.

"I can't just tell everyone in my family I want them to call me Grace from now on. They'll not take any notice."

"Try it," Kit said. "You'll be surprised. And if they don't take any notice, you'll just have to keep telling them."

I started with Vinnie.

"I don't want you to call me Mary Grace anymore. I just want you to call me Grace."

"All right," said Vinnie. "Kit's idea, is it?"

"No, it's mine!" I snapped

"Fine. Grace."

The rest of my family proved more difficult. It was not that they objected to calling me Grace; it was just that they kept on forgetting. Eventually I gave up reminding my father and mother that my name was no longer Mary Grace: it seemed easier to answer to it. But I began to sign myself Grace Brennan, I told everyone that was my name, and gradually it came to be accepted at school and, most of the time and at least by my brothers, at home.

Not long after my change of name, Kit invited me to meet her parents. She had already been to Hopwood Street several times and was on good terms with my whole family. I hesitated for a long time before accepting her return invitation, and then I kept finding excuses to put the visit off. Finally Kit lost patience with me.

"Don't you want to see where I live? I spend enough time at your house with your family."

"Yes, of course I do," I said. "It's just that your life is so different from mine."

"You mean because Daddy's a doctor and I'm an only child and we live in a big house with a real garden? All right, so it's different. But I'd rather have a family like yours, if you want to know the truth. There's always someone to talk to. And your father's so interesting."

"Daddy?" I was incredulous. "Interesting? All he does is talk about the docks and politics and the Labour Party and the Union."

"It makes a change from hernias and operations and whether we ought to run a Jowett or a Citroen."

Our family had never even considered the possibility of owning a car. I remained silent.

I couldn't sleep the night before the visit to the Morrissey's house. In the morning, heavy-eyed, I put on my Sunday skirt and brushed my hair a hundred times with Mammy's tortoise-shell hairbrush. I would have preferred to wear my school uniform; the navy gymslip and blue-and-navy tie gave me an identity that might have protected me from the unknown, but Mammy wouldn't allow it.

"They'll think you have no other decent clothes to your name. Now get on with it."

Daddy stopped me at the door.

"I'm not sure I like the idea of you mixing with the Morrisseys," he said. "I wouldn't want you paying too much attention to what Alan Morrissey has to say."

"But he's a doctor," I said, surprised. "Why shouldn't I pay attention to what he says?"

I held my breath. Had I been too impertinent? Sometimes I could say almost anything to my father, and he would laugh and pat my shoulder. But there were other times when he would bark at me for what seemed no reason at all. I never learned how to tell the good days from the bad days, so conversations between us were always unpredictable. Today seemed to be one of the good days, however.

"Doctor he may be, but he's also a Tory," my father said. "He's just managed to wheedle his way on to the city council. We've crossed swords a time or two."

"Do you want me to tell Kit I can't go?" I asked. Half of me was hoping he would say yes, but I also knew I would be furious if he refused his permission.

He considered for a moment.

"Go, if you must," he said eventually. "But don't be taken in by him. Will you promise me that?"

"Yes, Daddy," I said. I tried to squeeze past him, but he was blocking the doorway and I was forced to ask, "Is it all right, if I go now?"

"Yes, yes," he said. "But don't be late back. Your mother will worry."

"No, Daddy. Thank you, Daddy."

At last he stood aside to let me pass.

Kit met me from the trolleybus, and we walked across Pearson Park to her garden gate, which was white and newly painted and swung open upon oiled hinges with no effort at all. The garden itself was equally threatening: lawns and flowerbeds and a vegetable plot, all formal and neatly spaced, with bare weed-free earth showing between the rows of carrots and summer bedding.

"How does your father manage to keep the garden so tidy?" I asked. "I mean, he must be very busy, being a doctor and on the city council."

"Oh, Daddy doesn't do it," Kit said. "Mammy looks after the flowers and we have a man for the lawn and the vegetables."

A man. I wanted to turn and run home. The Morrisseys employed a gardener, and the house I was approaching was twice the size of ours and detached. I stopped, clutching Kit's arm.

"Are you sure you want me to come in?"

"I asked you, didn't I?" Kit said. "Now, stop being so silly, and come and meet Mammy and Daddy."

And I did.

At the time I could not tell whether I loved or hated the experience. I knew as soon as I saw her that I did not like Kit's mother, who was all silk dress and cold hands and painted fingernails.

I found Dr Morrissey intimidating too, particularly when he said, without smiling, "So you're Jack Brennan's daughter?"

"Do you know my father then, sir?" I asked, doing my best to make conversation.

"Everyone in this city has heard of Jack Brennan," Dr Morrissey said.

The way he said it made me think that perhaps my father's local fame was not, after all, something to be proud of. I looked down at my fingers interlocked on my knee, so that I would not disgrace my mother by biting my nails. I had no idea what to do next.

"Would you like to see my room?"

Kit intervened just in time. We excused ourselves and hurried upstairs. Kit's room, like all the other rooms in the house, was more spacious than I was used to. Kit obviously expected me to comment. I made the effort to do so.

"I like the walls – they're so light! Everything in our house is either dark green or brown. It's like living in a dungeon!"

"Dungeons are grey and made of stone," Kit objected. "Your house is more like an underground cavern."

"Or sea cave." We considered the limitations of the Brennan family home for a moment, in silence. Then I spread my arms wide and whirled around.

"When I grow up, I'm going to live in a house like this, with huge rooms and pale walls and windows that actually let in the light."

"Do you want to see my clothes?" Kit asked. It seemed a strange question, and I did not really know how to answer it. It hardly mattered. Kit flung open her wardrobe door and held up a variety of dresses, skirts, and blouses, all of them obviously expensive, and none of them looking as if they had been worn more than once or twice.

"Very nice," I said, aware that I had to say something, and not knowing how to express the dismay and envy I really felt.

"You can try them on, if you like."

I looked at Kit, tiny and trim in the light from the window. I was uncomfortably aware of my own solid body, which none of Kit's clothes could possibly fit. Perhaps Kit realised it too, for she suddenly threw down the skirt she was holding.

"Let's go and see if Mammy has anything for us to eat. I'm starving."

Her intentions were good, I thought. It was a thing my mother often said about people, and for the first time I understood what she meant. Kim did not mean to hurt me. But before I followed her downstairs, I picked up the skirt and put it back on its hanger, hung it carefully in the wardrobe and closed the door.

*

The following day I visited a very different sort of house.

"Get your coat on, Mary Grace," my mother said. "We're going out."

"What? Where?"

I looked up from my reading. Mammy was already at the door.

"Now, Mary Grace!"

I stopped, curious, one arm inside my coat sleeve.

"Where are we going?"

"I'll tell you on the way. There's no time to waste."

My mother set off down the street so quickly that I had to run to keep up. I had no breath to ask again, and it was not until we reached the corner that Mammy chose to explain.

"Vinnie came by with a message from Declan. He and Josefina need our help."

"What with?"

"It's complicated, Mary Grace. You know the new estate that your father has been working so hard on, on the housing committee? The Corporation estate? Well, the Pontis are due to move in there today. You heard their street was being knocked down?"

"Yes," I said. "But I don't see …"

"They can't get Signora Ponti to leave the house. The workmen are threatening to knock the house down with her still inside it if she doesn't move. Now, hurry!"

We had already passed St Charles's Church, and the streets were suddenly narrower. The houses too were smaller, huddling together on the very edge of the pavement, with no front gardens at all, and with doors and windows that seemed tiny, even to me. A sweet, sickly smell hung over the buildings, making me press my hand to my nose and mouth in an attempt to block it out.

"What's that smell, Mammy? Is it because it's the slums?"

Mammy turned back, frowning.

"What do you know about slums, Mary Grace? That's the smell of the brewery. You meet it everywhere this side of town. I grew up with it. So did your father."

"Sorry, Mammy." I ducked my head in apology, though I wasn't really sure what I was apologising for. In those few seconds the connection was made: the smell of brewing hops would always bring back to me those early slum clearances my father pushed through in the years after the Great War. I did not understand at the time how much it had cost him.

Soon we were in a street that had been almost entirely demolished. Only one end house still stood, its neighbour's faded wallpaper hanging in strips from the dividing wall. On the pavement near the door were Declan and his fiancée, Josefina. They turned, faces tense, as they heard our footsteps approaching.

"Thank God you've come, Mam. We can't do anything with her. Granny P's in there too, but she'll come out as soon as we can get Josefina's mother out. We've been trying for hours."

Mammy asked no further questions but made her way to the front door. It opened straight into the one cramped downstairs room, with its two tiny windows, dark red walls, and heavy, old-fashioned furniture. A stale smell of violets overwhelmed us. I noticed something that looked like a piano stool, a huge table surrounded by an assortment of chairs, the great black range that took up the whole of one wall. A stray gleam of light, catching on Granny Ponti's one-toothed grin, showed me where the old woman crouched in a corner, scant white hair scraped back from her forehead. But where was Josefina's mother?

A low moan made me turn: Signora Ponti, in the opposite corner, overflowing the armchair in which she sat. Neither Mammy nor I had ever seen Anna Ponti before, and the size of her staggered us. A goitre as wide as a washing-up bowl dragged her neck to one side; folds of flesh the colour and consistency of uncooked scones drooped over her wrists and ankles. A black shawl, blouse, and skirt did not disguise her bulk, but accentuated it. After two or three seconds of horrified silence, I stared down at my feet, which suddenly looked absurdly small but were, at least, familiar.

"Josefina, come here." Mammy spoke over her shoulder to the girl in the doorway. "That's right. Tell your mother that I have come to help her. She's not to be afraid."

Unintelligible speeches in what must have been Italian followed. To me they sounded a little like the Latin I recited at Mass, but easier on the ear. Josefina turned to us to explain.

"She has not been outside for fifteen years. She is afraid."

Surely, I thought, and was ashamed for thinking, the family doesn't have an inside lavatory. Mrs Ponti must go outside, if only to the privy in the yard at the back of the house. But then my eye returned to the piano stool without a piano, which might not be a piano stool at all, but a commode, and I began to think I understood. I could not stop myself from wrinkling my nose, but luckily Mammy was too busy to notice.

"I will hold one hand, Josefina. You can hold the other. Help her up. You, Mary Grace, push from behind."

Mrs Ponti's black knitted shawl stretched tight against her back. Reluctantly, I placed the heels of both palms against the spongy flesh and pushed. Mammy and Josefina pulled. Finally, Signora Ponti tottered to her feet. Little shuffling steps took her towards the door, though her whole body leaned back in protest. One foot, two feet, and she was nearly there and –

The door was too narrow. There was no way in which Josefina's mother could leave the house, even if she agreed to do so. She was simply too fat.

"Declan! Fetch two of the workmen here. Tell them to bring their sledgehammers with them."

Step by step, we led Signora Ponti away from the door. Mammy, Josefina, and I surrounded her – as best we could – holding fast to her trembling bulk. Minutes went by, and at last Declan returned with two workmen, who swung their hammers at the walls on either side of the door, being careful not to dislodge the lintel, but not bothering to hide their laughter.

"Shouldn't we have got the furniture out first?" I whispered to my mother.

"No time. I don't want to give her the chance to change her mind. We'll get it out later."

The gap, where the door had been, widened as stones tumbled, and dust and light entered the room. As sunlight fell on the table and chairs, I could see how worn and stained they were, how scuffed the paint work.

A sudden scuffling movement and Granny Ponti was outside in the street, gesturing with both arms to her daughter-in-law to join her. Mammy, Josefina, and I moved forward in unison, bearing Mrs Ponti still resisting into the unaccustomed light of the afternoon, onto the cobbled street, out into the air.

Declan was there with the handcart on which he and Josefina planned to transport the family furniture to the new corporation estate. The sight of the terrified woman in front of him was disconcerting; like the rest of us, he watched the swaying body as it threatened at every moment to collapse.

"Get her on the cart. Jesus, Mary, and Joseph, is everything to be left to me?"

Mammy was right, of course. The first thing to do was to get Signora Ponti back under the safety of a roof, any roof, if she were to survive with any sanity intact.

If she is sane, I thought.

And once she had been pushed and pulled onto the cart, Mammy and I left. There was, after all, nothing left for us to do.

"You make it sound really funny," Kit said when I described it all later. "Was it funny?"

"No. It was horrible."

"Then why didn't you make it sound horrible?"

"You know me," I said. "I never let the truth get in the way of a good story. That's what Mammy always says. And I wanted to make you laugh."

"I feel mean for laughing. That poor woman."

"Yes," I said. "That poor woman." But it was myself I felt sorry for. I had wanted to make her laugh. Instead I had reminded her once again how different our families and friends were, and just how far away Hopwood Street was from Pearson Park.

3

My father, Red Jack Brennan, was dying. He was, uncharacteristically, taking his time about it: death was one project he would not be tackling with his usual bite and vigour. I had seen him diminish since the failure of the General Strike, and now he was dying. I knew that for a fact. Vinnie and I heard Mammy tell him so.

Neither of us intended to eavesdrop. We'd simply decided that Sunday afternoon to tidy the box-room, knowing no-one would disturb us. We would have time to talk for once. We were leaning against the wall that separated the box-room from our parents' bedroom, arguing over who had owned the rag doll with the hideous pottery head, when I heard Mammy's voice.

"Listen to me, Jack Brennan. You're forty-six years old and you're never going to see forty-seven. Don't try to tell yourself that it's indigestion that's keeping you in bed. It's heart, and it will kill you as it killed your father before you. You know it. It's time to put your house in order."

Vinnie and I both started to speak, then stopped. Vinnie's face was strained as we listened for Daddy's reply.

"Don't talk nonsense, woman. My house is in order, and well you know it. Everything's paid for, four of the children are working, Sean has his apprenticeship at the cycle factory, and your nuns will take Grace as a pupil teacher when the time comes. What else do you want of me?"

The door of the box-room was open. Multicoloured rays of late afternoon sun slanted across the stairwell through the stained-glass window on the landing. Segments of yellow and green light illuminated my arm, Vinnie's face, the smooth bald head of the rag doll. I held my breath. My father and mother were in the next room, talking about my father's approaching death, and I was frozen in that one moment of time when my future stretched out, clear and achievable before me. I had never thought of becoming a teacher, had never thought at all of what I should do when the time came for me to leave school; but there it was, in its entirety, and it was right.

I turned to share the realisation with Vinnie, but he was still intent on the conversation in the next room, which had just resumed. Or perhaps it had never stopped.

"Well, then. If you want it straight, I want you to make your peace with God and the church. Let me send for a priest."

"Have an Irish bog-priest spouting his mumbo-jumbo under my roof? Are you daft, Nora?"

I caught my mother's controlled intake of breath.

"Look, Jack. You say it's all nonsense. If you're right and I'm wrong, what harm is it going to do for someone to speak a few words over you? For you to take Communion? None at all. And I shall be so much happier in my mind, when you're gone. Even if I am mistaken and it's all the mockery you say it is. Can't you do it for me, Jack? For my sake? And it needn't be one of your bog-priests. I could ask for an English priest. Father Sebastian. You know you've always said he had a head on him."

"Go on then." The proof of his love for her was so softly spoken that we barely heard it, but next moment the bedroom door opened, and Mammy peered in at us.

"Vinnie. Away now to the presbytery and fetch Father Sebastian. Father Sebastian, mind. And be quick about it. Tell him Jack Brennan is asking for him."

"I'll come with you!" I was ready and in the street before Vinnie had time to think of stopping me. Together we set off the half mile to the presbytery, half running, half walking, heavy with the importance of our errand.

"We've to tell Father Sebastian Jack Brennan is asking for him," I said as soon as the housekeeper opened the door to our knock.

"Lord bless us and save us!" The housekeeper crossed herself. "But Father Sebastian's not here at the moment. Will Father Ryan do?"

I was in despair.

"It must be Father Sebastian. Where is he? Will he be back soon?"

"He's here."

The voice behind us made me jump and whirl. Forgetting myself, I caught at the tall priest's hand, realised what I was doing and fell back, flustered, leaving it to Vinnie to pass on the message.

"You have to come with us, Father. My father – Jack Brennan – he's dying, and he wants to see you. My mother said to tell you so."

"Red Jack Brennan dying? And wanting to see me? Surely not?"

"Father, you've got to believe us." Vinnie was as desperate as I was. "Else he'll die with all his sins on him and we'll never forgive ourselves."

"We can't have that now, can we?" said Father Sebastian, turning and setting off towards our house on Hopwood Street so quickly that Vinnie and I were momentarily left behind.

"But, Father, the Eucharist …"

"I have it on me. Your father's not the only one sick and in need this day."

We heard Daddy's voice as we entered the hall and started up the stairs.

"That'll be your English priest now, God rot his soul. Is it yourself, Father Sebastian? I'm glad to see you, God damn and blast your eyes. Get yourself in here, why don't you? I sure as flaming hell can't keep you out."

"He's always like this when people come to the house," I said, tearful and embarrassed. It was true. I had often heard my father swear at a visitor under his breath while going forward to meet him with hand outstretched and a smile on his face. "He doesn't mean anything by it. Don't take offence, Father."

"I take no offence. Now downstairs, the two of you. I'll send for you later, Vinnie, if I need a server for the Last Rites. Or perhaps Sean would do it. He's more in the way of it, after all. No, you can't come in. This is between me and Jack Brennan – and his God."

The next morning Daddy came downstairs for breakfast.

"You're feeling better, then?" Mammy asked. "It'll be the Extreme Unction has done it. That, and feeling quiet in your soul."

"It will not! I'll be damned if I let any Catholic witchcraft save my life. It was just a wee bit of indigestion that had me laid low, and I'm over it now."

"It was not. Whoever heard of a man having indigestion down his left arm and through his shoulder? It's heart, Jack Brennan, and it'll kill you if you thump the table like that. Just be grateful God's spared you for another day of spleen and blasphemy. Now, what will you take for your breakfast?"

"If I'm as sick as you say, I'll have bread and milk. A light invalid diet. And then I'll be off down the docks to talk to Barney Yates about next week's Union meeting."

"I think we have a little milk left," Mammy said. "Mind you, I was saving it for the cat."

"Let the cat eat water," my father said.

They brought him home from the docks that evening in a cab. I wasn't there at the time, but Vinnie told me later what had happened: Barney Yates paying off the driver with stiff, unresponsive fingers, Pat and Mick stumbling into the hall with the weight of our grey-faced father, Sean silent in the kitchen doorway. There was no talk now of sending for the priest; that was over and done with. No attempt either, to get him upstairs. The makeshift bed in the front room that had been mine since I was twelve was turned over to him and he lay there beneath the blankets unable to speak, while his wife and sons watched over him. There was nothing else they could do.

I came back home from my piano lesson at six, out of breath from running, brown leather music case under one arm. I was still thinking about the left-hand fingering for Minuet in G, as I came through the door, but I felt the change in the house at once, the dreadful quiet, the emptiness. Mammy must have heard the door open, for she came out to take my hands and lead me into the room I still thought of as my own, but which was now my father's sickroom. Death Room.

He did not move or speak. He did not die. At ten Mammy sent us away, saying we must get some sleep. The boys went without a word, but I hesitated, not knowing what I should do.

"You'll sleep in our bedroom tonight. I'll stay with your father. No, don't argue."

It was strange and disturbing to undress in the big bedroom at the front of the house, to think of lying down in the double bed. I had not slept in that room since I was a little child with tonsillitis. The furniture seemed unfamiliar – some of it may have been new – but I remembered the fireplace where the coals burned the whole week of my illness, the pattern of the blue and white tiles around it, and the broad mantelpiece with the studio photograph of my Irish grandparents, my mother's mother and father, whom I never knew.

I put my clothes on the blue basket-weave chair near the window, and then moved them again, to have somewhere to put my father's pillow. I could not bear the idea of my head touching it: it was so tainted with his dying. I moved my mother's pillow into the middle of the long bolster and lay down in the exact centre of the bed, seeking my own space, away from my parents' habitual positions. I lay stiff, my hands at my sides, eyes wide in the dark. Sleep came uneasily and late.

I woke early, before the sky was fully light. Someone – Vinnie – was sitting on my bed, holding my hand which rested on the cotton bedspread. It seemed separate from me, somehow. Vinnie did not look at me.

"He's dead, then?"

"Yes."

"When?"

"About an hour ago."

"Did you see him when …?"

"When he died? No, but afterwards."

"What did he look like?"

"Like nothing. Like there was nothing there. You can see for yourself, later."

"No."

Perhaps it would have been better if I had looked at him then. I do not know. But I was so angry with him for dying. For leaving us alone.

For three days and nights my father's body lay in the front room, while the house filled with people come to pay their last respects and say they were sorry for our trouble. I grew to hate those two phrases almost as much as I hated my dead father. For three days and nights I resisted my mother's attempts to make me enter the room and say "good-bye". No, I insisted, I would not look at my father's dead body. The air in the house was clogged with prayer and reminiscence. I did not know half the people I made tea for and thanked for their condolences; even my mother seemed uncertain who some of them were. "From the Council," she said. "A Union man. A party worker." She did not cry but filled her time with arrangements for the funeral. We children followed her example, but I found later that parts of those days had disappeared entirely from my memory.

Suddenly one morning I was kneeling in the front pew at St Patrick's Church, and my father's coffin, borne in on the shoulders of his four eldest sons, was received by Father Ryan, with Sean as his altar boy.

I might have refused to see the body, but I could not deny its presence, there under the heavy oak lid. And the brass nameplate which bore not his name but a stranger's: John Brennan. "More respectful that way," Pat had said, and Mick had agreed. They always agreed on everything, those two.

John or Jack was there, and I would never see him again. I'll not cry, I told myself, but I did, sniffing and blinking and rubbing my eyes with the back of my hand. I'll not cry. And then the requiem mass was under way, and all I could think of was how much my father would have hated it.

"Jack Brennan was not a good Catholic."

My head shot up, as did every other head in the church. Father Ryan was seated at the side of the altar, and it was the English priest, Father Sebastian, who stood in the pulpit, speaking the unthinkable truth that everyone there knew but would never have spoken.

"No. Jack Brennan was not a good Catholic, but he was, most emphatically, a good man. In his short life, he did more for this city than anyone else I can think of. You are perhaps unacquainted with the poem by the English poet, Leigh Hunt: *Abou Ben Adhem*. Jack would have known it. He was, in his own way, an educated man. In that poem, Hunt speaks of a man whose name does not appear on the list shown to him one night by an angel, of "those who love the Lord". And Ben Adhem says to the angel humbly, but without apology, "Write me then as one who loves his fellow men." It is a plea Jack Brennan might with justification have made. "Write me then as one who loves his fellow men." We have only to look at the new Corporation Estate to see his legacy, the results of his work for the poor of this city. That bad-tempered, foul-mouthed, opinionated Irish docker, who worked tirelessly for justice and truth, was, above all, this city's Ben Adhem." Here, Father Sebastian stopped, leaned forward in the pulpit, gave himself enough time to draw the eye of every person present, in a pause so long that for the first time I realised just how full the church was. "I should like to tell you how Leigh Hunt's poem ends. The next night the angel appears again. He has with him another list: "the list of those whom love of God has blessed." The priest drew himself up, paused, looked round again. Then he threw out his arms in a theatrical, perfectly calculated gesture, and delivered the last triumphant line: "And lo – Jack Brennan's name led all the rest!"

Consternation. We were in a church, after all, so there could be no outcry. But on the faces of the congregation the disapproval of the devout vied with the jubilation of the Union men. I wanted to laugh and cry at the same time. I could see my mother's lips twitching – had she known what was coming? – and the horrified look on Father Ryan's face. And Daddy would have enjoyed it so much!

I think that was the moment when, remembering how he loved to shock, I felt my anger leave me. After that – a blur. I have no recollection of how we came to be standing in the cold windswept graveyard, with the family ranged around the crumbling sides of my father's grave. But the coffin was there, being lowered down, not smoothly, but in a series of jolts that made me want to cry out in protest. Then I heard the noise of Pat scattering the first handful of dirt onto the brass nameplate and polished wood. Shockingly, a dark form lurched forward – Sean, attempting to throw himself into Daddy's grave. Mick and Declan jerked him back by the arms, but he struggled and kicked and, for a moment, everything was in uproar.

And then Mammy had her arms about her youngest son.

Finally, it was over. Vinnie and I left the graveyard together.

"I never knew," I said. "I never knew Sean loved Daddy so much."

Vinnie did not answer me directly.

"It's not easy being Sean," he said.

"I don't understand."

"I don't suppose you would. Why would you?"

I knew better than to ask for further explanation, but I thought about it. I thought about it intensely. For a while.

The house had never been so full. All the people who came to visit in the days after Daddy's death were here now, but all at once so that there was no room to move. I squeezed my way through to the scullery to be out of reach of the red faces and sympathy. I busied myself at the sink, washing up plates and glasses as they were brought to me, but even so I could hear the noise rising, the laughter that kept creeping in and, eventually, the voices raised in song. The Fahy cousins, not one of whom had set foot in a church for years, sang their way through all the verses of "Father O'Flynn" seven times. Then there was no stopping the rest of the relations: the Mountains of Mourne, Galway Bay, politicians, and rebels all had their turn, as the O'Driscolls celebrated Mary, Eileen, and Cathleen, Roger O'Malley, John Mourne, Roddy McCauley, and, inevitably, Kevin Barry. It might only have been ten years since the Easter Rising, but already the rebel songs were sung at any wake or wedding.

As he went to death that morning,

He proudly held his head up high.

My brothers' voices: Pat and Mick's baritones, Declan's tenor. Vinnie and Sean were silent, Vinnie working beside me in the scullery, Sean nowhere to be seen. With a shudder, I remembered his behaviour at the graveside.

"Go and see how Sean is," I suggested to Vinnie.

"He wouldn't thank me for it," Vinnie said. He picked up a jug of porter from the scrubbed table and pushed through to the main room, ready to wait on Jack Brennan's family and friends and acquaintances, and the inevitable hangers-on, who loved a good funeral and went to every wake on the street.

I dried my hands on a tea towel. The tips of my fingers had begun to wrinkle, and my knuckles were red. It was hard to force my way through to the stairs and make my way up to the bedroom Sean shared with Declan and Vinnie. I opened the door and looked in: no Sean. I was sure he was not among the mass of people downstairs, eating, drinking, and, yes, enjoying themselves, but where else could he be? In the yard, perhaps? Once again, I pushed my way through the crowd to the hallway. Some of the guests were spilling into the scullery itself. I let myself out through the back door and ran down the path to the shed. I opened that door too, and again looked around. At first, I saw only the usual clutter of tools and bicycles, but then a slight movement behind the pile of wood in the far corner caught my eye.

"Sean?"

"Go away."

I hesitated.

"No, I won't go away. But I'll just sit here and keep quiet. You don't have to talk to me. I know how you feel. All those people in there, having a good time, when Daddy's dead."

"You don't know how I feel," Sean said, but he moved a piece of wood aside and now I could see him, crouched in the corner, his arms round his knees and head bent.

"I'll just sit here."

"You said that before."

Silence. Not usually particularly talkative, happy to sit for hours reading without saying a word, now I found it hard not to speak. I could sense Sean's pain, his impatience with me, his need for comfort, but I did not know what to do. In the end I could be quiet no longer.

"Shall I fetch you something to eat?"

"I'm never going to eat anything again."

"Now you're being stupid."

"What would you know?" and Sean pulled the piece of wood back into place, so that he was once more hidden from my view.

"I'm going to fetch Mammy."

"See if I care."

But there was a brighter tone in his voice, and I understood that I had, at last, hit on the only thing that could comfort my brother.

"I'm going now."

"Just go then."

I left the shed door open, half hoping that Sean might come out of his own accord, half trying to ignore him so much he would be forced to get up and shut it. It would mean he would have to do something, rather than just sit behind the wood, sulking.

"He's not sulking," Mammy said when I found her at last. "He's grieving."

"We're all grieving."

"In our own ways, yes. I'll go to him now. See if anyone needs anything more to eat or drink, will you? I'll not be long."

I was so tired of smiling at strangers that I would rather have gone with my mother to the shed, but instead I steered my way through the crowd, fetching plates of sandwiches, refilling glasses, responding politely when some distant relation or workmate of my father's recognised me.

"You'll be Mary Grace, Jack's youngest."

Yes, I agreed, I was. Where was Vinnie? When would they all go home? But it was worse when they had gone, with nothing left for me to do but tidy away the leavings and, with them, the last traces of my father's presence. Shortly before it grew dark, Mammy had persuaded Sean to come in. Perhaps he went to his room, for I did not see him among the departing guests, nor was he rearranging furniture with his brothers. Josie Ponti, Declan's sweetheart, stayed to help us set the house to rights, though it was long after midnight before we finished. Josie and I worked side by side in the scullery, sorting and washing crockery, and talking quietly. I was fascinated by Josie, whose dark eyes and full lips were so obviously foreign. Her mother and grandmother spoke almost no English at all, but when Josie talked, it was with the flat, local accent: there was no trace of her Italian ancestry in her voice.

"Declan and I want to get married soon," she confided. "But we'll wait for a while, until your mother's had time to get over your father's death."

"She wouldn't want you putting off the wedding for her sake," I said. "She'll be happy for you. I'll talk to her."

I had no idea what I would say, but the promise seemed to please Josie, who hugged and kissed me, leaving soapy imprints on the shoulders of my black dress.

"You don't know how much I am looking forward to having you as a sister-in-law," she told me.

"Oh, me too," I said. "Me too." But in truth I could not imagine how any of us could ever return to the sort of life where people laughed and fell in love and danced at weddings. Not with Jack Brennan dead and buried and – I could not push the thought away – rotting in his grave.

4

One weekday afternoon, a Tuesday probably, about a month after my father's funeral, I was standing at the upright piano in the front room. My bed – not the one that Daddy died in; I could not bear to sleep in that, and Declan had it now – was in the corner behind a screen. On the music rest of the piano was a book of English folk songs my music teacher had lent me, and with my right forefinger I picked out the melody of "Tom Bowling", occasionally adding a chord with my left hand. I should have been sitting at the piano stool, playing the full score, with the metronome to keep me in step, but I preferred the lazy touch of my finger on the yellowing keys, the quiet sound of my voice singing, slightly flat, the words of the song:

Here a sheer hulk lies poor Tom Bowling,

The darling of the crew …

The easy tears spilled from the corners of my eyes. I liked that sort of crying, self-induced almost, when my face remained calm and smooth, my nose did not redden, and all I could feel was the slow salt fall of teardrops on my skin. I tilted my head so that the tears ran back into my eyes.

No more he'll hear the tempest howling,

For death has broached him to.

I was not sure what that meant, "broached him to", but it sounded sad and important. It was so much easier to cry for someone I did not know, someone imaginary, than to cry for my father, who still walked my dreams and inhabited the house in which we, his children, lived. Even now I was half listening for his voice in the hall, cursing unwanted visitors underneath his breath while calling out a welcome. The high back and battered arms of his favourite chair still dominated the living room, although he was not there to use it; only Mammy ever sat in his place.

The door behind me opened and closed softly. I slammed the piano lid down, almost catching my fingers beneath it as I did so, and twisted round to see who had come in.

Sean.

"Grace, can I talk to you?"

"Yes." If I sounded surprised it is because I was surprised. Sean and I had never been close; I could not remember a time when we had talked as he seemed to be asking me to talk now. I sat down on the piano stool, my back to the piano, and looked up at the youngest of my five brothers. He was the closest to me in age and the one I knew least well.

"I want to talk to Mammy, and I'd like you to come with me."

I could not help myself. I was curious.

"What about?"

Sean hesitated. He was obviously finding it difficult to say what he had to say.

"Just come with me, would you?"

Intrigued, I agreed.

Mammy was in the scullery, just starting on the ironing. She had heated the big irons on the range and was testing them for heat, spitting on the base plate and then bringing it up to her cheek, listening to the splutter and hiss. The room smelled of heat, and damp linen, and the hot metal of the irons. Mammy stretched the sleeve of one of the boys' shirts over the sleeve board and began at the cuff, as she had taught me to do, working in short smooth strokes. She had not bothered to heat the small iron she would normally have used. I had noticed more than one omission like this since Daddy died, and it troubled me.

Sean stood beside our mother. He did not know whether to speak, I thought. He was frightened to disturb her concentration. Something in his stillness must have alerted her, for she stood the iron up on its heel, took the shirt off the board and put it back, only partly ironed as it was, in the washing basket with the other shirts and pillowcases.

"Well?" she said.

"We could come back later," Sean barely managed to say. I had never seen him so uncertain. I was looking at him now, though, seeing someone I did not recognise. My brother.

"Come through to the front room."

That showed how serious it was. For Mammy to use the front room to talk to one of her own children was unheard of. I followed them back. If the front room was anyone's territory, it was mine. It served as my bedroom at night, and I used it every day to practise my scales and the pieces my music teacher had set me to learn. I sat down on the piano stool, which was familiar and unthreatening, and watched as Mammy seated herself in the window, her back to the light, so that it was hard to see her face. Sean would have remained standing, but Mammy motioned him to be seated opposite her. The chair he chose was hard and upright; he perched on the edge like a child awaiting punishment. I wondered what he could have to say that had made him so uneasy. Inside my head I was willing him to speak, but he said nothing, merely looked down at his feet in their worn but well-polished boots.

"Well, Sean?"

Mammy's voice was patient. I wriggled on the piano stool, sliding my hands over the smooth handles and leaning back to feel the hard edge of the keyboard against my blouse, solid, reassuring in a world that was suddenly fluid.

"I want to be a priest."

He spoke so softly I barely heard him. Mammy leaned forward.

"Say that again, Sean."

"I want to be a priest." Louder this time, more certain. He has been considering this for weeks, I thought suddenly, and then, why does he want me here?

"Why?"

It was a stark question and there was no softness in Mammy's voice. Sean tried to answer her.

"Because …" He got no further.

"Because your father's dead and buried and an English priest put on a show that silenced the people who thought he should never have been buried in sacred ground. Is that it?"

"No!"

"Then why?"

The silence lasted so long I began to believe it would never be broken. I looked from my mother to my brother. But when Sean did speak, it was not the question Mammy had asked that he answered.

"You don't think I'm clever enough, do you? You don't think I've got her brains, or Vinnie's. You don't think they'll take me, do you? Say it!"

"I'm not the one who's saying it, Sean. You are."

He was angry by then, really angry, and the words came out so fast he could scarcely control them. He doesn't know what he is saying, I thought; he just wants to shock us. And that is all.

"I've never had a chance. Never. All my life I've looked up to Declan and Vinnie, because they're so clever, they know it all, and then she comes along, my little sister, who sails through the scholarship and goes off to the convent because she's Daddy's favourite and always gets what she wants. No talk of sending Declan or Vinnie to grammar school, oh no, and no help for me when you knew I was struggling, but she only has to think a wish and it's hers. It's not fair, Mammy; it's not fair."

Well, I thought, now I know why he wanted me here. Not for support. No; he wants me to feel guilty, he wants us all to feel guilty, but me especially. Well, I will not do it. It's not my fault he's not as clever as the rest of us. It's not my fault he failed the scholarship. He has no right to make me listen to this.

"He'd make an awful priest, Mammy," I heard myself say. "Even if they'd have him. And they will not."

"You don't know that, Mary Grace," Mammy's voice was harsh. "You can't know it. You don't know it and you have no right to say it. Now, Sean, take your time. Get a grip on your temper and tell me again what makes you think you want to be a priest. And you, Mary Grace, go and make yourself useful. Finish the ironing."

"Yes, Mammy," I said thankfully. I slipped off the piano stool and made for the door. As I shut it behind me, I remembered unwillingly what Vinnie had said to me. "It's not easy being Sean."

Well maybe it was not easy being Sean, but he didn't make it any easier for himself. I retrieved Pat's shirt with its one ironed cuff from the basket and put it back on the sleeve board. Then I began to test the irons, as my mother had done, happy to concentrate on the warmth against my cheek and the satisfying splutter of my bubble of spit on the hot metal.

They turned him down. Of course they turned him down. He did not have the right educational qualifications, he did not have the temperament for dealing with people; he did not, in short, have a vocation. That is what they told him. "You do not have a true vocation." And that was the end of it. What Sean did have, I thought, was a gripping desire to be different, to outshine his older brothers and his sister. He knew he could not do it on our terms. That was why he had to look for something else, some area where none of us would challenge him. Finding that something was not going to be easy. Since he was fourteen, he had had an apprenticeship at the local cycle works. Daddy had provided enough money to pay the one and threepence a week it cost, giving explicit instructions for its payment in the will he surprised us all by leaving. Sean would have none of it. He was not going to finish his apprenticeship, he said. If he could not be a priest, he wanted a real job with real money, and he wanted it immediately.

It was Vinnie who finally came to the rescue. Vinnie had left his own job with Fenners to join the Merchant Navy – before Daddy had been dead a week – and he had just returned home, after his first voyage as third engineer with the Blue Star Line.

"You remember I talked to Uncle Martin at the funeral?" Vinnie asked one Sunday afternoon. "The shop's getting too much for him and Auntie Eileen these days. Too much lifting and carrying for people of their age. He asked if I would be interested in joining him, but of course I am fixed up already. I wondered if you'd be interested, Sean. He'd like it to stay in the family – pity they never had any children of their own, but it's too late for that now. I can imagine it painted up above the shop: Brennan and Nephew. Sounds all right to me."

"No," said Sean, but without emphasis, almost as a matter of course. "I don't want to be a shopkeeper. Da wouldn't have wanted me to work in a shop."

"Da would have wanted you to complete your apprenticeship, and you'll not do that either. So it's no good using him as an excuse. Of course, you'd probably find it hard to manage without the rest of the family."

"What do you mean?"

"Well, you've always had us here to support you," Declan joined in. "You'd probably not have much luck surviving on your own."

"I don't need any of you to tell me what to do," Sean said. "I'm quite capable of making my mind up. If I wanted to work with Uncle Martin, I wouldn't need your help. I don't suppose he'd want me, anyway. Why should he? Nobody else does."

"We could always ask him," Mammy suggested. "He might at least give you a trial."

"I said I don't want to be a shopkeeper," Sean said. "I mean it. You just can't wait to get rid of me."

No-one said anything further. Mammy went on with her mending, stretching a sock over the polished wooden mushroom as she skilfully darned a hole in the toe. Declan took a stump of pencil from behind his left ear and returned to his calculations of exactly how much money he and Josie would need to live on when they got married, while Vinnie and I played a childish game of "Beggar My Neighbour" on the pegged rug in front of the hearth. Sean, who was, I suppose, angry at being ignored but was powerless to protest – hadn't he told us he did not need our help? – slammed out of the house to kick a can about the street with the Cahalin boys from next door.

"He'll come round," Mammy said. "Just give him time." She put her hand out for the scissors and, not finding them, bit off the grey worsted she was using to close the darn.

"You'll break your teeth," I said.

Sean came back shortly before tea, still scowling, but in a slightly more positive frame of mind.

"You can ask him, if you like," he said. "Uncle Martin, I mean. I might as well do that as anything else. At least it would get me away from this house."

A letter was written. It took some time, because everyone in the family had ideas about how it should be phrased, but eventually it was sent. Martin replied by return of post. He was willing to give Sean a month's trial. The youngest Brennan boy was to live over the shop with his aunt and uncle and have his meals with them.

"Auntie Eileen's a good cook," Vinnie assured him. "And think of the swimming. You'll be less than a minute from the beach."

"And the fishing," Declan added. "You'll be able to go out with the herring fleet. Well, I think you will. I'm not sure Withernsea has a herring fleet."

"I don't like swimming and I don't like fishing," said Sean doggedly. "But I'll give the job a try. It can't be any worse than living with you. Not you, Mammy," he added hastily. "I didn't mean you."

"We'll miss you, Sean," Mammy said. "We really will."

*

The wooden floor in Mother Bernard's room was glossy with polish. Shifting my weight from one foot to the other as Kit and I waited to be told why we had been summoned, I felt the left one slipping away from me. Hastily I regained my balance, but not before Kit had seen and failed to suppress a giggle. Perhaps that was why, in contrast to her words, Mother Bernard's voice was so stern.

"Well now," she said. "Here are my two cleverest girls standing in front of me with their leaving examinations less than a month away. I thought it was time we had a little chat."

I wondered wildly if we were there for a lecture on the moral dangers of dancing and cinema, or whether Mother Bernard was about to tell us what questions were going to come up in our examinations. Other than that, I could not see any reason for this interview. We were obviously not in any trouble, though you might have thought we were by the way Mother Bernard was looking at us. I began to feel I was expected to make some reply but could think of none. As ever, Kit was more direct.

"What did you want to see us about, Mother?"

"About your future, dear girl. Your plans. You, Mary Grace, have you thought what you will do once you leave school?"

"My father wanted me to be a teacher, Mother."

"Ah yes. But you, Mary Grace. Do you want to be a teacher?"

"It's what I've always wanted, Mother."

And, indeed, it seemed to me it was. The half-forgotten feeling of certainty which had overwhelmed me in the box-room came back to me, and I smiled with the delight of it. Mother Bernard's face softened.

"Then we must see that you receive proper training. Your mother would not want you to go away from home, I'm sure."

"No, Mother."

"Then we shall see what we can do for you at Endsleigh. And now you, Kit."

"I'm going to be a doctor, like my father," said Kit confidently. "I'll need to go to university, of course."

Amazed, I swivelled to look at her. Kit had never given any indication that medicine interested her. But then, I thought suddenly, we have never really talked about the future. Not in relation to jobs. Careers. Mother Bernard coughed, and I turned back to face her, but continued, from the corner of my eye, to watch Kit, who stood still and straight, her cheeks blotched with colour. She was a stranger. I looked away.

"Have you discussed this with your father, Kit?"

"Not yet. But he's bound to be pleased, isn't he? Having his daughter follow in his footsteps – isn't that every father's dream?"

It did not sound like Kit. It sounded false, almost sarcastic. I glanced up at Mother Bernard, noticing the red line across her forehead where the starched white linen of her wimple had cut into it, the slight bulge of ageing flesh above the coif. Most of all I noticed the tiredness in her eyes.

"I think you should talk to your father, Kit. It is possible that you are right, and that he would welcome a daughter who followed his own profession. But I have to say that the last time he spoke to me, a week or so ago, he expressed a wish that I should recommend a training college for you. He seemed to think that your future, like that of Mary Grace, lay in teaching."

"Teaching!" Kit reddened with anger. "No, thank you, Mother. Me, teach? I'd rather die. Teaching is for nuns and …"

And then she remembered me and was silent. Neither she or I spoke again until Mother Bernard dismissed us and we were on our way across the playground.

"Nuns and what?" I asked. "Goody-goodies? Nobodies? Drudges?" I was walking so fast in my anger that Kit's shorter legs had to quicken to keep up with me.

"I didn't mean it like that. You'd be a wonderful teacher. You will be a wonderful teacher. You're so calm – and organised. But me! I don't even like children. Daddy's got some silly idea in his head, that's all. I'm sure I can make him see things my way."

"Perhaps you can. You've always been good at that."

Even as I said it, I realised I was being spiteful. But Kit had hurt me. By her contempt she had diminished my pleasure, my certainty about what I wanted to do.

"We'd better get back to class," Kit said. "Let's talk about this later."

But we did not.

The subject was not even mentioned again until two days later, when Kit came to school late, with a sullen face and hooded eyes. She seemed shrunken somehow, and it was all I could do not to question her until we were safely on our way home.

"What's happened?"

Kit turned to look at me. Her face was suddenly plain, the skin tight above her short straight nose, her mouth thin.

"Mother Bernard was right. He doesn't want me to be a doctor. He says it's not a job for a lady. But I'm not a lady: I'm me, Kit Morrissey. And there have been women doctors for years! Just think how hard they fought, and now Doctor Alan God Almighty Morrissey says that the job he's done all his life isn't suitable for his daughter. It's not fair." Her voice failed and she mumbled the last few words. "I just don't understand."

I did not understand either. Medicine was an honourable profession, surely. I had no idea how to help her, though I did not, on this occasion, remind Kit of the consequences of taking the Lord's name in vain. I tried, instead, to show my support for her.

"Couldn't you just defy him and do it anyway?"

"Where would I get the money? He's absolutely refusing to pay for me to go to university. But I'll not go to training college. I'll leave home first. Or get married," Kit said suddenly. It was as if the idea of marriage had only just occurred to her. "Yes. He'd probably like that."

"You can't get married," I protested. "You need someone to marry first, and you don't know any young men. Neither of us do."

"Yes, we do," Kit said. "And I know one who might just have me. What about Vinnie, Grace? How would you like me for a sister-in-law?"

I knew I would not like it at all. I did not have to think about it: I knew. Vinnie and Kit were the two most important people in my world; the idea that they might form a pair, a unit that excluded me, was unbearable.

"Vinnie would make an awful husband," I said swiftly. "He's

always saying he doesn't want to get married. And he'll be away at sea all the time once he gets another ship. You'd hardly see him."

"Maybe that wouldn't be such a bad thing," Kit said, considering. "I'd be a married woman and free to do what I liked, and I wouldn't have a husband to worry about. The best of both worlds. Oh, we could have such fun, Grace."

"I don't want to have fun." I sounded sullen, even to myself, but I could not seem to change the tone of my voice. "I just want to get on with my training and start work in a school. That's all. Teaching wouldn't be so bad, Kit. Not if we worked together."

Kit was not listening. She had moved on.

"You mustn't warn Vinnie," she said. "I shall need to work on him, catch him unprepared. I'll need to work on my parents too. But that's it. That's the answer. I mean to be married by the time that I'm eighteen."

"You don't want to marry Vinnie," I said desperately. "There must be dozens of other boys you might like. Boys who are far more suitable. Boys your family would approve of."

"You were the one who said we didn't know any young men," Kit pointed out. "I think it's a wonderful idea. You'll come around to it in the end, you'll see."

"What about Vinnie? Will he come around?"

"Leave Vinnie to me."

I could think of nothing I wanted to do less. Surely Kit could not just decide, on a whim, that she wanted to marry my brother? My favourite brother. It was unthinkable. But I knew Kit. She might not be able to persuade her father to let her study medicine, but I had little doubt she could do anything else she set out to do. If she had decided that Vinnie was what she wanted, there would be little either he or I could do about it.

*

Secretly I enjoyed examinations. I could not admit it, of course; it was bad enough that Kit and I were Mother Bernard's "cleverest girls" without me making things worse. But I loved the whole process of revision and, in particular, the charts I made showing what I would revise when, with their neat underlining and colour coding. I could happily spend an entire evening deciding what revision to do, even if some subjects would receive a scant hour of study. Once the chats were complete, I would be ready to make a start. Days would go by in which I was completely unaware of the outside world. I was working alone this time. In the past Kit and I had studied together before end of term examinations, sharing books and notes, hearing each other answer questions, deciding on headings. But since Kit's quarrel with her father, she had been behaving strangely. Sometimes she claimed that she would not even bother to turn up for the examinations; what was the point, after all, in achieving qualifications that she could not use? So I made my own revision schedule and hid myself away in the front room to go through my notes. My exercise books and textbooks covered the green chenille tablecloth; my fingers flicked from the sharp edges of paper to the soft warmth of the chenille. Even without Kit, I was happy.

When at last I arrived outside the examination room for my first paper, I was relieved to see that Kit was already there. I made my way through the crowd of girls towards her. She was leaning against the door frame, studying her nails, while all around her our classmates frantically scanned their notes.

"Thought I might as well turn up," Kit said. "Nothing else

important to do today."

I smiled nervously. I did not know how to react to this new, nonchalant Kit, but luckily there was only a little time to wait before the doors swung open and we were allowed to enter in silence to find our desks. My desk was the first of all, at the front, in the left-hand corner. There was no Sheil Aherne, no Margaret Brady to precede me now, since they had left at the end of fifth year, but Eileen Colhoun was there on my right, just as she had been in my first year at the convent. Kit was somewhere behind. Just as well, I thought. If I could see her, I might waste time wondering how she was getting on.

Sister Scholastica, the nun with the frightening name and the fascinating history, stood at the front of the hall ready to invigilate. She was the only nun the girls in my year gossiped about – with the exception of Sister Clement, who was young, possibly pretty, and rumoured to flirt with the milkman. But Sister Scholastica had once been Eleanor Beaumont, dressmaker to the old Queen. I was not sure who the old Queen was, the King's wife or his mother. Both seemed old to me. In any case, I did not see why anyone should look on a dressmaker as something special, even if the clothes were made for royalty. (And since I was my father's daughter, royalty meant little to me.) After all, I was a dressmaker of sorts myself. And if I could do it, it was nothing special. But I was impressed by Sister Scholastica's upright posture and cultured voice, by the way she looked slightly down her nose at us – she was a tall woman – and by the calm folding of her long white hands.

"You may turn your papers over."

The pale octavo leaflet lay upside down on the desk in front of me, only the printers' name visible in tiny letters on the back. I picked it up and opened it out. There were twenty questions on this British

History paper, and I had to answer four of them. I settled myself to read.

To my right Eileen Colhoun was already scribbling. She had taken no time to examine the paper, choose her questions carefully, make up her mind as to the order in which she would answer them. We had two and a half hours for this examination. I knew I could afford to spend ten minutes planning what I was going to do. That left me thirty-five minutes for each question. Time enough.

Elsewhere in the hall pens scratched. I wrote my name on one of the sheets of creamy foolscap while I was deciding my plan of action. Four questions to do, and eighteen of the twenty I felt confident I could answer. I had almost too much choice. I spent some time looking for the ones that would not distract me by leading me into the little dramas and asides that were for me the heart of history, the stories that would not let me go. Lord Melbourne, standing with his back against the Cabinet Room door, telling his colleagues that it did not matter what they said, so long as they all said the same thing. Castlereagh. I could have written a biography of Castlereagh and filled it with quotations:

"I met Murder on the way. He had a mask like Castlereagh."

"Die, my dear doctor? That's the last thing I shall do."

I looked at the clock above the blackboard and realised with a start that I had wasted my planning time. Nothing for it now, but to start writing. Some of the others were already on their second sheet. Facts, I said to myself. Stick to the facts.

The Chartists first. Daddy had approved of them, even if they were English, but I had no time to think about my father. Then the Luddites, uselessly flailing against the future, not knowing the century had left them behind. I had never had any sympathy for them, and I saw them off crisply and conclusively. Next the Factory Acts, and three of my four questions were done. I had forty minutes left. It was time to make my final choice.

The word "Irish" almost threw me. There was such a temptation to answer the question about events in Ireland, that I had real difficulty in resisting it. The great names came rolling back: Daniel O'Connell, whom even my mother admired, and the other two, my father's heroes, Robert Emmett and Wolf Tone, whose names Mammy would not have spoken in the house. But another voice, a voice of caution, Sister Anthony's voice, was ringing in my head. "The English do not understand Irish history," I heard the nun say. "And remember, girls, it will be an Englishman marking your paper. If you want to pass, avoid the Irish question. It may seem like betrayal, but it's only common sense."

Common sense prevailed. I located a question on the extension of male suffrage near the top of the examination paper. I would have no trouble with that one: rotten boroughs, Dunwich, the property qualification. I began to write.

I hated it later when we gathered outside the examination room and everyone told everyone else how badly she had done, what a mess she had made of the paper. I knew I had not made a mess of the paper; I was not going to lie, but neither did I want to draw attention to myself. I kept quiet until someone asked me a direct question, when I mumbled something about not having done too badly. Kit, on the other hand, was magnificent.

"Superbly well, thank you," she said when asked how she thought she had done. "As usual, I shall stun the examiners with my erudition and fluent command of the English language. I expect I shall pass *summa cum laude*."

Because it was Kit, no one commented. They probably believed her. Together we walked away from the crowd.

"I'm glad you did well," I said.

"Not that well," Kit replied. "I shall have passed of course, but it may be a near thing. How about you?"

"Oh, I think I passed. At least I avoided the Irish question."

The two of us laughed softly together as we turned out of the school gates on to Anlaby Road. It felt strange to be going home in the middle of the day, strange and grown-up and exciting.

"You know," Kit said. "I like exams."

"So do I," I agreed. "So do I."

5

1930-1933

I met Xavier Quinn for the first time on the afternoon of Saturday 26th April 1930, two days after Amy Johnson had set Hull alight by landing in Australia. Amy Johnson is not the reason I remember the date. I remember it because it was the date of the Brennan double wedding. Declan and Josie had been beaten to the altar. My two oldest brothers, Pat and Mick, were marrying the Rafferty sisters, Teresa and Maureen. Secretly, I could see no reason why it should be Pat and Teresa, Mick and Maureen, rather than Pat and Maureen, Teresa and Mick. With such a tight foursome it could have gone either way. They were going to share a house, with Pat and Teresa upstairs and Mick and Maureen downstairs. It was a large house and they were lucky to get it, but it was not what I would have wanted. Still, the Raffertys had money, which was why the reception was being held in Hammond's Ballroom, rather than in St Patrick's Parish Hall. The shine and polish of the furniture were rivalled by the dancefloor; the dark, velvet curtains made richer by the whiteness of tablecloths and napkins. It was not Brennan home territory, Hammond's, but it was a fitting setting for the brides and grooms that Saturday. Identical, narrow white dresses and lace veils. Almost identical Irish faces beneath the veils, fair skin, freckles, and blue-green eyes. At their sides my brothers, big and dark as Daddy had been, handsome as Mammy still was.

I stood back from what I saw, admiring the picture, watching the reddening faces, listening to the rising laughter. Then there was a swirl of skirts on the dancefloor, as the two newly married couples led the first waltz. It all seemed far away to me, but perhaps that was because Vinnie was not there. His ship had been expected to dock that morning, but he had not made it to the church. And was that perhaps intentional? I knew, or at least I hoped I knew, what Vinnie thought about weddings.

Then there was a shift in the crowd, and I could see the stairs that led up from the ground floor. Someone was coming up them; it was Vinnie and someone else. I did not recognise the other man, but ran to meet Vinnie, with no eyes for anyone else. It was strange because, when I did look at his companion, I realised I had known him all my life, though I had never seen him before that day.

"Xavier Quinn. My sister, Mary Grace. Though she prefers to be known as Grace."

The eyes met mine. The lips smiled. I could not have begun to describe them. To describe him.

"Mary Grace. Ave, Maria, Gratia Plena," and he bent over my hand and his lips just touched my knuckles and I was rigid with fear and happiness and never mind if what he said was blasphemous. It is as it has to be, I thought; this is what happens when you fall in love; this is what I have been waiting for; love at first sight; how could I have doubted it?

"Do you dance?" said Xavier Quinn.

"Oh no. Well I do, sometimes, but not now ... I couldn't."

I knew I sounded foolish, but I could not help it. The idea of being touched by this man was too overwhelming. Vinnie laughed at me, but I turned away just in time to see Xavier Quinn whirl Josefina on to the floor. He led her expertly among the more inhibited couples, while Declan looked on approvingly. I was furious with myself for allowing Xavier to escape, furious with Vinnie for doing nothing to help me. I could feel my face setting into its most unbecoming expression, lips pursed and pouting in what Daddy used to call my "little trunkeen". I made an effort and stretched the corners of my mouth into a smile so broad it hurt. I lifted my head and opened my eyes wide. That was a mistake: tears of anger and frustration spilled over, and I blinked rapidly, not daring to wipe them away.

"My little sister struck dumb," Vinnie said. "Never thought I'd live to see this day. Well, if you'll not dance with Xavier Quinn, will you dance with me?"

I struggled with a desire to slap him. I could not dance. Vinnie knew I could not dance. But at least, if I were on the floor with Vinnie, no one else would see my tear-stained face.

"All right."

Vinnie was more devious that I had realised. We circled the floor once, and then, with a sudden unexpected change of direction, he swung me into Xavier Quinn's path, claiming Josie as his new partner and delivering me, stiff with disbelief, into Xavier's arms.

"So Vinnie changed your mind?"

Was it possible to feel any more stupid than I did just then? I doubted it. I concentrated on the steps and did not answer his question. What a child he must have thought me! But he did not seem to notice that I had not answered him. He was telling me a story about why he and Vinnie had missed the wedding ceremony. It sounded unlikely, and I was certain he had not been invited anyway, but I was fascinated by his voice, which was warm, like his hair. For I noticed his hair now, red-gold and curling and flopping over his left eye in a way he surely encouraged, if he did not contrive it. I still did not dare to look at his face, not from so close. It would have seemed an intrusion. Then the music came to an end. He walked me back to the table where I had been sitting. I slumped gratefully into a chair, then pulled myself upright because my partner had sat down beside me and was looking at me in amusement.

"That wasn't so bad now, was it?" asked Xavier Quinn.

Days later, I was sorting through the boxes in which I kept the photographs Vinnie had sent me since he joined the Merchant Navy. I looked again at the names scribbled on the back, ships' names, s/s "Araguaya", s/s "Darro", s/s "Descado", s/s "Nogoya", s/s "Somme". And the places: Livepool, Zulu Reserve (Natal), Valley of a Thousand Hills, Table Mountain, Miami Beach, Durban, Port-au-Prince (Haiti), Kingston (Jamaica). All the places were labelled, but not the people. They were people I would never know; perhaps Vinnie had known them so well, he had not felt the need to name them.

Near the end I found two photographs of Xavier Quinn, one on his own, one with Vinnie, both taken on rowing boats and obviously on the same day. It was the one with Vinnie that caught my eye. It was off-centre, not out of focus, but as if the photographer on the riverbank had had trouble keeping his footing. Or perhaps it was not a riverbank. Maybe it was the side of a lake or canal. The two men were so large in the frame that the tops of their heads had disappeared. All I could see behind their shoulders was water, or perhaps trees. Vinnie was on the left, his head turned over his right shoulder, looking away from the camera. A wave of dark hair fell over his forehead. He was frowning with effort. I could see from the muscles of his upper arms that he was pulling hard. Beside him, Xavier leant forward, smiling into the camera, both hands with their long bony fingers gripping the oar. But I could tell there was no commitment in it. He was shirking his share of the work. His eyes and teeth were smiling. I could just see the faint outline of his Adam's apple above the strong sinews of his neck, the hollow at the top of his breastbone. Both he and Vinnie were wearing black one-piece woollen costumes, which just covered the tops of their thighs. They looked young and healthy and vital and, in Vinnie's case, angry.

I had seen the photograph before, but until now had seen only Vinnie. I reached for the second photograph, the one in which Xavier was in the rowing boat on his own. I must have passed it over when it arrived. But then, I told myself, there was no reason why I should have taken an interest in someone I'd never met. Many of Vinnie's photographs showed him with people I did not know, but here was Xavier Quinn on his own. And now I had met him, I could not imagine ever passing him over. He was laughing in this photograph, not just smiling. His eyes – what colour were they? They were staring directly at me. They were laughing too. I had seen that look at the wedding. Could he really always be laughing like that? It seemed possible then.

The next photograph was of Declan fishing, half concealed in the reeds at the side of a canal. There was a bridge in the background. It looked familiar, which did not surprise me: Declan had never, to my knowledge, been any further than Leeds. Vinnie was the traveller in the Brennan family, and how I wished I could go with him. And with Xavier Quinn.

The next time Vinnie and Xavier came home from sea, Mammy offered to let Xavier stay at Hopwood Street.

"There's no point in your man going off to the Seamen's Mission when there's beds empty here."

There were beds empty, now that Pat and Mick and their wives had their own house, and now that Sean was living with our aunt and uncle in the flat above Brennan's Corner Stores in Withernsea. I had already moved into the four-foot bed Pat and Mick used to share, in the little bedroom that looked out over the back yard. Declan had abandoned his single bed for Vinnie and Sean's double, while Vinnie now had the single. While they were at home, Mammy said, Vinnie could share with his brother, and Xavier could have the bed under the window that was formerly Declan's. It was a satisfactory arrangement all round, unless you happened to be me.

The first night Vinnie and Xavier stayed in Hopwood Street, I could not sleep. I was too busy worrying about what I would do in the morning. Because of course I could not go down to the bathroom in my nightdress and dressing-gown, not when the door opposite mine might open at any minute to disclose Xavier Quinn. I ended up rising very early, before Mammy even, but still did not risk going downstairs until I was fully dressed. So, I put on my underwear and my stockings, and over them the high-necked blouse and long dark skirt I wore to Endsleigh Training College. I even put on my shoes. Then I opened the door of my room as quietly as I could, inched my way down the stairs with one hand on the rail to make sure I did not miss my footing, and fled through the scullery and into the bathroom under the stairs. For a moment I looked at the bathroom through Xavier Quinn's eyes, noticing how worn the towels and rag rug were, how shabby my toothbrush with its limp and tired bristles.

I put my blouse back on, with some difficulty (because I had skimped on the drying, and my hands were still damp), unhooked the waistband of my skirt and smoothed down the tails of my blouse so that it lay neatly. I looked at myself in the foxed mirror over the washbasin. Lack of sleep had left me drained of colour; my heavy hair hung over one eye. I noticed my parting, which was as crooked "as a dog's hind leg" (Mammy's words) and attacked it irritably with my mother's comb, which was on the windowsill.

I was in despair. How could I face Xavier Quinn at that time in the morning? Once he saw me over the breakfast table, that would be it. He would never want to look at me again.

"Are you going to be in there all day?" Mammy's impatient voice sounded outside that bathroom door. Hastily I put down the comb, ran the forgotten scummy water out of the basin and rinsed it. Then I slipped my thumb into the catch on the door and slid it back. Mammy was waiting outside.

"Sorry, Mammy."

"And what got you up so early?" Mammy asked. I blushed.

"I thought I'd get out of the bathroom before the boys needed it."

"Those two boys will not be out of their beds for hours yet. And why should they be? They work hard enough; they deserve a bit of rest."

There was no sign of Vinnie and Xavier as I glanced at the clock and realised I would have to go now, or I'd be late for college. Now that I was at Endsleigh, I walked there along Beverley Road, except when it was raining. It was a fairly long walk; the temptation to catch a trolleybus was often strong, but so far I had managed to resist it.

Halfway along Hopwood Street, I turned back to wave good-bye to my mother, who was watching, as she always did, from the front room window. She went in there every morning to clean through, whether the room had been used or not. Mammy was not obsessed with housework, not the way some women at St Patrick's were, but she was always working. More so now, I realised, since Daddy's death.

My day at college passed slowly. Lectures, seminars, two lessons in the demonstration school: it was easy enough to deal with, though my mind was not entirely on my work. Were Vinnie and Xavier up yet? I wondered at half past nine. How would they spend their day? I imagined them walking down to the docks or to Victoria Pier, stopping to make fun of King Billy on his horse, buying chestnuts in the marketplace from Josie's grandmother, or ice cream from Massarelli's Parlour. It seemed a leisured, self-indulgent sort of day, an enviable way to pass a few hours. Normally I loved the college, the smell of polish, the high leaded windows of the 'Dem School', the well-behaved children, who sat in rows and gazed at me wide-eyed. I loved to hear them address me as Miss Brennan, to see them shoot up their hands in answer to my questions. But that day, the work was just something to be got through, a stretch of tedium before I could get back to my real life.

It was the first time I had felt like that. I was shocked by the conviction that where I was and what I was doing were irrelevant, that my real life was elsewhere, walking down Whitefri'gate or the Land of Green Ginger, laughing with my favourite brother. It reminded me in some ways of the time when I had first found Kit as a friend, but then again, it was nothing like that. I did not even know why I had made that connection. I hurried back along Beverley Road to the house where Xavier Quinn was waiting for me.

But he was not waiting for me: he was far too busy charming Mammy to notice me when I smiled tentatively at him. Oh, he acknowledged me, smiled back even, but it was Mammy he was concentrating on.

"And where do you usually spend your time when you are between ships, Mr Quinn?"

"Xavier. Call me Xavier," he protested, as I had heard him do every time he was addressed more formally. "Here and there, Mrs Brennan. Here and there: Belfast, Southampton, Liverpool. All the big ports. Anywhere I can pick up another ship."

"You don't have a family to go to?" Mammy asked.

"Alas, I am alone in the world." He smiled, the long mobile lips curling upwards. "But you don't want to hear about me, Mrs Brennan. Tell me about yourself. Where did you get that wonderful red hair?"

I watched in disbelief as my mother smoothed back the lock of her hair that always escaped from her old-fashioned bun to fall over her right eye. I had never seen Mammy so disarmed, so excited by anyone. I understood the feeling, of course I did, since it was what I was feeling too. But Mammy was so old. Over forty. What was she doing talking to Xavier Quinn when I was there waiting?

"From my mother's side of the family. I was a Fahy before I was married, and my mother was an O'Driscoll."

"Two good Irish names," Xavier said. "Were you born in Ireland?"

"No, but my mother was. She came over as a babe in arms, during the Famine."

I began to set the table for tea. I had heard all this before many times, and although I was usually interested in the story of how young Nancy O'Driscoll came to live in West Street, next door but one to young John Brennan, whose son would marry her daughter, I could not see what it had to do with Xavier Quinn. I could feel myself pouting. I was setting out the knives and forks on the table with altogether too much force, but no one noticed. They were all paying attention to the newcomer, who was paying me no attention at all.

I am envious of my mother, I realised. The idea was ridiculous. Slowly my lips relaxed. I took and deep breath and began to smile.

"That's more like it," said Xavier Quinn, who must have been watching me all the time.

*

Friday evening. Six o'clock. I lay gloomily in three inches of lukewarm bathwater, refusing to think about the night ahead. When I lifted my right arm to soap it, my fingers knocked against the sloping ceiling of the bathroom under the stairs. If I were to sit up, I should have to protect not only the top of my head, but also my left cheek, dangerously close to the handle of the three-legged posser. It leant at an angle in the dolly-tub next to the bath because there was no room to stand it upright in the cramped space.

In an attempt to cheer myself up, I began to list all the things I could do well, a ritual I went through whenever I was feeling depressed. I liked lists. They satisfied me and made me feel I was in control. I began with the things I had been sure of for years: reading and writing; spelling and mathematics. In my last year at the convent I had won the prize for religious knowledge, and I could follow and understand – and even enjoy – the Latin of the Mass. I was the only one in the family who could speak confidently on a telephone, and I knew how to send a telegram, though I had never had to do it. Because I was Mammy's daughter, I was a more than competent needlewoman who could hem and quilt and darn and faggot and smock. I could look after children and keep them amused; at the 'Dem School' I had also learned to control and teach them. Since meeting Kit, I had learned how to be a good friend. That was a fairly good total, I thought. And then there were the things I could do at least adequately: cook, paint a room, ride a bicycle, knit without dropping stitches, sketch, play the piano, read music.

I examined the tips of my fingers, which had begun to pucker. I had been in the bath too long. But, no matter how hard I tried, I was unable to stop a third list from forming in my head: the list of things I could not do. I could not meet someone new without blushing. I could not dance. I was not witty. I could not tell jokes. I had never been able to bring myself to give my hair a permanent wave, and I hated buying clothes. I did not know how to mend a puncture. I had never been able to skip. I could not play Whist or any other card game except the ones I had learned as a child, because I could not remember the rules.

So why, I asked myself, as I began to rub dry my arms on the threadbare towel, why had I agreed to accompany Xavier Quinn to St Patrick's Hall for a Whist Drive and Dance?

6

"Anyone can play Whist," said Xavier. "Anyone can dance. Come here till I show you." He caught me by the wrist and pulled me from my chair by the range, where I had been sitting with Mammy, the two of us pegging opposite ends of a rug. Now I found myself sitting across the table from Xavier, too startled to protest, as he called out to my brothers: "Declan! Vinnie! Come and take a hand at Whist, will you? This girl's in urgent need of a lesson. Mrs Brennan," and now the smile and the charm were directed at Mammy, "Have you a pack of cards handy, by any chance?"

There was no need for Mammy to move from her seat. She bent to her left and opened the door of the boot cupboard beside the range. Out came the stained leather card case, its original pale pigskin darkened by years of use. I knew every inch of it with the tips of my fingers, from the indentations that traced out the shapes of the Jack of Diamonds, the Queen of Hearts, and the Ace of Spades, to the wrinkled straps, which still snapped satisfactorily open when Xavier pushed his thumbs beneath them. The two packs of cards were there as they always were, the blue and red backs, the blue with its easily identifiable Seven of Clubs, the corner bent where Vinnie once pushed it under the mat in temper. It was always the blue pack we used for Snap, Beggar My Neighbour, and Clock Patience, though I do not remember why.

Xavier eased the red pack out of its holder, ran the cards through his fingers, spread them on the table in a perfect fan, picked them up, and shuffled them with gusto. Showing off, I thought, and was not displeased.

"These have been well used." I was not sure whether the note in his voice was one of approval or displeasure. I did not have time to consider it further, because he was off again, dealing and talking like a professional card player. "Watch my hands. Now. Pick up your cards. Make a fan. Yes, you can, Grace. Thirteen cards are nothing. You can span an octave, can't you? Well then. Good. Hearts are trumps. Because I say so. For the purposes of this demonstration. Don't quibble, Vinnie. It's your lead."

Vinnie threw down a card. It was my turn. I stared at it, uncertain what to do. The fan of cards drooped in my hand.

"Keep your cards up. Don't worry about it. Just follow suit. No, you can't trump it, not if you've got a Spade. Well of course I knew you had one. I dealt the cards, didn't I?"

Something was not quite right, though I hesitated to call it cheating. I watched the cards fall, threw down the first one that caught my eye, occasionally won a trick without understanding how it had happened. Declan and Vinnie became bored, started to talk, paid no attention to what they were doing. I was amazed and dismayed to see Xavier suddenly furious, the muscles in his cheeks tightening, the skin round his mouth growing whiter and whiter. I had never seen him angry before, and this seemed such a trivial occasion for anger. After all, what did cards matter?

After twenty minutes he threw down his hand, sucked in his

cheeks, relaxed his face, smiled.

"Enough of that. You'll do, Miss Brennan. You won't disgrace me entirely. Now as to the dancing …"

Vinnie fetched the wind-up gramophone and the small box of needles. He and Declan bickered over which record to play.

"A waltz will be fine," Xavier told them. "Have you 'The Blue Danube' at all?" They had, and Declan wound up the gramophone with enthusiasm, Vinnie warning him not to overdo it, he'd strain the mechanism.

"Listen to the engineer talking," Declan said, and he let the arm fall carelessly onto the record, so that for a few moments all we heard was the hiss and scuff of the needle on the edge before it reached the groove. But soon we were off: Xavier grabbed my right hand in his own, while I rested my left on the crook of his elbow, and he started to propel me round the room. Vinnie pushed the table back, Mammy rolled up the rug she was working on. And to begin with, it was bearable. I could do it, if I concentrated, one two three, one two three, and turn and step, and now I was on Xavier's toes, the whole weight of me, and I stumbled back, apologising.

"Never mind it," he said, and swung me away again, but I had lost the rhythm, could not remember which was my left foot and which my right, and my hand in Xavier's was sweating wet. It did not help that Vinnie had taken Declan in his arms, and the two of them were solemnly circling the room, perfectly in step, making ridiculous small talk, Declan simpering, looking up under his eyelashes at his taller brother. I stopped, broke away.

"I can't," I said, afraid that I would cry with frustration as the words forced themselves past the obstacle in my throat. Xavier turned to my mother with a flourish.

"Mrs Brennan, would you do me the honour?"

Mammy rose, walked into his hold, back straight, shoulders relaxed, slim as I had never been slim, confident as I had never been confident. All I wanted to do was run and hide, leave the room, and escape from this humiliation before I screamed with rage and despair.

The music slowed. Declan stopped dancing, moved to wind up the gramophone again, but Xavier stopped him.

"You'll be fine," he said to me over his shoulder as he handed Mammy back to her chair. "Don't worry about it. You'll have a wonderful evening. The Belle of the Ball, isn't that right, Vinnie?"

Vinnie hesitated, and it was difficult for him; I could see that. We knew each other too well for him to lie, even to make me feel better. It would not have made me feel better anyway, because I would have known he was lying. I always knew when Vinnie lied.

"It'll all come out in the wash," Vinnie said, and he rubbed the end of his nose with the back of his hand. "Is there any tea in the pot, Mammy?"

"There soon will be." Mammy nodded, and the awkwardness was passed over and forgotten, though not by me.

"I'll see to it," I said. "You sit down, Mammy." And, by the time the tea was ready and poured, my embarrassed flush had receded, and I could sit down with the others and talk. Because talking was the one thing I was increasingly good at since I'd started at training college, even if I could not play Whist. Or dance.

What had begun as an excursion for Xavier and me alone had developed into an outing for the whole family. As we made our way down Hopwood Street to St Patrick's Parish Hall, I found myself walking in the gutter. True, I was arm in arm with Xavier, but then so was Mammy, and it was Mammy who had favoured the inside position. I could find no footing on the narrow pavement. The rest of the family followed behind: Pat and Teresa, Mick and Maureen, Decan and Josie, and, finally, Vinnie and Kit.

Vinnie and Kit. It was Kit's fault they were all here to witness my misery. If she had not made such a fuss about it, about the need for a new frock, if she had not walked me half around the city centre to find it, no one would have noticed. That is what I told myself. I had not forgiven Kit for wanting me to look at the dresses in Hammond's. Hammond's! I would not have dared speak to one of the shop assistants, let alone try anything on. It was bad enough being pulled into Edwin Davis's and made to buy something that was twice as much as I had intended to pay, when really all I had wanted to do was find a new blouse to go with my old skirt. I did not like the dress Kit had chosen for me: it was new and stiff and attracted far too much attention. Kit would not let me save it for the dance; I had to try it on and show it to the whole family the day we bought it, and somehow I could not work out how, exactly, the whole family had ended up being invited to St Patrick's Flannel Dance.

The wind was cold. When we arrived at the hall, I wanted to keep my coat on, but it was whisked away from me. Xavier placed one hand on the small of my back and steered me in ahead of him. The hall was set out for Whist, forty tables arranged around the room. A few were still empty. We Brennans almost filled three amongst us. At least that had one advantage: when I moved on I was still with people I knew, and Xavier was still my partner. I was not sure how this had happened. One of the few things I knew about Whist Drives was that you were supposed to change partners at the end of each hand, but Xavier paid no attention to that convention. Nor did the rest of the family, who cheered him on as he rescued me yet again from my wild, distracted play and won the trick. It did not take me long to realise that he was cheating again, and that, if I had seen it, then surely others must have done so too. But again no one seemed to care. It was Xavier, after all. The Brennans did not judge him by their usual standards.

Things changed when we were finally separated from the family. Hard eyes watched Xavier's hands as he dealt; there was no scope for creative shuffling here. We lost a trick, and then a hand, and Mrs Rourke from St Wilfrid's had no intention of allowing Xavier to ignore the rules. So it was that I found myself cast out among strangers, my play deteriorating all the time, until in the end I could only blush and stammer and drop my cards, and, eventually, excuse myself and hide in the cloakroom.

It was fortunate that the Whist did not last much longer. The tables were cleared away, and Xavier sent Kit in search of me. She found me huddling against the cloakroom wall, biting my balled-up handkerchief and then rubbing my eyes with it.

"Now, what's the matter?" Kit said. "Pull yourself together. I could be dancing with Vinnie, not wasting my time in here."

"Why aren't you, then?" I asked crossly. "I didn't ask you to come for me."

"No, but Xavier did. He wants you to dance with him. Heaven knows why – I've never met someone so feeble."

Kit's rudeness, calculated perhaps, was enough to propel me back into the hall. I was reassured when Xavier came to greet me, but as the band took their places, I froze again.

"The Syncopations? That's a jazz band, isn't it?"

"Right first time," said Xavier. Catching my hand, he began to twirl me back and forth.

"Stop it! I can't – I won't – no, Xavier. I mean it. I don't mind trying a waltz – well, I do mind, but I'll try anyway – but not this. You'll have to find someone else to dance with."

And he did. He bowed, mockingly, and then was off in search of another partner. Mammy first, keeping up the show of manners he had put on since he first met her. I chewed my nails and tried not to look. The he took a brief turn with Kit, the pair of them stylish but distant, neither of them much impressed by the other, as far as I could see. Then it was on to Teresa and Maureen, and finally Josie. I watched Declan's eyes follow them as they whirled past. I could see for myself that Xavier danced better with Josie than with anyone else. It was something to do with the way their bodies dipped and flowed towards each other. It made me uneasy, and I was glad when Declan cut in and took Josie off to the other side of the hall. After a moment, Xavier sat down by my side. There was a faint flush along his cheekbones, and he was breathing deeply and fast with the enjoyment of the dance.

"Come on now, Grace," he said. "Let's show them, shall we?"

"I don't like dancing," I muttered. "I can't dance," and then to my horror I was crying. He pulled me to my feet and drew me into his arms, so that my face was pressed up against his shirtfront, and all I could think of was that my nose was running. I sniffed hard, and suddenly the band struck up a waltz – could it be the last waltz? I prayed it was. And Xavier moved me gently round the floor, so calm and steady I could not protest any more.

"Don't enjoy it then," he said. "But it's time you learned. After all, how could I consider marrying a girl who can't dance?"

"Well?" Kit said. "Aren't you going to tell me what happened?"

I did not raise my eyes from the bed sheet I was turning side to middle. My foot kept up a steady rhythm on the treadle of the old Singer. My hands eased the material beneath the needle.

"He wants to marry me."

"What? Grace Brennan, are you telling me that Quinn has asked you to marry him?"

I did not like the way Kit said it, the mocking tone in her voice, but I had to tell someone.

"He said I had to learn to dance. Because how could he consider marrying a girl who doesn't dance? Actually, he didn't ask me as such. He just said he was considering it."

"Thank God for that," Kit said. "Why would you want to get married? Haven't you got your career mapped out? And don't say anything about me and Vinnie. That's something else entirely."

"I think he will ask me though," I said, resolutely ignoring the reference to Vinnie. "If not now, maybe next year." I came to the end of my seam, swivelled the sheet round to overlock the stitching. Kit leaned forward in her chair.

"Then you must say no. You can't marry him, Grace. I won't permit it. He's a – a chancer."

It was not a word either of us normally used, but as soon as Kit said it, I knew it was the right word for Xavier. That was exactly what he was: a chancer. What I could not explain to Kit, who was something of a chancer herself, was that that was part of the attraction for me, the sense of something dangerous beneath the charm. I cut the thread, slid the finished linen from beneath the presser foot and stood to fold the sheet.

"He's very good looking," I said, hating myself because I sounded so apologetic.

"Good looking?" Kit laughed. "The man has red hair."

"He's Vinnie's friend. Vinnie wouldn't take up with a chancer."

"Where is Vinnie, anyway? I wanted to see him. That's why I came round."

Hurt, I was brusque:

"You're too late. He and Xavier are off to Paragon Station to catch the three o'clock train to Liverpool. They're picking up a new ship tomorrow."

"Three o'clock? It's only just half past two. Come on, we've just got time."

"Time for what?"

"Just get your coat."

We raced along Spring Bank and into Prospect Street, for once passing Thornton Varley's without stopping to look in the windows, then we turned right into Brook Street just before Hull Infirmary and ran into the station through the Paragon Square entrance opposite the war memorial. The clock above the entrance showed ten to three. It did not take us long to find the platform for the Liverpool train, but locating Vinnie and Xavier was less straight forward. I took two pennies from my purse and bought platform tickets, and then we were running the length of the train, looking for any sign of Vincent Brennan and Xavier Quinn. We had almost reached the end of the platform before we found them, but suddenly there they were, in the front carriage, leaning out of the open window, Xavier's red-gold hair vivid in the greenish air below the cast iron roof. Kit forced her way past him and onto the train. Already she was whispering to Vinnie while I stood on the platform afraid to board in case the train drew away with me still on it. Xavier stepped down to stand beside me.

"No, you mustn't. What if it went without you?"

"I've an eye open for the guard," Xavier reassured me, and then, "I hadn't thought to have the pleasure of your company to see me off."

"Oh, it wasn't my idea," I said before I realised how rude it must sound. "That is, Kit wanted to see Vinnie, and I thought it would be nice to see you, so I came along."

"I'm flattered."

Was he making fun of me? Along the train the doors were shutting; I could just see the guard with the green flag in his hand. Kit and Xavier changed places, the whistle blew, and suddenly steam rose up in a cloud as the pistons began to move and the Liverpool train pulled out of the station.

"Was it worth the hurry?" I asked.

Unexpectedly, Kit hugged me.

"It most certainly was. Just you wait and see!"

Kit wanted to go into the ladies' waiting room to adjust her hat. We crossed the dowdy room grey with cigarette smoke and stood in front of the speckled mirror in the corridor outside the lavatories.

The corners of the frames enclosed advertisements for skin products and shampoo. I watched Kit as she unpinned her cloche hat with its upturned brim, smoothed her short dark hair, and replaced the hat even more jauntily than before. A further wait while she renewed her lipstick, and then we left the station through the side entrance, coming out onto Collier Street beside the canvas booth where you could buy the Hull Daily Mail and The Yorkshire Post, and passing placards announcing Ramsay MacDonald's new National Government, before we headed back to Hopwood Street and home.

These days the front room was just that, a place for piano practice and welcoming important visitors. So when Vinnie next came home from sea and wanted to talk to me in private, the front room was where we went.

"I want you to look at this," he said as he pulled something out of his pocket and handed it to me. A box. A small leather box with a slightly domed lid, four triangular feet and a tiny catch. "Go on. Open it."

I did not want to open that box. My fingers were clumsy as I depressed the catch, swung back the lid. For a moment I managed not to look at what was inside, focusing instead on the white satin lining with its fine black script. I read it aloud.

"Watchmakers and Jewellers. J. Hudson and Sons Limited. The Old Establishment. 95 South Main Street, Cork. And Tralee. Made in England."

"Not the box," Vinnie said impatiently. "The ring."

The ring. I could not avoid it any longer. A solitaire diamond in a delicate gold setting. It looked quite big to me, expensive, but I knew nothing about diamonds.

"What is it for?"

I knew I sounded off-hand and ungracious, but I could not help it. I did not want to hear what Vinnie was going to say.

"It's for Kit, of course. Do you like it? Try it on!"

It just fitted the little finger of my right hand. I pulled it off hastily, put it back in the little box.

"Very nice."

"Very nice? Is that all you can say? I thought you'd be pleased."

"Then you thought wrong."

Vinnie took the box back from me and put it in his pocket.

"I don't understand. I thought you knew that Kit and I planned to get engaged."

"I knew she'd planned it. I didn't think you'd be so spineless. I didn't think you'd marry her."

"Why shouldn't I marry her?"

No stopping now, I thought, but I did not look at him when I answered, busied myself with rubbing away at the little finger of my right hand with the thumb and forefinger of the left.

"Because you don't love her. Not that way."

"I don't love anyone else. That way. I never will. I'm – not made that way. You have to understand, Grace. A good Catholic boy like me needs to be married, unless he's destined for the priesthood. It's what everyone expects. I can't go on any longer the way I am now. And I like Kit. It could be worse."

I did not know what he meant by "the way I am now" and I did not want to understand. Whatever he was suggesting, it was something outside my experience, something I was sure I would be better off not knowing. I moved to the window and looked out into the street, which was empty.

"I don't want you to marry Kit."

"All right. Tell me why not."

The paint on the windowsill was worn and cracked. I worked my nail into a crack, nagging until a flake came away and lodged, green, on the ball of my thumb. What I wanted to say made me feel petty, self-centred. Did I have to say it? Yes, I decided, whatever it sounded like. I had to be truthful.

"You and Kit, you're the two most important people in my life. She's my best friend – no, let's be honest, my only friend outside the family. And you – we've always been closer than the others. The idea of the two of you together, and me left out … I don't want to come second," I finished, ashamed.

Vinnie did not answer me directly. He came and stood beside me, both of us looking out on the street we knew so well, side by side, not touching.

"How much do you know about Wordsworth?"

"William Wordsworth? The poet?"

"Yes."

"Enough," I said.

"What was his wife called?"

"His wife?"

"Yes," Vinnie said. "Don't keep repeating everything I say. Just tell me what Wordsworth's wife was called."

"I don't know."

"Mary. Mary Hutchinson. What about his sister?"

"Dorothy?"

"That's right. Now do you see? William and Mary, that means nothing, unless it's an English king and queen. But William and Dorothy … Everyone's heard of William and Dorothy."

I looked at him, confused but somehow happy. If I had understood what he was saying correctly, at least I would not come second with him.

"So it's to be William and Dorothy? Vinnie and Grace, not Vinnie and Kit?"

"Vinnie and Grace," he confirmed.

"Not," I paused, then said it anyway. "Not Grace and Xavier?"

"Dear God, not that!" His fingers closed about my wrist and he turned me to face him. "Not Grace and Xavier. Never that. I wouldn't wish that on either of you."

I did not know what he meant.

"I'm not serious," I said. "Just testing that's all."

Both of us knew that I was lying.

7

"Vinnie's asked me to marry him," Kit said.

"And?"

"And I said yes."

"Congratulations."

"You might try to sound pleased for me."

"I'm not. I'm not pleased for you, and I'm not pleased for Vinnie, and I'm certainly not pleased for me. I don't want you as a sister-in-law, Kit. I want you as a friend."

"Well, you'll be getting both. Do you like the ring?"

"Yes, it's lovely."

"Oh, for God's sake," said Kit. "Can't you show any enthusiasm?"

We were in Savile Street, outside Gough and Davy. I was on my way to Browns to buy books for my course. I had been looking forward to it. Kit and I had always liked Browns, ever since we had been sent there from the convent to choose our end-of-term prizes. But this talk of an engagement spoiled everything.

We crossed the road in silence. I was hovering between anger and guilt; perhaps Kit and Vinnie did love each other, perhaps their marriage would be successful, and I was just being sour about it all because it was almost a year since St Patrick's Flannel Dance, and Xavier had said nothing further about marrying me. He had not even kissed me properly – not that I was sure what "properly" meant, my experience did not extend that far. Yet the family album now included several photographs of us hand in hand, or lying, daringly embraced, arms about each other's waists, and gazing up at the camera from the lawn in front of Burton Constable Hall.

"We're going to tell your mother tonight."

"What about your mother? And your father? How do you think they'll take the announcement?"

"Doesn't matter," said Kit dreamily. "I've made up my mind. They'll come round eventually."

I remembered another occasion when the Morrisseys had not "come round". But then, perhaps marriage was not as important as Medicine? Or maybe, I thought, Doctor Morrissey will feel safer with Kit married off and answerable to someone else. "When do you think you'll get married?"

"As soon as we can arrange it. You'll be chief bridesmaid, of course."

That was typical of Kit, the way she assumed rather than asked. But much as I was against the marriage, I could not have borne it if I had been left out. I knew Kit was right; I would be a bridesmaid. I changed the subject.

"Is Vinnie going to get a shore job?"

"Heavens, no," Kit looked horrified. "I don't want him at home all the time. I shall be far too busy to bother with cooking and cleaning and all the other things that husbands expect."

"Then why are you marrying him?" It came out as a cry of despair, but Kit seemed to take no notice.

"So that I can have a home of my own, of course. What other reason is there for getting married?"

"Love?"

"Well, of course, I love Vinnie," Kit said. "Otherwise I'd be marrying someone else."

Savile Street was not the place to be having this conversation, but now we had started, I had to go on.

"Vinnie doesn't really like women," I said. "I don't know why he's marrying you. He did try to explain, said he had to be married. I'm not sure what he meant."

"Yes, you are," Kit said. "You're being deliberately stupid or else you're a great deal more naïve than I thought. But it doesn't matter, because it will be different with me."

I really did not know what she was talking about, but I knew better than to attempt a reply. Over the last two years I had grown used to the new, cynical Kit. I did not like her as much as I used to do, but who else was there? After all, she was still special, still had that air of glamour about her that had first attracted me all those years ago when we were children at school together.

Kit opened the bookshop door, and together we stepped into the dark interior that smelled so excitingly of paper and polished wood. But there was no pleasure in being in Browns that day; I was glad when we returned to Hopwood Street, where Vinnie and the rest of the family were waiting. Together he and Kit broke the news that they were engaged.

"Jesus, Mary, and Joseph!" Mammy cried. "Not another wedding! You wouldn't like to make it a double one with Declan and Josie?"

No, Kit would not like that at all. Too long to wait, for a start. Declan and Josie had decided on June 1933 for their big day; Kit wanted to be married before 1932 was out. Anyway, I thought, she would not want to share her glory. It was funny how thoughts like that, unthinkable a year or so before, kept on resurfacing.

"I thought of asking Xavier to be Best Man," Vinnie said. "Unless you thought it should be Pat or Mick or Declan or Sean, Mammy."

Mammy shook her head. "Better not to have to choose. Xavier will do you proud, I'm sure. Where is he, anyway?"

"Gone to see about another ship. We should be away before too long if I'm to make it back before the wedding."

"You're surely not going to go on with this travelling around the world?" Mammy objected. "What kind of married life would that be?"

"For the time being," Vinnie said. "Though I might look into getting a job at the aircraft factory. They're always short of engineers."

I glanced quickly at Kit and was not surprised to see that she was scowling. Vinnie permanently in residence was not part of the plan.

"I'm sure Kit would appreciate that," I lied. "Wouldn't you, Kit?"

Kit did not trouble to reply.

*

Of all the Brennans, I suppose I was the one who was least impressed by what was happening at St Charles's. Of course I was pleased that the first Catholic service to be broadcast over the wireless was to come from Hull, and it was only right that it should take place at St Charles's, which was the oldest Catholic church in the city and my own favourite. But the combined Catholic choirs did not require my undistinguished if serviceable alto; at best I could look forward to being part of the congregation, which was likely to be enormous, for who would want to miss the historic opportunity of taking part in a broadcast?

Declan, however, was indispensable. There was not a tenor in the city to touch him, Josie said, and I had to agree with her. Vinnie and Xavier, who were between ships, were also needed in the choir, as were Pat and Mick, and even Teresa and Maureen. Of us all, only Mammy, Kit, and I made our way into the body of the church at half past seven on Low Sunday, 3rd April 1932. St Charles's was already full, although not, I noticed, with the usual Sunday congregation. Where were the Shawlies, who usually filled the front pews? There was no sign of them; everyone present was dressed in better than their Sunday best. It was the hats I noticed first, extravagant, deliberate hats, hats more suited to a wedding or a garden party than to a church service that no one outside the church was ever going to see. Hammond's hats, in short, hats to which I could never aspire, all of them making a statement about their wearer's social status and right to be there. Just in front of me, a navy-blue straw with a shallow crown draped in blue chiffon, its wired brim veiled with embroidered silk-organdie. Next to that, a pink velvet beret with its satin ribbon trim. I was glad not to be an observer of my own sensible, unobtrusive hat. I knelt at Mammy's side, peering through my fingers at the women in the neighbouring pew. No, I did not know them. I recognised few of the congregation, though I frequently attended Mass there. Clearly, they had come from every corner of the city.

"How many of these people belong to St Charles's parish?" I hissed to Kit.

"No idea. We don't, for a start."

"Yes," I began, but Mammy turned to me with such ferocity in her eyes that I was silenced. I might be twenty years old and almost a schoolteacher, but I was still Nora Brennan's wee girl.

The church had been specially wired for the occasion. I could see two of the three microphones that were being used for the broadcast. One was near the pulpit and one was in the space between the front pew and altar. The other one must have been up in the choir, where my brothers and Xavier were singing. But the first thing they heard at eight o'clock precisely was the Organ Voluntary, followed by the voice of Canon Hall reading the Night Prayers. He must have practised using the microphone, for although the words were magnified, they came out clear and comprehensible. Mammy and I followed in our prayer books, but Kit was gazing round unashamedly, watching the sound engineers from the BBC, who lurked in the side aisles, ready to step forward should disaster strike.

The congregation stood while Father Brunner read the Gospel of the day. Even Kit did not venture to speak during the Gospel but, once we took our seats for the sermon, she nudged me.

"Hasn't he something to do with the BBC Religious Service?"

I did not reply. I was trying to listen to the sermon, but my mind kept wandering. I thought about Xavier up in the choir. He and Vinnie were both in their Merchant Navy uniforms, so they would look impressive, but did they even know the Easter Anthem they were about to sing? Declan did: I had heard nothing else around the house for the last month. Vinnie had been humming it too, now I came to think of it. I was only unsure of Xavier. No doubt he would bluff his way through if he had to.

The sermon was over, and I had not heard a word. I glanced at the faces around me, all of them satisfied if not actually smiling, and I decided it must have gone well. Kit, of course, was looking bored; she was playing with the fingers of her pink silk gloves, pulling them up so the dropped over the ends of her nails, then pushing them back until they wrinkled. I stretched my legs under the kneeler, wriggled my toes inside my shoes. Then the choir was singing "Haec Dies". I could hear Declan's voice above them all; he must have been standing right in front of the microphone. If I listened carefully I could hear another, lighter tenor, less powerful but still true. Xavier. He did know the words, and I wondered why I had ever thought that he would not. He was not one to pass up the chance to show off.

The thought had come upon me unawares. How had I allowed myself to think of him so critically? But I had no time to question myself further. The whole congregation was rising to its feet, ready to obey the exhortations in the Catholic Press to "respond heartily to the prayers and join in the singing of the hymns and the Benediction service".

"Soul of my saviour, sanctify my breast…"

We all knew it, we had sung it a hundred times, and a great wave of sound flooded the airwaves, my voice, and even Kit's, joining with the rest.

It was all over in forty-five minutes. Nothing had gone wrong; the equipment had functioned perfectly, and if the wireless audience could not see the hats, at least everyone at St Charles's had. It took a long time for us all to leave. People were exaggeratedly careful not to trip over the cables, and it was amazing how many of the congregation wanted to look at the microphones close up. The BBC engineers were patient. It must be like this everywhere they go, I thought, as I waited at the end of the pew to make my way into the aisle. Progress was slow. As soon as a group of friends left the church, its members stopped on the steps to exchange views about the occasion. No one else could get out. Mammy, Kit and I, having finally reached the front doors, squeezed round the side of the crowd on the steps and stood in the road waiting for the rest of our party.

"That was a waste of time," Kit said. Hers was perhaps the only dissenting voice in the general excitement and self-congratulation.

"Oh, I don't know," I said. "It's a historic moment, isn't it?"

"It is," Mammy said. "Thank God the BBC has broadcast a real Catholic service at last."

Kit sniffed.

*

Right then, there we were. This was it. Happy, happy wedding day, all important hats and glacé-kid shoes, the Brennan brothers uncomfortable in suits, shirts, and ties. Vinnie alone at ease, but uncharacteristically dour, not a twitch of a smile. Bridegroom to the slaughter, I thought. I held my bridesmaid's bouquet (rose buds and baby's breath) over the stain on my beaded bodice. It was a tear stain, left that morning by Kit, a Kit who by this time was no more ecstatic to be marrying my brother than Vinnie was to be marrying her. Not now the day was finally here. Had she suddenly realised it was a mistake: she did not love him, not really, and he did not love her? If so, she was not saying. And anyway the dress had been bought – indeed, Kit was wearing it – the flowers had arrived at the Morrissey house in Pearson Park, the reception had been arranged and paid for, and the day had come. If the whole thing was a mockery, the guests were not to know. Only the three of us knew, and we were going through with it; there was nothing else to be done. Perhaps it was all for the best, for Kit, and maybe for Vinnie too.

We began the slow procession up the aisle. There was standing room only on the groom's side, with crowds of Brennans, Fahys, and O'Driscolls, school friends and neighbours, two nuns from St Patrick's, a couple of Pontis invited for Declan and Josie. Such hats, such smiles, such triumph. A handful only on the left: Ethel Morrissey in the front pew, tall and cold in green silk. An unlucky colour for a wedding, I thought, and particularly for this wedding. Then, keep your mind on Kit, I told myself, as though my thoughts could buoy Kit up, carry her through. Still I kept glancing to left and right, unaccustomed heels tapping on the cold stone floor of the aisle, throwing me forwards onto my toes. I could not keep this up. Look at the flowers, Grace, great swathes of lilies, so white they were shading into green, blooms stained with pollen, their heady scent at war with the memory of incense. I wanted to sneeze but managed to stifle it.

The church was all light, colour, smiles, tears, just what Kit had wanted, a storybook, fairy-tale wedding that would be remembered for years, happily ever after. I doubted it. I looked at Vinnie, so beautiful my throat hurt; I looked at Kit, tiny and determined and be damned to her family, to grey Doctor Morrissey and his cold unmotherly wife. Kit would marry Vinnie: she had chosen it. I looked at Xavier in the front pew beside the bridegroom, saw the pair of them step out into the aisle as Kit neared the altar, hand lightly on her father's arm, fingers just resting on the dark cloth. No real contact there. You could tell Doctor Morrissey did not want to give her away, though he could see no way out. There was no way out for Kit and Vinnie either, not then or ever. "Whom therefore God hath joined together, let no man put asunder." I stood beside Xavier Quinn, Kit's bouquet clutched in my fingers next to my own, not daring to look at him. From the corner of my eye I glanced up, saw the long bones of his face, the faint gold thread of stubble on his chin. Xavier Quinn and Grace Brennan together before the altar. In front of me the slow dance of the marriage ceremony, in my ears the light voice of the young priest. Give them a show, I begged Vinnie silently. Hide the fact that you do not want this. Dazzle them, Kit.

Words like a blur, and the ring handed smoothly from Xavier to Vinnie, slipping, relentless, onto Kit's slender finger. The vows must have been made, though I did not hear them; the whole thing was over in minutes. Off now to the vestry to sign the register, Kit and Vinnie side by side. Xavier and I followed them in. A sudden gleam of satisfaction in the midst of the misery: he was there at my side. Where I wanted him. Where was Mammy? She must have been there surely, but I had not seen her. Here were the four of us and young Father Daly and the open pages of the register. I signed my name. And then we were back out into the church again, where all the time the organ had been playing, and on and out down the shifting aisle, out into the sunshine for the grave unsmiling photographs amid the scuffing of heels on the gravel.

And on. Half familiar territory now, Hammond's ballroom. We Brennans were good at celebrating, and Kit was a Brennan now. She would out-dance them all, and Vinnie with her, and I would dance with Xavier Quinn. I would not need to be asked twice this time. And perhaps, after all, this disaster of a marriage would make it, would surprise them all and make it yet.

*

I was not so very keen to get married. After all, there were things I had to do. There was a training college course I needed to finish, a whole generation of children on whom I must make my mark. I owed it to myself, and to that long-ago moment in the box room at Hopwood Street, when I first realised that I was going to be a teacher. I did not want a house and housework, and an end to my ambitions.

All the same, it worried me that Xavier had said not one thing further about marrying me. I did not know where I stood at all, and there seemed to be no way, short of asking him directly, to sort it out.

Added to that, I was worried about the photographs. It was over a week since the last set had arrived from Vinnie. I had studied them with even more interest than usual, because one of them showed Vinnie and Xavier on either side of a long-legged girl, her hair darkly glamorous under a wide-brimmed sun hat, her body barely concealed under a bathing costume like none I had seen before: it was strapless and smothered in tropical flowers. She had her arms around both of them, but surely her head was inclined more towards Xavier. Why should Vinnie be interested in her when he had only just married Kit?

As usual, there were no names under the photograph, only the place where it was taken: Miami, Florida. I could make out palm trees in the background, though it was not the background that interested me.

"Who do you think she is?" I asked Kit, who glanced briefly at the snap.

"His landlady's daughter? An American cousin? The love of his life?"

"She's standing just as close to Vinnie."

"Why shouldn't she?"

"Aren't you worried?"

"What Vinnie does when he's away at sea is his business," Kit said. "Just as what I do here when he's away is my business. If you want to worry about what Xavier might be up to, go ahead: worry!"

"Do you think I've got anything to worry about?"

Kit lost patience.

"Wait until he gets back and ask him then. Always supposing he does come back. I always said he was a –"

"Chancer," I finished for her. "Yes, I know. I'll have to make do with lectures and lesson plans."

"That's a much better idea. Now let's go and have tea at Trippett's."

Tea at Trippett's was, as far as I could see, Kit's one concession to being a married lady. It was a tradition her mother had kept up for years, meeting her friends for tea and cakes at Trippett's in Prospect Street, and Kit saw no reason why she and I could not build on that tradition. I still felt uncomfortable sitting among well-off matrons who formed the large part of Trippett's clientele but, as usual, I gave in.

Luckily, it was fairly empty that afternoon. I watched Kit eating an éclair and unashamedly sticking her tongue between the two layers of choux pastry to extract the cream while licking her small fingers, which were smeared with chocolate, and still managing to look more sophisticated than I had ever done in my life. But then I would not have dared to eat a cream cake in public. Instead I cut a small portion from the plain scone I had ordered and lifted it carefully to my mouth. Even so, crumbs sprinkled across the cloth. Kit stretched out a licked finger and scooped them up.

"What's it really like?" I asked. "Being married, I mean."

Kit was no help.

"What exactly do you want to know?"

"You know."

"No, I don't."

"Well, then. Kissing and the other stuff. You know what I mean."

"How should I know?" Seeing my stunned face, Kit elaborated,

"You don't imagine that Vinnie goes in for that sort of stuff, do you?"

"But you're married!" I protested. "When I told you that Vinnie wasn't interested in women, you said it would be different with you."

"I miscalculated," Kit said. "Another cup of tea?" She reached out for the teapot.

I did not know how to continue the conversation. We had never really talked openly about Kit's motives for marrying Vinnie, though I had been prepared to believe she loved him. There had to be more to their relationship than a shared surname and a rented house on Beverley Road. I dabbed at a crumb Kit had missed and sucked it off my finger.

"Can we go now?" I asked.

8

No one in my family was surprised when I came top of my year in the final written examination. Because everyone expected it, the compliments I received were low key, perfunctory. It did not feel like much of an achievement.

What none of the Brennans, apart from me, knew was that my performance in the teaching practice had been graded as only satisfactory. I had passed, but only just. Sister Tutor had quite a lot to say about my delivery, which was too loud, and the fact that the content of my lessons was sometimes pitched too high for any but the brightest to follow. She also remarked that, while I was perhaps too ready to tolerate poor handwriting, I had shown little sympathy for those of my charges who were not able to spell correctly. Sister Tutor remarked that my own handwriting was not always as legible as it should be, and that spelling came easily to me; she suggested I might be a little more understanding in one area while raising standards in the other.

I thought about this almost-failure while I was cleaning my shoes. The two activities were equally distasteful to me. For some reason, I had never been able to clean my shoes without gritting my teeth and holding my breath, and this idiosyncrasy made the whole process very uncomfortable. It was worse when I was using the brush, but Mammy never let me buff up a shine with a rag alone; each shoe, and especially each toecap, had to receive at least two minutes of focused brushing. The routine was ingrained in me. Yet, funnily enough, cleaning my shoes on this occasion made thinking about my mediocrity in the classroom more bearable. What upset me most was that I had not been aware of my inadequacy, had believed myself a model student, when obviously I was no such thing. Still the more agitated I became, the more my shoes shone.

On that particular day there was a purpose to my fevered polishing. I had an interview at the new school at St Peter's. It had been open less than a year, but already the school board was looking to take on three new teachers that September. Every time I opened a copy of the Hull Catholic Magazine, I saw the square brick outline of the school in the Robinson and Sawdon advertisement. It was a threateningly efficient-looking building with its main entrance flanked by two new metal dustbins. A no-nonsense sort of school, the sort of school in which I felt I ought to be working. It was a school, perhaps, where I could learn to be as effective in the classroom as I was in the examination hall.

If I had given the matter much consideration, I might have been surprised that my interview was conducted not by the headmaster, but by the parish priest. My confidence was low: I had told no one, not even Kit, about my marks for teaching practice, and all my energy was now channelled into appearing competent and capable. I kept my feet in my carefully polished shoes side by side and firmly on the floor. I clasped my gloved hands in my lap and held my head up straight as I recited in a clear voice (but not too loud) my examination grades from the convent and my results in the college written papers. I said nothing about teaching practice.

The priest's first question caught me off guard.

"You'll be Jack Brennan's daughter?"

I had to admit it. There was no point in doing otherwise, but I was not sure that this fact of life was going to help my application. I did not know a single priest, with the possible exception of Father Sebastian, who had ever had a good word to say about my father. It did not seem fair that his quarrel with the church should keep me out of a job in a Catholic school, but that was exactly what might happen.

"Yes, Father," I said. "But I'm Nora Brennan's daughter too."

He laughed, and I relaxed a little, only to be unsettled by his next question.

"Tell me," he said. "Are you thinking of getting married at all?"

I should have expected it, of course. School boards took the view that married women would put their husbands first and neglect their duties to the school; they refused to employ them. I searched for the exact truth.

"I've no plans for marrying at present."

It seemed to satisfy the priest for, after a few cursory questions, he offered to show me around the school, which was in session. In one classroom I heard tables being chanted – "four elevens are forty-four pence: three and eight" – while in another a whole class of children were practising a hymn to Our Lady. Everywhere else the pupils were working in silence, a calm, purposeful silence; I liked the sound of it. In the top class two successful scholarship candidates were pointed out to me, and I was reminded that they had been at the school for less than a year. Privately I thought that they might have been well taught at their previous school, but I made the right responses and began to hope that, yes, I might be one of those three new teachers who would be working in those classrooms in September.

The priest had one more question for me, but he waited until we were back in the headmaster's office, before he inquired as to whether I thought I had sufficient authority to deal with the bigger boys.

"Yes, of course," I said, startled. "I have five older brothers, Father. I know what boys are like."

He happened to know, he said, that there was a post going at St Gregory's Girls' School, if I would like him to put in a good word for me.

"Thank you, Father, but I'd rather work here. Such a lovely new school, and a new thriving parish besides. I can't think of a better place in which to start work." I held my breath. The priest scribbled down something in a notebook; he tapped the end of his pen on the desk.

"All right, Miss Brennan. We'll see what you can do."

I breathed out. Immediately, I was exhausted. For the first time I realised what a strain the interview had been. The priest leaned over the desk and shook my hand.

"Welcome to St Peter's," he said.

*

"Miss! Miss, there's a man outside the window!"

"Not 'Miss'," I sighed. "It's 'Miss Brennan'. How many times do I have to tell you, Eddie? What is it you want to tell me?"

"Miss Brennan, there's a man outside the window."

Gradually I realised what Eddie Ryan was saying. I turned from the blackboard to the high windows along the outside wall of the classroom. There was indeed a face at the window, and it was one I knew: Xavier's.

"Carry on with your work, children," I said quietly. "I'll go and see what the man wants. You're in charge of the class while I'm gone, James Kennedy. If anyone speaks, you're to write his name on the board. Or hers," I added belatedly, though I knew from experience that if there was going to be trouble in this classroom it would come from the boys. That was why I was leaving James Kennedy in charge. He might not have been the brightest boy in the class, but he was certainly the biggest.

"Yes, Miss," he said, pleased. I opened my mouth to protest – not 'Miss' – but thought better of it. I had more important things to do now than make a fuss about being given my full title.

"What are you doing here?" I asked Xavier angrily, once I had rounded the corner of the classroom and was within a few feet of him. He turned to me, smiling.

"I've come to see Miss Grace Brennan at her work. Shall we go in?"

"You can't do that!" I protested. "This is a school. You can't just walk in. What will the children think? What will the headmaster think?"

"Lead me to him. There'll be no problem."

He did not listen to my protests, and in the end I watched him walk away from me, his red-gold hair undimmed by the shadowy air in the corridor, his stride easy and assured as he made his way towards the classroom where the headmaster was teaching. For a moment I stood there and then, as he opened the classroom door, I turned and ran – yes, ran – to my own room.

"I kept them quiet, Miss," said James Kennedy proudly.

"Thank you, James."

"Eddie Ryan wanted to come and help you, but I wouldn't let him."

"You did right. Now, children…"

"Have the police taken the man away?" Eddie Ryan asked.

"No. Everything's in order, Eddie. There's nothing for you to worry about. Now, if we can get on with our –"

But I did not manage to finish the sentence. The breath was caught in my throat and I swallowed, for the door was open and Xavier was in the doorway. He was smiling. "Good afternoon, Miss Brennan," he said. "I'm here by special request of the headmaster to help with your class's geography lesson. Now what would you like me to do?"

I felt my skin go cold. My hands gripped the edge of the desk; I did not know what to say and could not even begin to think how to continue with the lesson. I looked down the room at the children, all of whom were sitting in surprised silence, their eyes on the tall, smiling stranger by the teacher's desk.

Eddie Ryan put up his hand.

"Are you a teacher?" he asked.

"No. I'm a merchant seaman. A sailor," he added when it appeared that some of the children did not understand him.

"On a ship?" That was Mary Ellen Gallagher, the boldest of the girls.

"On a ship," Xavier confirmed gravely. "I've just come back from the United States of America."

"Were you in Hollywood?"

"New York?"

"No," Xavier said. "I was in Florida. They have beaches there the like of which you've never seen, and palm trees, and the sun shines all day every day."

There was no stopping any of them now. Xavier and the children travelled the world, his stories becoming more and more unlikely, more outrageous, but they loved it. They were leaning forward in their seats, hands up, questions coming one after the other, and I sat at my desk forgotten, not knowing whether to laugh or scream, hot with a mixture of shame, pride, and disbelief. I was also biting my nails, I suddenly noticed, and I stuffed my hands beneath my thighs.

At last the bell rang. I collected myself, stood, dismissed the children crisply. I picked up my basket, walked past Xavier, down the corridor to the staffroom. When I emerged in my coat, my beret sitting squarely on my head, not a trace of nonsense about me, Xavier was waiting. I did not speak, but he kept in step with me as I left the building and began to walk home. Once we were outside the school gate, he took my arm. I tried to shrug him off, but he was holding my elbow too firmly, and there were children about. I did not want to draw more attention to myself. So, I quickened my step, but there was no hope of leaving him behind – his legs were so much longer than mine. Besides, he was laughing and determined, and part of me was glad to be with him.

"Aren't you going to ask me how I talked your headmaster round?"

"No," I said. I kept on walking.

"You'd have been proud of me. Such a story I spun him! Are you sure you don't want to hear it?"

I did want to hear it. I could not help myself. The stiff corners of my mouth unbent even as I refused to speak. He saw it.

"It was this way. He's a reasonable man, your headmaster. When I told him I was your long-lost Irish cousin come to see how the schools were run in this enlightened corner of the earth – why, he welcomed me in."

"You're not my cousin."

"No, I'm not, am I?" he agreed. "So who am I, Grace, if I'm not your cousin?"

"My brother's friend."

"Come on, now. I'm more than that, surely?"

I stopped. Turned to look at him. I could not be sure of what he was saying. Perhaps he was saying nothing at all. Just playing with words, as usual.

"Who are you then?"

"Why, Grace," he said, and his voice was easy, his smile more charming than ever. "Aren't I the man you're going to marry?"

In the silence that followed I heard the soft hiss and swish of a passing trolley. I heard the sharp tap of my own heels on the pavement, the softer, more slurred sound of Xavier's rubber soles at my side. I heard my own breathing, which was quick and shallow. And I could not think of a word to say. Had he proposed to me? No. He had asked me a question, but it was more of a statement. I did not know how to deal with it. I imagined telling Kit about it, because that was still the way I made sense of things: rehearsing them in my mind as a story to tell Kit. It did not help. All I could think of was Kit laughing. Mocking, even. What sort of man was Xavier that he could not speak plainly? I wondered suddenly what he made of my silence, whether her read it as acceptance or dissent. I tried to open my mouth to speak, to say something, anything, but I could not. I did not know what to say. I did not even know what I wanted to say.

It did not take us long to reach Hopwood Street. Neither of us had spoken again. I imagined myself walking in, telling my mother that Xavier and I were engaged, were to be married. A small voice deep inside me made itself heard. He had not even kissed me yet, it repeated.

It was an academic question anyway. When we walked in, the family was already celebrating. I wondered what they were all doing there, my brothers, at half past four on a Friday afternoon, but I had no time to ask. Declan and Josie were there in the centre of it all, smiling radiantly, ecstatic. No need to ask what their news was: I could see it in their faces. No need to ask, but they told me anyway.

"We've named the day!"

I tucked my own news (if it were news) away at the back of my mind, where I could find it later, and think it over for myself, in my own time. I watched Xavier congratulate Declan and Josie, noticed Vinnie sitting by the fire in the armchair that used to be Daddy's. That was something new, something I had not expected. I made a note of it. But where was Kit?

"Where's Kit?"

"Not here."

"I can see that."

"At her mother's. She'll be here later. Probably."

I turned to Josie and hugged her.

"I'm so glad."

"We are too. Would you think of being a bridesmaid?"

Twice a bridesmaid, then a bride. It seemed an inevitable progression. I glanced at Xavier, but he was looking the other way.

He was laughing with Declan, relaxed, at ease. There was no sign of turmoil in his face, and why should there be? I knew what he was thinking.

"You're very quiet," Mammy said to me as we met in the scullery, Mammy to cut sandwiches, I to make tea. "Cat got your tongue?"

"I'm tired. That's all. It's been a hard week, and now all this excitement."

"Another wedding," Mammy sighed. "Still, at least Declan has his job with the Insurance. They'll not go short. Though what sort of wedding the Pontis are going to be able to provide, I don't know."

"Will Josie's mother come to the wedding?" I wondered. I had not seen Mrs Ponti since the family had moved to the new estate. She had never been to Hopwood Street, that was for sure.

"She'll not miss her own daughter's wedding!" Mammy stopped, the bread knife upright in her hand. "I tell you now, Mary Grace, nothing will keep me away from your wedding, though I hope it's not just yet a while."

What did she mean? Did she know how it was between Xavier and me? If she did, she was better informed than her daughter. I shook myself. This was no time to be brooding on my problems. I picked up the kettle and filled the brown teapot to the brim and covered it in the singed but brightly striped cosy. It was one I'd made myself years ago. I could see the hole where I had dropped a stitch and had had to cast one on.

"Don't forget the sugar," Mammy said. "No; use the good bowl. What can you be thinking of?"

*

Another week passed. Xavier said nothing further. I wilted both at school and at home. I told myself it was not knowing that was the problem, but in bed, at night, blankets drawn up dark around my head against the cold, I acknowledged my deepest fear: what if he were teasing?

I said as much to Kit on the Saturday morning, when she and Vinnie arrived on their way to the Co-op. Vinnie and Xavier – who still stayed with us when he was on shore leave, even though Vinnie was married with his own rented home on Beverley Road – went off somewhere together, shopping forgotten. Kit had come with him only because it was an excuse to call in at Hopwood Street, anyway. It seemed to me that my brother and Kit no longer enjoyed each other's company as they once had; they would rather be with the family, even Kit, even if it was not her own family. But I had no time to worry about their marriage just then. It was all I could do not to burst into tears over the increasing unlikelihood of my own. Not that I wanted to be married, I reminded Kit. After all, I had a career.

"Do you want to marry Xavier Quinn? Yes or no?"

I thought about it. "Yes," I said at last. "But not yet. Some time."

"When?"

"The year after next, maybe. When I've had time to make a success of my job."

"Well," said Kit. "I don't know what you see in him or why you think you want to marry him, but if it's really what you want, we'd better do something about it. I'm tired of seeing you look like, like …"

"A dying duck in a thunderstorm?" suggested Mammy, as she came into the room.

"Mammy! This is a private conversation."

"Sorry, I'm sure," Mammy said, not in the least sorry, and she went through into the scullery with her head held high, her back straighter than ever.

"Now look what you've done," I said unfairly, but Kit ignored me. Vinnie and Xavier had just reappeared in the doorway.

"We thought we might go to the match this afternoon," Vinnie said. "They're playing at home."

"Fine," said Kit. "But Xavier's not coming with you. We need him with us. We're going for tea at Trippett's."

"Trippett's? Xavier?" Vinnie was scornful. "What on earth for?"

"We have things to discuss," Kit said, and I looked round desperately for somewhere, anywhere to hide. I ran through into the scullery. Suddenly it was vital that I apologised to my mother for my rudeness, and by the time I came back it was all settled. And although Vinnie was still disbelieving, Xavier seemed more than a little pleased with the idea of afternoon tea.

"Two beautiful women on my arms," he said. "What more could a man want?"

Kit chose a table next to the glass-fronted cake counter. Xavier, who had stopped just inside the door to hang up his coat and trilby, was too late to prevent Kit squeezing me into the position nearest to the glass, and then sitting down beside me. He pulled out a chair opposite me and was about to sit down when Kit stopped him.

"I want you sitting opposite me. It's me you'll be talking to."

Xavier shrugged, smiled at me and sat down where he was told to sit down,

"Well?"

Kit ignored him, turning her attention to the ancient waitress in her frilled white apron, who had come to take our order. Xavier was about to speak, the waitress was already turned towards him, pencil poised above her note pad, when Kit cut in.

"A pot of tea for three, please, and a plate of fancy cakes."

Not the cakes, I thought. Please, not the cakes. At that point I could not cope with eating a cake in public, negotiating the pastry fork and then the cream that spurted out just as you were raising a carefully measured mouthful to your lips. Trippett's with Kit was bad enough, but Trippett's with Xavier, and with Kit in this mood was much, much worse.

"No cake for me," I said. "I'm not hungry."

But the cakes arrived immediately as did the tea. Kit used the cake slice to transfer an ornate, raspberry-topped meringue to my plate.

"There. Your favourite."

I picked up me fork and gloomily broke off a portion of meringue, which immediately crumbled into fragments across the cloth, scattering my coat with tiny white flecks of sugar. Cream began to ooze from the cake's interior; I blocked its advance with the cake fork. I could not begin to understand what I was doing there.

"Are you intending to marry Grace?" Kit's clear voice carried through the room. Trippett's was unusually empty for a Saturday afternoon, but at least twenty people turned and looked at our table, where this interesting conversation was taking place. I thought about slipping under the table and hiding under the long folds of the cloth, but there was not enough room. I had to stay where I was.

"Why don't you ask Grace?" Xavier said, surprisingly at ease. He poured out three cups of tea, since no one else had thought of doing so, then added milk and sugar to his own.

"Why don't *you* ask Grace?" Kit repeated his words. "If you want to marry her, why don't you just ask her?"

"It's understood," Xavier began. "Grace knows how I feel about her."

"No, I don't," I could not stay silent any longer. "How should I? It's all a big game to you. You talk about marrying me all the time – well, you've talked about it twice – but you've never asked me. How do I know if you're serious?"

"Yes," said Kit. "How does she know if you're serious?"

"Right. You want to know whether I'm serious." He stood up, hitched up the knees of his trousers and knelt down.

"What are you doing?" I asked, horrified.

"I'm showing you whether I am serious or not. Here in front of Kit and all these good people, who came in for a quiet cup of tea. Mary Grace Brennan, will you marry me?"

It ought to have been the most wonderful moment of my life. That was what I had read in all the books. And in a way it was. It was also the most embarrassing.

"Get up!" I hissed.

"Not until you say yes."

"For God's sake," said Kit. "Say yes, and let's get on with our tea. I've had enough of this floor show."

"All right," I said. "Yes. Yes, I will marry you."

Xavier rose to his feet. He looked around the tea-room as if expecting applause. The other customers looked away, so he clapped his own hands. Twice. Slowly. I was shocked into silence. Was he mocking me?

"I'll have the banns put up next week," he said.

I took a long slow breath. "No. Not yet. I can't marry you yet. Don't you see? I have my job. I'll have to resign. I'm not ready."

"You'll lose your job if they know that you're married? Is that what you're saying?" Xavier asked.

"You know Catholic schools don't employ married women teachers."

"Then don't tell them that you're married," Xavier said.

I knew I should protest, draw attention to the dishonesty in his words, but that was not what came out.

"They'd find out," I said. "Someone would tell them. Someone who was at the wedding. The priest even."

"You'll not be getting married at St Peter's," Xavier said. "There's a risk, I agree. But if you want to go on teaching, isn't it worth it?"

"Yes. I suppose it is."

Inside I was terrified. I was wondering just exactly what I had agreed to when I said I would marry Xavier Quinn.

9

(1934-1939)

There were so many Brennan weddings during those years that it is sometimes hard to remember my own. After all, many of the same people were present at each one, though the patterns they made varied. I can no longer be sure which reception it was where the Fahy cousins commandeered the floor for Irish dancing; it was, nevertheless, the highlight of that particular day. But if one bride had only one bridesmaid, while another had six, I cannot now remember which was which. Some memories, though, I know, are of my wedding.

On my wedding morning, I woke up in my four-foot bed to feel the weight of another body against my own. Someone's breath was stirring the hair at the back of my neck, and an arm was flung across my waist. The bedclothes held a dark, unfamiliar smell. For a moment I stiffened, bewildered, until I remembered that it was Kit who was sharing my bed, Kit who had come to play matron-of-honour at my wedding to Xavier Quinn.

The friendship Kit and I shared had never been physical: we had never walked arm in arm or hand in hand, or with our arms around each other's waists, as some girls did. We had rarely hugged or kissed, rarely touched except by accident. This sudden closeness of another person's body, and particularly the intimacy of her smell, startled me – frightened me even. I edged my way from Kit and slid out from under her arm. She muttered in her sleep and turned over onto her back. Then the door opened and Mammy came in carrying two cups of tea. Tea in the best cups, the cups that were never usually used, white bone china with a gilt rim and a pattern of tiny rosebuds. I had never had tea in bed before, not even when I was ill. I nudged Kit awake, and we sat up together, elbows knocking, side by side in my three-quarter bed. On my wedding morning.

Later, at St Patrick's Church, my veil was blown from my head by the Boxing Day wind as I climbed the steps to the front door. Up it went, whirling away, until a further gust of wind slammed it against the façade of the church and it lodged on the statue of the Blessed Virgin Mary aloof and smiling in her carved niche, at her Son's right hand. What a hurrying and scurrying there was then, and a final desperate fetching of ladders from behind the church hall, while I stood on the steps of St Patrick's in my wedding dress and the December cold, waiting for someone to retrieve my veil. Vinnie would have done it, but Vinnie was best man and could not risk his suit, so it was Sean, home from Withernsea for good and lodging with Pat and Mick while he looked for work, who grudgingly climbed the ladder. It was too short, of course, and he had to reach up for the top rung, edging his knee into the niche which housed the statue, before he could divest the Virgin of her unaccustomed finery. He came down covered in dust and pigeon droppings. Mammy darted at him with little cries of horror, brushing his knees and the front of his suit and then the precious veil with a dampened handkerchief. Kit pinned it back into place with long black Kirby grips, anchoring it more firmly this time in my heavy fall of hair. Then she placed her small hands on my shoulders, looked at me for a long moment and kissed me on the cheek. For luck.

These things I remember from that day. And I remember too how my thoughts were wandering when Xavier was asked if he, Francis Xavier Quinn, took me, Mary Grace Brennan, to be his lawful wedded wife. How strange to think of him as Francis. Had he been a Brennan, he would have been Frank or Frannie, so who had chosen Xavier for his use name? Xavier himself, perhaps, as I had chosen Grace. It was one more link to bind us, like the look of achievement which passed between us when he manoeuvred the ring onto my finger.

"There are no two people I would wish to see happier," Vinnie said as he made his speech at the reception in St Patrick's church hall. Kit raised her glass in agreement; even in the midst of my own dazed happiness I was pleased to see this little show of unity between my favourite brother and his wife, who was still my best friend. It was unrealistic to think that their marriage would ever work, but at least they could be peaceable together. I felt Xavier reach for my left hand. I placed my right hand on top of his: the fine red-gold hairs on his fingers tickled my palm, while the warmth of his skin welded us together. Again, I marvelled at the length and elegance of his bones, at my amazing good fortune in being, at last, Grace Quinn.

There was no wedding night to look forward to or dread. I was not sure which it should be. We were going to Dublin for three days, my first time in Ireland ever, and there was the whole breadth of England and then the Irish sea to cross first.

Most of the guests accompanied us to the station. I wore my new blue costume, while Xavier still looked formal and unfamiliar in his wedding suit with its fine white stripe and fashionably wide lapels.

Someone stuffed a handful of confetti down his neck as he followed me into the compartment, and we spent the first few minutes of the journey brushing away the small pieces of coloured paper after settling our luggage on the rack above the holiday posters. But it was a long way to Liverpool and the boat train: there were still hours to go. Suddenly, I panicked. The momentum of the day was gone and I had nothing to say to him.

We were not alone in the compartment. As the train rattled on, we sat opposite each other in corner seats, watching the long sweep of the Humber estuary grow narrow as we travelled inland. The other occupants of the carriage were caught up in their own business and, at the first stop twenty minutes later, the compartment emptied. Xavier and I looked at each other, he in hope, I suppose, and I in fear, but we were not to be left alone. New people got in, sat themselves down. I leaned back my head and closed my eyes. Time and stations went by.

At Liverpool Lime Street we saw nothing of the city, transferring immediately to the boat train. It too was packed. It was evening by then; I was too tired to watch Wales slide past. There were no corner seats for us on this train. Xavier and I were squashed between two sleeping passengers. We held hands, my right hand in his left, arms bent between our adjoining thighs. It was not comfortable, but it was reassuring. I had never known Xavier so silent.

Holyhead. The sea was rough; most people were below deck, in their cramped communal cabins with rows of bunk beds and the all-pervasive smell of sick. Xavier and I stood at the stern, watching the white curve of the wake on the dark waters of the Irish Sea. I was cold but some of the magic of the day had returned: Xavier's arm was around my shoulders, his warmth against my side.

"Xavier," I said, "Do you love me?"

"Why else would I have married you?"

"I need to hear you say it."

"I love you, Grace Quinn. There, will that do you?"

"Say it again."

But he did not. Instead he kissed me, so gently I barely felt it.

I wanted the crossing to go on forever.

"Are you afraid?" Xavier asked me.

We were standing in the bedroom of the boarding house in Baggot Street, our suitcases, still packed, at our feet. I stared at the double bed, which seemed to take up the whole room. I had never seen anything like the blue silk eiderdown before, or the way it was ruched up in the middle to make a kind of circle on the candlewick counterpane. I reached out to touch the eiderdown. It was not silk after all, though it looked like silk. The bed was tall and imposing, mahogany perhaps; I was not sure. The only familiar thing in the room was a picture of the Sacred Heart on the wall.

"Sweetheart," Xavier said. "It's all right. There's no need to be frightened."

I turned to look at him. My husband. It was barely nine o'clock in the morning, and we had not slept at all. I felt dirty and unreal; the floor was still swaying under my feet from the motion of the boat. Xavier was used to travelling, of course, but there were shadows on the thin skin below his eyes, red-gold stubble on his chin and his long upper lip. I felt it graze my cheek when he bent to kiss me. My hands dangled at my sides, useless.

"Yes," I said. "I am afraid."

"I'll go out," he said. "I'll go and fetch a paper or something. You have a wash and get into bed. Go to sleep."

Before he left, he drew the curtain across, so that the room was in semi-darkness. He did not touch me again, but left immediately, closing the door behind him.

I took a deep, deep breath. I could feel myself trembling. The marble-topped washstand behind the door held a large bowl and an ewer of cold water. I poured the water out, took off my jacket and blouse, then my skirt. There was a chair by the bed. I folded my clothes neatly, laid them over it. The water was unexpectedly soft on my skin. It smelled different too from Hull water. The soap in the china dish was finer than the soap I was used to at home; it lathered easily as I turned it over and over in my hands. I dried my hands and face on the rough white towel which hung from a rung at the side of the washstand.

My new nightdress was in my suitcase, near the top, with my hairbrush. I put the nightdress on, brushed my hair and climbed into bed. I did not know on which side I should sleep. The night before the wedding, Kit and I had giggled as we decided who would lie on which side of my bed. This was different. In the end, I chose the right side, then got out of bed again to straighten the eiderdown. I could not sleep under its ruched surface as it was. I could not sleep anyway, though I closed my eyes as I curled up on my side, my back to the centre of the bed. I closed my eyes and shut them tight and kept them closed while I said my prayers. I hoped God would forgive me, would understand why I could not kneel down beside that bed.

I did not move at all when Xavier returned, but lay still, deepening my breathing, pretending I was asleep. I heard the snap of his braces as he undressed, felt the lurch of the bed as he sat down on the side.

What was he doing? Taking off his socks, possibly. He stood up again. I heard the click as he opened his case. A pause. The sound of cotton going over skin. When he climbed into bed beside me, I smelled first the newness of his pyjamas, and then his own faint agreeable foxiness. He touched my right shoulder.

"I know you're not asleep."

Afterwards, I wondered what I had been expecting. I was not totally ignorant. I knew – roughly – what went where. Josie had seen to that. It was bad enough, she said, that I should have such a long wait after the wedding, so much time for expectation to build up, and dread. Better I should know what I was waiting for. But the reality of it was another thing entirely. The weight of him, first of all. Xavier was long and muscular, his bones weighed heavy on me. I did not know how I could continue to breathe as he worked on top of me, even though he had taken some of his weight on his elbows. Josie had told me it would hurt, and that there would be blood, but it did not hurt that much, and there was no blood, just a sort of dry stretching, a kind of soundless pop. Then the unexpected accelerating rhythm, which I feared would go on forever and, finally, to my amazement, the quiet sunrise inside me, of which he seemed completely unaware.

"It'll be better next time."

But it was not.

*

The first thing I saw when we returned to Hopwood Street was the rag rug, complete at last and spread out in front of the range in the living room.

"You must have worked hard to finish it," I said to Mammy.

"What else had I to do? There's no work in an empty house. I'm glad to have you back, the pair of you. It will liven the place up."

"We were thinking of looking for somewhere to rent, Mammy," I said. "You'll not want to be bothered by us."

"No bother at all. I rattle round here on my own. This is a family house; it needs people in it. And what's the point of you two spending good money on rent when you can live here for free?"

"We wouldn't do that, Mammy." I glanced at Xavier, who nodded. "Well, if you're sure…"

"That's settled then. Which room would you like?"

I was about to say my old room would suit us fine when Xavier interrupted.

"We'd like Vinnie and Declan's room, if that's all right with you, Nora. It's got the big double bed and, with the windows on either side, it's light, even in winter. If it's all the same to you," he added.

"I'll see to it now," Mammy said. "No, I don't need you to help me, Mary Grace."

"Why do you want that room?" I asked, once I had heard Mammy's feet on the stairs. I was curious, nothing more.

"I've no wish to share a bedroom wall with your mother," Xavier said. "And it's true, what I said. That room is always light. It will suit us fine."

I did not really care which room we had. Abandoning the subject, I flung myself down on the rag rug. It was new, but the multicoloured strips of fabric were old; there was already a slightly dusty smell that prickled the back of my nose.

"Here," I said. "Look. See that splash of deep red? That's from the velvet dress I wore for my first photograph. We went to a photographer's studio. I must have been about six, I suppose. Here, I'll show it to you."

I scrambled to my feet, crossed to the heavy wooden sideboard beneath the window. The photograph album was on the left-hand side, along with the tablecloths which were too good to use, the best china, and Mammy's workbox. I laid the album on the table and began to turn the pages. Xavier came to lean on my shoulder.

"Who's that?"

"That's my daddy, the year he was made Alderman. And that's Uncle Martin. Oh, look, here we are. Sean and I on our best behaviour."

"You had curls?"

"Ringlets. Yes. Mammy made me sleep with my hair tied up in rags the night before. She didn't take them out until we left the house. They hurt dreadfully. I wonder what happened to the lace collar and cuffs Mammy made me. I thought I was so grown up."

"And Sean in a suit with short trousers. What's that he's holding?"

"It could be a book, I suppose. I don't know. I don't even remember Sean being there that day, though he was – he's there in the photograph, so he must have been. What I do remember is being asked to sit on that carved oak bench, and the seat being so high and slippery I thought I was going to fall."

"Your mouth hasn't changed."

"My mouth?"

"Your lips." He traced them with his forefinger. "Come on. Let's go and help your mother get the room ready."

*

The day after Epiphany, I went back to teach at St Peter's. I wore an engagement ring, but my wedding ring, suspended on a fine gold chain, was hidden beneath my high-necked blouse. When my colleagues congratulated me on my engagement and asked when the wedding would be, I prevaricated. No. I lied.

"Not for years yet. We need to save for a house."

It did not feel like lying at the time.

Meanwhile, Xavier made himself useful in Hopwood Street. He repainted the front room for Mammy, and he proved to be surprisingly meticulous about covering the piano and the rest of the furniture with old sheets while he worked. But as the days went by, and Vinnie was on what was to be his last voyage before he moved on to aeronautical engineering, Xavier showed no sign of looking for a ship. There was no hurry: I had my salary coming in every month, and Mammy had to be persuaded to take even nominal rent from us. Still, I could not help wondering how long it would be before he went back to sea. Eventually, I asked him.

"What's the point?" Xavier said. "We're married, after all. Surely you don't want me gone already?"

"No, it's not that. I just thought …"

"I'll maybe get a shore job."

"You could go to the aircraft factory with Vinnie. They're short of engineers."

Xavier laughed. "I'm not an engineer."

"But I thought …"

I did not know what I thought. In the three years I had known

Xavier – if "known" was the right word – I had just assumed that he must be an engineer like Vinnie. Somehow, we had never talked about it. How could something so important have gone unexplored?

"I could have been an engineer. I'm good with mechanical things. If I'd stayed at school longer, perhaps that is what I would have done."

I had so many questions to ask him. How old was he when he left school? Why did he leave early? What else did I not know about him? What I actually said was, "So if you're not an engineer, what are you?"

He glanced at me. Did I imagine it, or was there a flicker of fear, or perhaps shame in his eyes?

"I'm a steward."

I did not say anything for a moment. It was silly, I knew, but suddenly he seemed diminished, because what sort of job was that for an intelligent man? Fetching and carrying, smiling and accepting tips? I did not say what I was thinking; I knew I had to make the best of it.

"I'm sure there are all sorts of things you could do on shore."

"Yes," he said. "But it has to be the right thing."

"There's no hurry." I could not leave it like that, even though I tried to say no more. "You could always get casual work on the docks until something more permanent comes along."

"Me? A docker?"

"It's what Mick and Pat do. It's what my daddy did."

That was not the whole truth, of course, and Xavier knew it. Pat had taken over Daddy's role as Trade Union secretary; Mick had moved on from loading and unloading cargo to a position as a supervisor. Both of them were in regular employment.

"We'll see. As you say, there's no hurry. Not when I've a hardworking wife to keep me."

The comment startled me – it was not one any of my brothers would ever make. I said only, "You'll look out for something?"

"I'll look out for something. I've said so, haven't I? And now, how about a night at the flicks? They're showing Boris Karloff in "The Mummy" at the Cecil."

An unnecessary waste of money. That is what I wanted to say in reply. It was the kind of luxury we could not afford, at least until Xavier found himself a proper job. But the alternative was another evening spent in with Mummy, playing cards or listening to the wireless, with its news of French riots and German politics.

"I'll get my coat," I said.

Late in February 1934, the newspapers were full of Ramsay MacDonald's refusal to meet the Glasgow hunger marchers. I was glad Daddy had not lived to see how far the first Labour Prime Minister had strayed from his ideals, glad too that Xavier had finally gone down to the docks to look for work. He was gone all day; when I came home from school there was no sign of him. I began to wonder where he was and what could have happened to keep him out so late.

It was dark when Pat and Mick brought him home. He was wet through and stinking, a streak of oil on the left side of his jaw, his hair dark and flattened on his forehead. Mammy was out, gone to make the Stations of the Cross at St Patrick's, but still I would not let him into the house in that state. I pushed the three of them out into the yard, where Xavier stood shivering and dripping on the tiny patch of grass. We wrapped him in an old blanket, and he tugged off his clothes underneath it, like a little child changing on the beach. I had the cold Brennan fury on me, but even my mouth twitched at the heavings and jerkings and soft continuous swearing that took place beneath the old grey blanket.

"What were you doing?"

"I fell in the dock."

"He did not. He jumped in."

"The man's a hero."

"A lifesaver."

"Not a bit of it. Wasn't I only after…?"

"Jumping in the dock to save a pig!" said Mick.

A pig. I could not believe it. Pat and Mick were silly with laughter, but it was to them, not to Xavier, I addressed my question.

"Had he been drinking?"

They shook their heads, Tweedledum and Tweedledee, united in this as in all things. "Catholic twins" – with only ten months between them.

"Not a drop."

"As God is my witness."

I hustled Xavier into the scullery, where I boiled the kettle and filled the old white enamel basin – the one I used for washing my feet – to its chipped blue rim.

"Here. Wash yourself down and then perhaps you'll explain."

But all Xavier would say was that it was a well-known fact that pigs could not swim. They would cut their own throats with their trotter in the attempt, and he had never been a man to see a poor dumb animal suffer. Besides, it was the man's only pig, he added.

Later, with the help of Mick and Pat, and while Xavier was upstairs finding himself clean clothes, I unravelled the whole incident. Pat and Mick were preparing to walk home together after work, as they always did, when Xavier appeared. He had had no luck in finding work, he told them, though he had been looking all day. He had not said where he had been looking, but there would have been no point in staying in the dock area once the morning hiring was done. So perhaps he had been in town, they did not know. They did not ask. The three of them, Pat and Mike with Xavier between them, were walking along the side of Victoria Dock when there was a sudden squealing, and a little runt of a pig, no bigger than a small dog, ran across their path and over the edge of the dock. It landed with an unexpectedly loud splash in the oily water six feet below. A wail of despair, the like of which neither Pat nor Mick had ever heard, went up from an old man, crouched on a coil of rope in the shadow of the dock wall, and Xavier dived to the rescue. Which was when the trouble really started.

"We couldn't get him out. There he is, pig struggling under one arm, trying to swim with the other and going round in circles. Eventually we fling him one end of the rope the old one is sitting on; he ties it round him and the pig – which is a job in itself when you've only the one arm free – and we manage to haul him to the side. He still can't get out, so we borrow a basket off an old Shawlie and lower it down on the other side of the rope, Mick here acting as the counterweight. Into the basket goes the pig, up it comes, squeaking and snorting, and the old one clasps it in both arms as if it was a baby. And before we know where we are, there's Xavier scrambling up the rope like a monkey up a stick, and the old one raining down blessings on his head the way you'd think he was every saint in the calendar."

"He might have drowned," I said. I refused to smile.

Later still, in bed, with Xavier reading beside me, I wondered if I had been too censorious. I touched him on the shoulder.

"It was a brave thing you did," I said. "But foolish. To jump in the dock after a pig!"

Xavier shrugged me off.

"Did I ever tell you," he said, "about the time Vinnie and I pushed a policeman into a dock?"

"Jesus, Mary and Joseph!" I said before I had time to think, and for a moment it could have been Mammy speaking. "How could you do such a thing?"

"We had no choice," said Xavier. "The man was ablaze."

"I see," I said, not seeing. "So why was he ablaze in the first place? And how did you know he could swim?"

"As to the first, why, I set fire to him myself, and as to the second – it would be a poor policeman who couldn't swim."

"You did what?"

"I couldn't resist it. There he was wrapped up in toilet paper –"

"Toilet paper?"

"It's not everyone uses squares of old newspapers to wipe their behinds," Xavier said. "You go into one of those posh hotels in the city, and you'll find rolls of the stuff hanging behind the privy door, and not threaded on bits of string either."

"I know what toilet paper is," I snapped. "I just want to know why the policeman was wrapped in it, and why you set fire to him. What in the name of God possessed you?"

"The toilet paper was Vinnie's idea. I had no part in it."

I was exasperated.

"Xavier, tell me. Why did Vinnie wrap a policeman in toilet paper? Why did the policeman let him? Are you sure this isn't another of your stories?"

"As God is my witness. It was last summer. Vinnie and I had gone ashore in Buenos Aires, and we had a drink in the bar of one of the big hotels not far from the waterfront. I forget what it was called, some fancy name, but it was a pleasant enough place. We got talking to one of the local policemen in there. As you know, Vinnie's fluent in Spanish, and I don't do so badly myself. And, of course, the policeman had a word or two of English."

"Was he on duty?" I asked. I knew it was irrelevant, but I had to ask.

"He had his uniform on if that's anything to go by. Well, we bought him a drink, and he returned the compliment, and when we were ready to go back to the ship, he insisted on coming with us to see us safe aboard. As it happened, I had a bottle of Irish in my pocket, and we stopped at the dockside for another drink. Your man can't have been used to the hard stuff, that's all I can say, because when Vinnie decides to turn out his pockets and they're stuffed with toilet rolls he picked up in the men's room, the policeman doesn't turn a hair. And Vinnie says he's going to decorate him for services to visiting foreigners, and he wraps him up, like a mummy, head to toe, in yards of the stuff, running round and round him, and all the while your man's standing there with a smile on his face as bright as Sunday. And when I put my hand in my pocket, what did I find but my lighter? What else could I do but use it?"

"You deliberately set light to him?"

"It was a joke, that's all," Xavier said. "Only he flared up like a rocket, we'd nothing to put out the flames, and so there was nothing else for it. He went in the dock."

"He was all right in the end?"

"Right as rain," said Xavier, and he turned away from me, on his side, and was asleep in seconds.

I lay awake. Mostly I was wondering what sort of a man I had married. One thing I knew for sure: I had not even begun to get the measure of him.

10

In the weeks that followed Xavier moved from one job to another so quickly and easily that I lost track of them. He had more luck than Sean, who took weeks to find an opening at the Co-op on the other side of the city. Sean had not told us why he had left Withernsea, and we had heard nothing from Uncle Martin. We guessed there must have been a disagreement of some kind. Already Sean had quarrelled with Pat and Mick and their wives; he was staying with Vinnie and Kit, though Mammy kept asking him to move home. I could not see Sean staying with Vinnie for long, but neither did I think he would come back to Hopwood Street while Xavier and I were living there.

As for Xavier, I knew, of course, how he was getting work. His sort of charm was a powerful force, even in those days of rising unemployment. I was not so sure how each of his jobs came to an end. It seemed unlikely that he had been dismissed, since he remained on excellent terms with his former employers. It was more as though he tired of doing the same thing day after day, and just had to move on.

Once he spent just over three weeks in the marketplace, tending Granny Ponti's chestnut brazier while she kept to her bed with bronchitis. I went down to see him every night after school, fascinated to watch him work his pitch by Holy Trinity Church, his long hands busy with the squat iron shovel to scoop up hot chestnuts. He could not overcome his natural impatience, though; if a chestnut fell, he would snatch at it with his fingers, so that for the first fortnight his hands were pink and shiny with burns. After that they became hardened to the heat, and by the end of the third week no one could have been defter at twisting cones of newspaper and filling them to the brim. Mammy and I had cold chestnuts for supper three or four nights running, some sweet and floury, others wizened and burnt. The scent of them hung about Xavier night and day.

And then, suddenly, Granny Ponti was well again, and Xavier was somewhere else, doing something else, which was probably illegal. Never having been interested in any sort of gambling, I knew little of betting law, but even I suspected that being a bookie's runner was not a respectable occupation. I was embarrassed by it. When a colleague at school asked me what my husband-to-be did for a living, I lied, saying he was a Merchant Navy officer waiting for another ship. I was good at lying; I stuck to something near to the truth for me to remember and for other people to believe. When someone asked me if Xavier was considering a shore job, I was able to say that yes, he was thinking about it, but he was waiting for the right one to turn up. It was only a white lie after all, a venial sin, the sort you confess generally rather than having to be specific: "It is six weeks since my last confession, Father. Since then I have told some lies, been inattentive at Mass…" There was nothing so terrible in that. It did not even merit a decade of the rosary. I preferred not to think about the other lie, the lie of omission I told every day to the school authorities.

Soon there was no more talk of betting shops and betting slips. Instead, Xavier was behind the bar in the local pub. Once or twice

Vinnie called in on him early in the evening, leaving Kit at home with Sean or in Hopwood Street with Mammy and me. Neither Mammy or Kit or I had ever been in a pub; I could not even begin to imagine what a pub was like, although I could imagine Xavier accepting drinks and laughing with the customers. It was yet another occupation that I could not talk about at school, though it seemed to suit Xavier. He liked the hours. No need to get up early in the morning and working late at night seemed to appeal to him as well. I saw very little of him over that period. I left the house before he was up, and by the time he came home from work I was in bed, and usually asleep. Perhaps it was this lack of contact between us that led Mammy to ask me her question.

"You've no news for me yet, sweetheart?"

"News?"

Coyly, Mammy cradled an imaginary pregnant stomach. I flushed, shook my head and tightened my lips.

"You've a mouth on you like a hen's bum," Mammy said. "It's not such a strange question to ask. Unless, of course, you're hiding something from me."

"What would I be hiding?" I asked, bewildered.

"It's as well you don't know," Mammy said darkly. "We'll say no more about it."

On Saturday afternoon I repeated the conversation to Kit, who began to laugh.

"What's so funny?" I asked. We were standing in Paragon Square, looking into Hammond's windows. I pretended to be interested in a skirt and jacket on display on a headless mannequin. It meant that I did not have to look at Kit while I spoke to her. "Would that do me for school, do you think?"

"No. You'd look a fright. Do you really not know what your mother was suggesting?"

"I wouldn't ask you, if I did," I said. I had an uncomfortable feeling that, once again, I was going to appear naïve, but it was too late to do anything about it now. The question had been asked and it was going to be answered. I stared fixedly at a pair of brown court shoes at the base of the display. They looked sensible and in control, which was how I desperately wanted to feel.

"Hunnish practices," said Kit, quoting a scandalous court case that had made even the sedate papers of the Hull Daily Mail. "Or worse. Interfering with the course of nature. Family Planning."

I was scarlet. "I never…. How dare she? I wouldn't know how. And, anyway, we're Catholics."

"Stranger things have been known," Kit said. I stared at her.

"You haven't?"

"No need, not with things the way they are between Vinnie and me. But have you never wondered why I'm an only child?"

"I don't believe you," I said.

"It's an interesting possibility, though, isn't it? After all, my father is a doctor." She must have seen how uncomfortable I was with the conversation, for she suddenly changed the subject. "Come on. Let's go and have tea."

We walked down Jameson Street, Kit darting ahead, pausing occasionally to look in a shop window, but never to let me catch up. It was her favourite way of spending a Saturday afternoon: window shopping and tea out. Real shopping – and that was only for clothes and shoes – took place every two or three weeks.

"Don't you get bored, not working?" I asked, when we were finally sitting down in Trippett's, a pot of tea and a plate of fancy cakes between us. "What do you do all day?"

"Read. Call on my mother. Call on your mother. Cook. Occasionally lift a duster. I even wash once a week. Clothes, I mean, mine and Vinnie's."

I did all that, as well as a week's teaching. I was not impressed.

"It's such a waste, Kit. You were always cleverer than me, cleverer than anyone at school. You could have done anything."

Kit frowned, her small face suddenly ugly. "You're forgetting Dr Ian God Almighty Morrissey, aren't you?" It was how she always referred to her father; I was no longer shocked by the words. I pressed on.

"There are other things you could do."

"I don't want to talk about it. How's your husband, the barman? Mixing with a nice class of person, no doubt."

"At least he's working."

"That's what men are supposed to do, isn't it? So how much is he contributing to the rent?"

I used Kit's words against her. "I don't want to talk about it. It's nearly five o'clock. Shall we go?"

We left the café in silence.

*

I did not have time to think much about Kit and her lack of meaningful occupation. School was spilling over into the evenings. I was bringing more and more work home, spending more and more time preparing for the next day's lessons. I knew I was being overconscientious, but I could not stop myself. It was something to do with my near failure on teaching practice, and perhaps more to do with my guilt at not telling the school authorities that I was married. (Surely, they would find out soon. Somebody was bound to say something, if not now, then next week, next month. Next year if I was lucky.) But mostly it was to do with my own stubbornness. Nothing would stop me making a success of this job, not even the demands of cooking, cleaning, and washing for the two of us. I refused Mammy's offers of help. After all, I had chosen to carry on working; I had to prove I could cope. Once Xavier's bar job fell through – which of course it did after a few weeks – I found it even harder to fit everything in. It did not matter how much work I had to do: if Xavier wanted to go out, he expected me to accompany him. "So I can show you off," he said. I dd not believe him, but still I was flattered. The Cecil was our favourite cinema; sometimes he would insist that we saw two films there in one week. Other times he just wanted to walk through the city. He liked the pier and the old town, not the centre; sometimes I wondered if he wished he were back at sea. He seemed drawn to the docks, though not to work there. When he did find another job, it was as an assistant in a corner shop. It would not last.

*

I knew something was wrong as soon as Kit suggested tea in Hammond's restaurant. Hammond's was for weddings, major celebrations, and funerals, and not for every day. Not at their prices. But I met Kit anyway, on the pavement outside the shop at exactly three o'clock. Kit was on time, another sign that things were not as they should be. She was wearing a navy costume I had not seen before, her hair had just been set and, altogether she made me feel large, untidy, and somehow dowdy, as she so often did.

We sat at a small round table in the window. Hammond's restaurant was very modern, with glass topped tables covered with heavy lace tablecloths – they had to be heavy or they would slip off – and spindly gilded chairs you hardly dared sit on. The waitress looked down her long nose at me, decided I was unimportant and turned to Kit for the order.

"China, with lemon."

I did not like lemon in my tea, and I did not like China tea much either, but I was not in the mood for an argument. We sat in silence until the tea arrived, with Kit deliberately looking past me every time I tried to catch her eye. The waitress brought the tray: two pots, one filled with hot water – not real silver, I thought, though I could not be sure – and two delicate gold-rimmed cups and saucers. I poured, automatically, as later I would pay, automatically. Kit expected it.

"Well?"

Kit did not answer at first. She took out the small silver compact Vinnie had bought her from Rio, the one with the picture of the River Plate done in blue butterfly wings. She inspected her make-up. A flick of the powder puff, a careful application of lipstick, then she was finally ready to speak.

"I've got news."

"What news?"

Would she ever get round to telling it? I fidgeted with the lacy edge of the tablecloth. What could require such a long preamble?

Kit coughed a small, unnecessary cough. Then she spoke.

"I'm pregnant."

For a moment I did not quite understand; for a moment I was joyful, excited.

"You mean you and Vinnie …?"

"Don't be naïve."

I felt the blood leave my face. I put up my hand to cover my lips.

"Then how? Who?"

"You know how. You've been married long enough. It doesn't matter who."

But it did matter. Suddenly it mattered more than anything had ever mattered, because possibly, just possibly … I knew it was ridiculous, but I asked anyway.

"It's not Xavier's?" My voice cracked on his name.

"Of course it's not Xavier's. What would I want with the likes of Xavier Quinn?"

I felt another sort of hurt then, something that felt like rejection. How could Kit dismiss Xavier so contemptuously? What was happening here? I should have gone on, pushing her to tell me who the baby's father was, but I did not. I am not sure why; perhaps the combination of relief and affront was too strong for me to think clearly.

"Why, then?"

For the first time that day Kit looked straight at me.

"I'll tell you why," she said. "I'm twenty-two years old. I'm married to a man who doesn't love me, for whom I'm merely a useful – accessory. I'm not complaining. I went into it with my eyes open, even if I did hope things might change, once we were married. It was a convenient arrangement and it suited us both at the time. It still suits Vinnie. But me…. I wanted, just once I wanted to know what it was like to have someone love me. Can you understand that?"

I could understand it. What I did not know yet was whether I could accept it.

"So," I said at last. "Was it worth it?"

"Was it hell!" said Kit. Her green eyes narrowed, but she gave no other sign of what she was thinking or what she was feeling. For a few seconds, neither of us spoke. But there was one more question to be asked. I asked it.

"Does Vinnie know?"

"He had to, didn't he? He's not pleased. But I think he'll come around."

"Pass the child off as his own, you mean?" I was shocked by the bitterness in my voice. Looking down, I saw my hand splayed out on the lace tablecloth, fingers tense, thumb gripping the glass tabletop.

"This won't make any difference, will it, Grace? To us, I mean. We'll still be friends?"

Godmother to your bastard, too, probably, I thought, shocking myself. Aloud I said, "Of course it won't make a difference. We've always been friends. We always will be."

As I spoke, I knew I was lying. Perhaps Kit did too because she reached out and grabbed my hand.

"You're all I have left, now, Grace. Don't desert me. I couldn't bear it."

I lifted Kit's fingers from my wrist, squeezed her hand, placed it back on her own side of the table. I picked up my handbag from the floor and opened it, ready to pay the waitress. "I'm here, if you need me," I said.

It did not mean anything. It was not what Kit wanted to hear, and

I knew it. But it was all I could bring myself to say. We left the restaurant in silence and separated almost at once, Kit returning to her rented house on Beverley Road, and I to Hopwood Street.

Only Mammy was at home when I returned. Xavier was out somewhere with Vinnie, perhaps at the match. As usual, Mammy was eager for the details of my outing and, as usual, I supplied them. Or at least the ones that I could bring myself to share.

*

Julia Grace Brennan was born in the Central Maternity Home on Spring Bank West in early June 1935. Mammy joked that was why the baby had been given the name Julia but, no, Kit told me, it had been Vinnie's choice, as Grace had, of course, been hers. And no one was more surprised than Kit at how attached Vinnie had become to the baby. He held her on his knee, carried her around in his arms, warmed her bottles, and even fed her in the night.

"He couldn't be more besotted if he was her father," Kit said the day before Julia's baptism. As I had known I would, I had agreed to stand as godmother. Declan and Josie were the other two godparents. Mammy and Ethel Morrissey had fallen out over who should provide the christening robe and the all-important cake. Kit had been happy to let them get on with it – "They can claw each other's eyes out, for all I care," she said – but Vinnie and I both wanted Mammy to be happy with the outcome. So it was agreed: Mammy would stitch the christening gown and bake and ice the cake, and Ethel would hold the christening party at her home in Pearson Park. This suited Kit, who would not now have to think about what to provide for people to eat and drink or worry about tidying up afterwards. It struck me that Kit herself was paying very little part in the preparations for the baby's christening, but I said nothing. That tea in Hammond's restaurant had left a distance between Kit and me that I could not have envisaged the year before.

At the font, I took Julia from Vinnie's arms. The baby was sleeping, a wild tuft of dark hair curling above her forehead. Her eyelids were so pale – almost translucent – that I could see the tiny blue veins. I looked at the small fingers with their smaller nails, the little pouting mouth and the surprisingly well-formed nose.

"I wish you were my baby," I whispered to her as I prepared, on her behalf, to renounce the devil and all his works. It was an impossible wish, an inappropriate wish, and I knew it, but I promised silently that I would make up to her all the love that Kit seemed so unwilling to give.

There was no devil to be driven out in Julia; she did not cry or even wake, when the priest traced the sign of the cross on her forehead with holy water, but slept on, long eyelashes dark against the pale cheeks.

The Morrisseys had brought their car, a new Jowett, to take the baby back to their home near the park. As chief godmother, I was allowed to climb into the back with Kit, Vinnie, and the baby, while Ethel Morrissey sat triumphantly in the front. Mammy and the rest of the family had to make their way by bus, which gave Ethel time to arrange the welcoming party. Dr Morrissey loaded his camera under cover of the chenille tablecloth in the dining room, and Kit went off to reapply her make-up. Vinnie and I were left alone with the baby.

"What made you decide to call her Julia?" I asked. Vinnie was surprised.

"Have you forgotten? Da's mother was a Julia, Julia O'Driscoll before she was married. I thought it was something he would have liked."

"Does Mammy know that's why you chose the name?"

"I haven't spoken to her about it if that's what you mean. But she'll know."

There were other questions I wanted to ask, questions about his obvious fondness for a child who was not his own, but I did not dare. It might have involved a discussion about how he felt about Kit, and I did not want to know. Even so, I could not keep away from the subject.

"Are you sorry you married Kit?"

He looked at me for a long time before he answered. "It was that or be a priest, and that wouldn't have suited either."

"You could have married someone else."

"Who else would have taken me on?"

Having started the conversation, I now did not want to continue with it. I was about to make an irrelevant, godmotherly remark about baby Julia's blue eyes, which were now open, when the doorbell rang – I still could not get over the fact that the Morrisseys had a doorbell – and the Brennan contingent arrived. In that big empty house, they seemed even more numerous than they did when they gathered in Hopwood Street, and I was glad to be part of a sprawling family which overwhelmed the emptiness with laughter and warmth, leaving Alan and Ethel Morrissey prim and colourless.

We posed for photographs in the garden. I held Julia in my arms, while Vinnie and Kit stood on either side. Then it was the turn of the grandmothers. A moment's awkwardness because both of them wanted to go first, but then Ethel Morrissey must have decided that, since they were at her home, she could afford to be gracious. She stepped back to let Mammy seat herself in a deckchair, the sleeping baby on her lap. Such grave eyes Mammy had! She did not look down at the child in her arms but stared out at the camera and the watching family, her still bright copper hair about her face. Ethel Morrissey, who chose to stand when it was her turn, dragged Kit into the picture but ignored Vinnie. Ethel smiled, and the smile sat uneasily on her face, which was more accustomed to pursed lips or a frown of disapproval. At last it was over. Julia was returned to Kit, who was already looking round for someone to hand her to. Vinnie, of course.

"That's a beautiful baby," Xavier said as we made our way home on the bus this time. "A beautiful baby. But ours will be twice as handsome, won't they, sweetheart?"

It was the first time Xavier had spoken about the possibility of our having children. I wished he had not raised the subject. Mammy was already looking eager and interested.

"No, I'm not," I said crossly, before my mother had time to speak. "Haven't you enough grandchildren already? I'm finding it difficult enough being a godmother. The real thing can wait a little longer."

Mammy leaned over from the seat across the aisle. She grasped my wrist between her cool forefinger and thumb, squeezed the bone.

"As God wills," she said.

11

For two days I had alternated between despair and terror. Now a postcard of the Royal Albert Hall lay on the mat inside the front door. I bent to pick it up. The edges had been chewed by the letterbox, and the coarse fibre of the doormat prickled my fingertips. I turned it over. On the reverse, along with my name, the Hopwood Street address and the stamp were three words and an initial: "Gone to Spain. X". Curiously, the card was postmarked Holyhead.

I gave one short and furious scream. As Mammy appeared, startled, at the door from the scullery, I rushed past her to the outside lavatory. There I slammed the door and jerked the bolt home. Then, teeth set, I tore the postcard into halves, into quarters, and then (with some difficulty) into ragged eighths. Tearing satisfied something inside me. I seized the wodge of newspaper strung upon a nail on the lavatory door, and ripped the squares from I, crumpling and scattering them on the floor. It was not enough. I had never been so angry in my life, nor as desolate. I bent my head, bit the window-ledge, leaving my teeth marks in the paint. Then I banged my hands against the walls and scraped my nails along the bricks. For the first time, I wondered if it would be preferable to be dead.

My bloodied knuckles and fractured nails hurt. I became aware of the state of my hands. I sucked the back of a finger, the iron taste of blood immediately familiar and therefore comforting in my mouth. All this frenzy had taken perhaps two minutes. I heard Mammy's voice outside the door.

"Mary Grace, are you all right?"

"Of course I'm not all right," I snapped but, at once remorseful, I opened the door. "Oh, Mammy!" I was ready to throw myself into Mammy's arms, but the arms were not offered. Instead a hard hand stung me across the left cheek, and I fell backwards to sprawl on the lavatory seat.

"Pull yourself together," Mammy said, "And tell me what all this play-acting is about."

I could feel my anger returning, but this time it was cold and controlled. I could deal with it.

"Nothing important," I said. "My husband has left me, as you supposed he had, that's all. You don't have to worry about me. I'm going for a walk."

"You've no time for walking. You've a job to go to, or had you forgotten? Away with you and wash your face; you can still be on time if you make an effort."

"I'm not going to school today. Let them think I'm sick." I could hear the self-pity in my voice, but there seemed to be nothing I could do about it. Did I not deserve at least my own pity?

"You're going, if I have to carry you there myself, you silly child. Be practical for once in your life. If he has gone, you're going to need your teaching, and not just because it brings in the money you need to live on. It will keep you sane."

I did not answer, but I washed my face at the scullery tap and dried it on the scullery towel. I put on my jacket and good shoes then took a moment to find my hat. Silently Mammy handed me my school bag. I left, still without speaking.

The trolley ride and walk to St Peter's school had never seemed so long. Or passed so quickly. I saw the faces I saw every morning. I smiled and greeted them, commented on the weather. But when I reached the school gates, I had forgotten whom I had met on the way there. Though I was not late, I was later than usual, and the children were already lining up in the playground. I told the small girl at the head of the line to lead in. Only in a very tiny place in the corner of my mind did the screaming go on.

Spain.

The name haunted me. Could he have really gone to Spain? There was a civil war going on. He might have gone to join the fighting. He could be killed. I could not even guess on which side he would be fighting. Franco, a Catholic, had the Church's backing. But Daddy would have backed the Republicans, no doubt about that, which meant that I would back them too. Xavier and I had never talked about politics. If a general election were called, I had no idea how he would vote. I had just assumed that my priorities would be his priorities. Anyway, I thought, who went to Spain by way of Holyhead? No one. Of course he was not in Spain. So where was he?

*

"Can't you stop crying?" Kit nudged my elbow. "You're embarrassing me." It was Saturday afternoon. We were sitting in the furred darkness of the Cecil cinema, in the middle row. I had been crying ever since we came in. I gripped my wet handkerchief more tightly and stared stubbornly at the screen. Kit nudged me again.

"No, I can't stop crying. Now are you satisfied? Why can't you pretend that I'm crying over the film?"

"No one cries over Old Mother Riley," Kit replied.

Silence. I had not noticed which film was playing. I gulped, bit my lip, rubbed my eyes.

"It's no good. I'm going home. You stay."

I edged my way past indignant knees. Kit followed me. We stumbled up the raked floor to the swing doors at the back. In the foyer the usherette looked at us suspiciously. I commented on it.

"No, she didn't," Kit said. "She just wonders why anyone should be stupid enough to waste their money by leaving as soon as the film starts."

"I'm sorry," I snapped. "I told you to stay and watch. You didn't have to come out with me."

"I never wanted to see the film in the first place," Kit said. "I just thought it might cheer you up."

"Well, it didn't cheer me up. I'm not in the mood for laughing. And you needn't say that I'm better off without him. I don't want to hear it."

"I wasn't going to say –"

"Yes, you were!"

We walked on in offended silence, not sure where we were going, each of us determined not to speak first. Xavier had been gone eleven days and, apart from the postcard, I had heard nothing. I'd continued to go to St Peter's and teach my class; I'd accompanied Mammy to Mass and to the market; I had stared at the pages of a book and read nothing. When my brothers called in at the house, they treated me as if I were an invalid, or invisible. Only Mammy and

Kit nagged at me, reasoned with me, tried to make me think of other things: the future, the exercise books I had to mark, the local gossip. I looked at Kit, diminutive and fierce at my side.

"Sorry," I said, and this time I meant it. The wind from the river dried my tears; I could feel the taut dryness of my skin beneath their tracks, taste the trace of them on my lips. Our furious walking had brought us to the high railings beside the Victoria Pier. Below us, the brown tidal waters of the Humber slapped against its wooden pillars. I breathed in. Behind my eyes a quietness descended, and I looked out across the river, across to Lincolnshire, just visible on the far bank. The short blast of a ship's hooter caught my attention. I turned to see the ferry boat pull away from the pier, and I watched its wake as it creamed into the distance.

"He'll come back," Kit said, her tone no longer sharp. "You just have to wait."

"I know." I straightened up and smiled, even though it was an effort. "Let's go home and find Mammy and Julia. We could take her for a walk in the new pushchair."

The new pushchair was a splendid vehicle, all green leather and chrome, folding and unfolding smoothly without a squeak. It was, of course, a present from Dr and Mrs Morrissey, as Julia's pram had been. I had been surprised that Vinnie had not objected, but since Julia's birth, he had been getting on increasingly well with his in-laws. Better, perhaps, than he did with his wife.

"Haven't we walked enough already?" Kit grumbled, but she too turned away from the river. "All right then, but not far. These shoes are new."

*

"Miss Brennan?"

I looked up from the Co-op counter where Maurice, a pencil behind his left ear, was pouring sugar into a blue paper bag. I wondered for a moment who had spoken my name, and then I saw the store manager in the shadowy doorway behind the counter, thumbs in his waistcoat pockets, his gold watch glinting across his chest.

"Mr Harding?"

"If you could spare me a moment?"

I stepped behind the counter and followed him through into the stock room at the back of the shop. Maurice, who had been deftly packing my sugar, hesitated for a moment and then placed it to one side, behind the brass scales. He went on to serve another customer as Mr Harding closed the door behind us.

"Yes, Mr Harding?"

The store manager turned to look at me. Even in the dimness of the stock room I could see that he was uncomfortable, but I had no idea what he was going to say.

"This isn't easy for me, Miss Brennan. I'm sure you'll appreciate that …"

"What isn't easy?"

"Your account. I'm afraid I have to ask you to settle your account."

"My account is settled monthly," I said crisply. "Why would you want me to change the arrangement now?"

"Because – forgive me for mentioning this, Miss Brennan – your account is three months in arrears. We can't allow it to go on like this."

"That's nonsense," I said. "Mr Quinn settled the account for us not three weeks ago."

But even as I said it, I knew it was not true. Of course he had not settled the account. He had taken the money with him.

"I hesitate to contradict you, Miss Brennan, but –"

"How much is owing?"

He told me and I paid him from money in my handbag. Both of us were embarrassed by the transaction.

"Today's purchases," Mr Harding began. "Will you be wanting them on account?"

I should have liked to tell him that I would never buy anything in his shop again but that was not practical. Mammy had always shopped there; since I had taken over buying food for the three of us, I had done the same. If Jack Brennan's family did not support the Co-op, who would?

"Yes, thank you, Mr Harding. You need not fear any repetition of this incident." I was amazed at how pompous I sounded.

"I'm sure everything will be in order now, Miss Brennan."

He followed me into the shop once more. Maurice totalled up the amount I had spent, asked me for the dividend number – 146 – wrote it down on the slip of paper, licked the back, and stuck it in the book. Like the children in my class, he licked the end of his pencil before he wrote, pressed hard, breathed harder. The actual calculations he did in his head, faster than I could, but writing them down was another matter entirely. I picked up my shopping and left, back straighter and head even higher than usual: I knew this was only the beginning. I ran through the bills Xavier had offered to pay "to save time". The Co-op, the coal man, the insurance. (The insurance. I would have to check that with Declan.) Those were the bills I knew about, the ones we had agreed to pay for the household in lieu of rent, but there might be others, bills he had run up and left unpaid and unacknowledged. At least, now I had found out, I could pay the bills myself. Mammy would not need to know.

I visited the coal man on my way home.

"Sorry to trouble you, Mr Addison, but Mr Quinn has been called away – a family emergency. I know he meant to settle our bill before he left, but there was so little time. Perhaps you could tell me …."

Three months. He had not paid the coal man for three months. Now it was not just the shame of being in debt that bothered me but also the fact that Xavier must have been planning for his absence. Or had he simply got into the habit, of betting perhaps, realised what he had done, how the debts had mounted up, and then run away? I had no way of knowing. That was the worst of it, that I did not know and did not guess what was happening.

I paid the coal man. I was left with little money, but at least it was nearly the end of the month. I realised that Mammy was right. Without my work at St Peter's, I would have found it hard to survive.

*

"He's not half the man your father was."

Anger made Mammy heavy-handed: she slammed the cup and saucer down so hard on the table where I was marking that the tea slopped over into the saucer, and then onto the copybook in which Eddie O'Donnell had made his best attempt yet at cursive script. I said nothing, but merely pulled out the drawer in the side of the table and extracted a quarter sheet of pink blotting paper. I laid it gently down on the pool of tea then, as the liquid soaked through, raised the page with my nail to examine the one below. That too was blurred and wrinkled. I picked up a second sheet of blotting paper and inserted it between the two pages, put the copybook to one side.

"So you keep saying."

"You'll not take him back? If he comes back?"

That was the heart of it. I picked up another copybook, corrected the length of the descenders, kept my head bent over it.

"Probably."

"I'd have thought you'd be looking for an annulment."

Now I was shocked. The pen stopped in my hand. I looked up at Mammy.

"On what grounds? Not non-consummation, that's for sure. Neither of us was under duress, neither of us was drunk – what other grounds would you suggest? I'm married to him, Mammy. I want to stay married to him. You liked him well enough once."

"Once!" Mammy was scornful. "That was before I knew him for the rapscallion he is."

"Mammy," I said, as my fingers gripped the edge of the table and a sour ache rose in my throat. "Xavier is my husband. When he comes back – when, not if – I shall expect you to treat him as such and welcome him as I do. Otherwise, we shall move from this house and you'll not see either of us again."

How momentous, that first defiance. Mammy wilted before it.

"Let's hope you're right. Let's hope he does come back."

We were not easy with each other for the rest of that Saturday. I was glad when mid-afternoon approached, and Pat and Mike called in.

"Teresa and Maureen would like it if you could come round for your tea, Grace. If that's all right with you, of course, Mammy."

Mammy nodded. I hurried into my coat, jammed my hat on my head, and walked with them the length of Hopwood Street, through the back alleys, to the big house on Beverley Road. Tea was to be downstairs at Pat and Teresa's, a very English tea, with ham and mustard, and bread cut thin and sliced from corner to corner.

"Party bread," observed Vinnie, who was there with Kit, Julia in his arms. The door opened again, and in came Declan and Josie, followed by Sean, back on speaking terms with his older brothers and here to take part in the family conference. For that, I realised, was what this gathering was. I knew too what its subject would be.

A sleeping Julia was laid down in the back bedroom with her cousins Paddy and Tess, both toddling now and with barely two months between them. Sometimes I forgot which child belonged to whom. Their ages gave it away: Paddy, slightly older, was Patrick's son. Tess was Mick and Maureen's daughter. I was surprised but grateful to find the children sleeping. A house full of Brennans and babies was altogether too lively a place for me that afternoon.

Teresa seated us around the table in pairs: Pat, then herself, at the head, then Mick, Maureen, Declan and Josie along one long side, with Vinnie and Kit at the bottom. Sean and I, the only two without wife or husband to support us, took the other long side. We had far more room than the others, who ate with their elbows squeezed in – when Teresa gave them permission to start. I was not used to a moment of pause before a meal, none of us were, but Teresa and Maureen were great ones for praying over meat, and, since the double wedding, Pat and Mick had apparently joined them.

"Bless us, O Lord, and these Thy gifts, which we are about to receive from Thy bounty, through Christ our Lord, amen."

"Amen."

If I had not been so on edge, I would have been amused by the shame-faced way in which Declan, Vinnie, and Sean ducked their heads and muttered their 'amens', by the sketchy sign of the cross, barely covering nose and mouth, let alone extending from forehead to breast and from shoulder to shoulder, and by Kit's open refusal to take any part or interest in the proceedings, whatsoever. As it was, I noted it all, but could not enjoy it as I would normally have done. I was waiting too apprehensively for Xavier to be mentioned.

Maureen began it, when we had finished with the ham and moved on to the cake.

"Have you heard anything from Xavier yet, Grace?" The question, designed to sound casual, fell portentously into the silence created by full mouths and a general desperation to avoid the one subject that had to be talked about.

"No."

"I'm sure you'll hear something soon." That was Teresa, supporting her younger sister. "I've prayed for you every night. I've prayed for him to come home."

"To St Jude, no doubt," Sean muttered beside me, and I turned to him in disbelief, uncertain whether to be annoyed or amused.

"What did you say?"

"Well, it's a lost cause, isn't it? Five Hail Marys and a Glory Be aren't going to bring that one back."

"You know nothing about it," I said. I was angry, but not angry enough to cry. For that I was grateful. "Can we change the subject?"

"Sean has a point, though." Pat, at the head of the table, was the head of the family in his own mind. "We have to consider the possibility that Xavier may not return. You'll have to consider what you'll do in those circumstances."

"That's easy," I said bitterly. "Mammy will get my marriage annulled, and I'll live out my days as a spinster schoolteacher, devoted to her brothers and their wives and her nieces and nephews – and her ageing mother. And everyone will be happy, except me."

"That'll do, Grace," Vinnie said quietly. "Is there more tea in the pot, Teresa? I'm suddenly thirsty."

Teresa conceded that the ham was perhaps a touch salty. Josie leaned across the table, took my hand in her own and squeezed it.

"You must come to us tomorrow," she said, in the flat Hull accent that surprised me, coming from those full Italian lips. "Just the three of us."

I thanked her. The conversation went on to other things. Paddy and Tess woke and wondered through to meet their adoring aunts and uncles. Vinnie went to fetch Julia, who had been woken by her cousins, and for a few minutes I sat and held my goddaughter, managing to block out the noisy family banter about me so long as I had the weight of the baby in my arms and the dark curl of her hair beneath my fingers.

"I'll walk back with you," Declan said unexpectedly as everyone was leaving. "All right, Josie?"

"Of course." She hugged me. Nothing had been solved, but suddenly I felt better. It was out in the open at last; I knew who my allies were. Declan and Josie. Vinnie and Kit. Who else did I need?

To begin with, Declan and I walked in silence. Then, just as we were turning into Hopwood Street, he spoke,

"I shouldn't worry about Xavier," he said. "He'll be off with the IRA."

I did not understand at first. I had heard of the Irish Republican Army, of course I had; I had heard the men of the family singing the old songs, which were not really so old. But Xavier an IRA man? Surely not.

"What makes you say that?" I asked carefully.

"Wasn't his brother Larry one of Eamon de Valera's volunteers? Joined up for the Easter Rising and was there in '22. Killed in the fighting. It's only natural that Xavier would want to continue his work."

"Xavier had a brother? An older brother who was killed in '22?"

"Didn't he tell you?"

I realised once again that here was another area of Xavier's life about which I knew nothing. He had never told me anything about his past, the time before he met me. For all I knew, he might never have had a family, never had a mother even. I remembered him telling Mammy he was alone in the world, the first time he came to the house. I had not wished to pry and so I had asked him nothing.

"He may have mentioned it." I moved on to surer ground. "But it's all over, surely. There's an Irish Free State, de Valera's Prime Minister – why should Xavier need to go and join the IRA? If he has joined them." I still did not believe it. I could not possibly be married to a man who dealt in guns and violence.

"He'll be in the north," Declan said confidently. "The IRA won't rest until the whole of Ireland's free, Grace. You should know that."

I looked at my brother, the insurance agent, the sensible one, and thought: I do not know you. I did not know my husband, if what Declan was saying was true. Did I even know my own family? I began to doubt it.

*

Two weeks later I came home from school to find Mammy waiting on the doorstep.

"He's back."

"Xavier?"

"Who else? He's in the front room. I thought you'd want to be private."

"Thanks, Mammy."

But it was the last thing I wanted, I realised, as I put down my school bag and hung up my coat and hat on the pegs in the hall. My fingers were clumsy; it took much longer than usual to find the loop inside the neck of my coat and slip it over the peg. For a moment I considered asking Mammy to come with me, but I was a married woman, an adult: I had to face him on my own.

I pushed open the door. He was sitting on the piano stool, stretching his long fingers over the keys – he could span nine of them easily, I remembered – and he swung round when he heard me, lifting his legs over the handle at the side of the stool. The movement was comic, and I had to struggle not to smile but to retain the grave face appropriate to the occasion.

He did not notice, just leapt to his feet and took me in his arms, hugging me close and high so that my feet left the ground and I was dangling in air.

"Put me down!"

He did so.

"It's good to see you, Grace."

"Where –?" I began, but he interrupted me.

"Not now. Let's just enjoy the moment. I've money in my pockets for once, so get your glad rags on. We're going dancing."

"No." I was firm on that. Eventually we settled on a visit to the cinema. If Mammy was surprised to see us go out, she did not say so.

The film turned out to be the same one that Kit and I had left so abruptly two weeks earlier. Once again, I took in none of it. Beside me, however, Xavier seemed intent on the screen, leaning forwards with his hands on his knees.

"That Kitty ..." he said at one point, when Kitty McShane had done something particularly daring, and he took my hand to squeeze it. My fingers lay limply inside his. I did not resist, but neither did I respond. Dance hall or cinema, both would have served the same purpose, to prevent me from asking him where he had been and why he had left.

And the longer he made me leave it, the more difficult it would be. He knew, of course. He was counting on it.

Sometimes, as you start to walk uphill through a wood, perhaps, you know you have chose the wrong day for such exercise: last night's rain has left the path treacherous with mud and fallen leaves; half-buried roots and crumbling logs make you stumble; briars reach out from the bracken to snare your ankles, catch at your hands, whip across your face. And even when you are out of the wood, the hill goes on another fifty feet of near vertical grass, and you have no idea what will be waiting for you at the top.

None of my questions took me a step further up the steep path of my ignorance of where Xavier had been or what he had been doing.

"Did you go to Spain?"

"No."

"Why not?"

"I ran out of money."

"In Holyhead?"

"Somewhere like that."

"So where have you been?"

"Round and about. Here and there. There and back again."

I did not ask him if Declan had been right, if he had been with the IRA. I could not find the words, and, in any case, I did not believe it. I did not ask him the questions I had asked Kit, so he never knew how I had wondered if he had found someone else on his travels. I did not tell him what Kit had said in reply, though I hoped it was true. "Your Xavier has a keener eye for a horse, than a woman," Kit had told me. Though I found it slightly insulting, I wanted to believe it. I carried on with my questions, though I was not good at confrontation and never had been, and I was afraid I might cry if I looked at him. I looked down at my hands as I spoke.

"What about the bills?"

"What bills?"

"You know what bills. The Co-op. The coalman. The butcher, the baker, the candlestick maker. I don't know."

He considered.

"I had things on my mind."

"And money in your pockets, my money. Where did it all go?"

"Grace, you know where it went." His voice was surprisingly tender. I blinked away tears.

"Why won't you tell me what went wrong?"

"Nothing went wrong."

I lost control. "In the name of God, why did you leave me?"

"I went away in order to come back."

It sounded profound, but it meant nothing to me. I did not understand why he would not answer my questions, questions I felt I had a right to ask. But I knew when I was beaten. The subject was closed.

12

I found it hard to understand my family's reaction to Xavier's return. I had forgiven him, of course, but I was his wife: I had to forgive him. Vinnie was his best friend, so of course he was glad to see Xavier home again. But Declan? Declan astonished me. Before Xavier had been home a week, Declan had come round to welcome the wanderer, and offered him a job as an insurance collector.

The round Declan arranged for him was in Beverley, two miles from the racecourse. Xavier left home early, taking a trolley bus into the centre of Hull, followed by another out to the suburb where the insurance company had its headquarters. What happened after that I put together from Xavier's own account, from what Declan told me, and from what I thought I knew of my husband.

The first trolley arrived on time, with a slick hiss and a shower of sparks. When the conductor came to collect his fare, I could imagine Xavier looking longingly at the brown leather shoulder bag and ticket machine. His fingers would have itched to turn the wheel and set the fare, to press down the lever which released the ticket: he always loved gadgets.

Well, at least he would have a brown leather money bag, provided by the company, along with a pencil and a ruled notebook in which to record the details of the payments he would take. All three items would be waiting for him in Declan's office – for Declan was too important to collect money himself; he had an office in which he sat all day.

Xavier was one of a crowd of people going to work and, for once, he told me, it felt good. He was a working man. Important. He found a seat on the trolley, but immediately leapt to his feet to offer it to a bewildered cleaner coming from her early morning shift at the hospital. He turned his smile on her, the one I had seen him practising, the one with which he had planned to charm the ladies on his round. He had told me he was glad to be working during the day, rather than in the evenings as some collectors did. After tea, when the husbands were at home, smiles such as his could not work their magic. The thought made him give the cleaner a second smile, a genuine one this time, a smile of pure delight. She lowered her chin and coloured up but could not resist smiling back at him. It seemed to Xavier that the whole bus was smiling.

Declan was waiting for Xavier in his office. He sat behind his desk, solemn, unfamiliar, not looking like Xavier's brother-in-law, but like a man who knows the ways of the world and grieves over them. He gave Xavier the leather bag, the pencil, and the notebook, and also a list of the clients he was to visit. So many names, and that was just for one day.

Xavier put the pencil behind his right ear, at an angle so that it lifted the brim of his borrowed trilby. For balance, he slung his leather bag over his left shoulder, but soon found it uncomfortable and swapped it over to his right. Then he tightened the belt on his overcoat, drew himself up to his full height, shook Declan by the hand, and strode out into the street. He knew that the coat and hat were not as glamorous as the Merchant Navy uniform he once wore, but he still felt confident and at ease with the world. As he walked along, he admired the gleaming toes of his shoes, which I had polished the night before. It was, it seemed to him, a beautiful morning.

His first call at precisely nine o'clock was on Mrs Brenda Nolan, wife of James Nolan, greengrocer. Plenty of money in this house, Xavier thought, as he turned in at the gate, past the lilac tree and the six rectangular flower beds with their intersecting turf paths. He made for the side entrance to the grey, semi-detached house. ("Never go to the front," Declan had warned him. "They'll think someone's dead.") He stepped into the porch with its three doors – water closet to the left, coal cellar to the right, scullery straight ahead – and knocked cheerfully.

"If that's you, Mr MacDonald, you can come straight in."

He was not Mr MacDonald, but he went in anyway. At the far side of the scullery a tiny woman was leaning over a dolly tub more than half her size, pounding away at a pile of sheets with a wooden posser.

"What you must think of me I don't know. I'm all behind this morning, what with our Valerie and the children staying here for the weekend, and then Dougie coming out in spots and I'm sure it's chicken pox, but there you are, these things always happen when you're away from home …"

She looked up, saw a stranger in her scullery and was momentarily silent. Xavier gave her the smile.

"Dear lady, allow me to introduce myself. Xavier Quinn, at your service: your new insurance agent."

He would have been proud of that word, agent, which sounded so much more important than collector. Proud too of his little speech of introduction, so formal and English, though with a name like Nolan it could not have been long since that one's family came over. Still, first impressions.

"Pleased to meet you, Mr Quinn, and what has happened to Mr MacDonald? Such a nice man, been coming for years, since Mother was alive, and always so polite. A Scotsman, of course, well, you'd expect that with a name like MacDonald, wouldn't you? I'm surprised he didn't say he was leaving. I hope he's all right."

Xavier did not know what had happened to Mr MacDonald. It had not occurred to him to ask. He relieved Mrs Nolan of her silver threepenny bit: two pence for James Nolan, a penny for herself. It was not every man who would insure his wife when all she had to do was to keep house, Xavier thought, and "Haven't you the thoughtful husband?" he suggested to Mrs Nolan, and she agreed.

"A darling man like yourself, Mr Quinn, or I'm very much mistaken," and she offered him a cup of tea, which he did not refuse.

Four hours and twenty clients later, he told me, he had begun to refuse the tea, but the smile would have been as ready as ever and coming more easily by then. He had already persuaded two of the ladies to top up their premiums, writing down the details in his strong cursive script in his little notebook, tucking the pencil back behind his ear, using his Irish charm on these Englishwomen while the pennies in his brown leather bag began to weigh heavy at his side.

By lunchtime he had taken six shillings and fourpence. He could not resist counting it, couldn't quite believe that he could go to so many doors and have money given to him. By right. That is when he must have told himself that he deserved a drink, and stopped off at the Maid of Erin, which would be sure to have an Irish landlord who served stout the way he liked it. He ordered a pint and stood drinking it at the bar. I do not think that he was really that surprised when the street door opened and Tommy Haughey, whom he had last seen years ago in Buenos Aires (also, incidentally, in a bar) came in. They would have had a drink together, swapped stories of where they'd been and what they'd done since they last saw each other in Argentina, and then they'd have had another drink in honour of Xavier's marriage and, somehow, when the first pint was just a distant memory and Xavier knew he should be back at work, he had found that he had agreed to accompany Tommy to the races "just for half an hour".

He would have recognised the smell of the racecourse even before they reached it: dust and horse sweat and a faint reek of onions frying. He liked the noise, the laughter, the swift indecipherable movements of tick-tack men, and it must have been very easy for him to wager all the money he had in his pocket on a horse with a winning name and no speed at all.

And when that money was gone, there was the big brown leather bag at his side, with its weight of copper and, before he knew it, five shillings had disappeared into the bookie's big cold hand, and the horse that was going to make his fortune did not even finish.

There would have been no point in saving one shilling and fourpence he had left. He put a few coppers by for his bus fare home, and he and Tommy bet all they had between them on a horse, whose eyes, Xavier probably said, reminded him of me. It came fourth. Then there was nothing for it but to go back and tell Declan the company's money was gone and he could not pay it back, and he had no idea at all, at all, how he was going to explain this one away.

He was sitting on the trolley-bus – less crowded at this time since it was mid-afternoon – with the brown leather bag sadly empty on the seat beside him, when it occurred to him how easy it would be to get up and simply leave it there. Obviously, Declan was not going to keep him on as an insurance collector, not with a whole morning's takings vanished who knew where, but at least if he thought Xavier was careless, rather than criminal, it might avert a family rift. At the last moment he stuffed the bag under the seat, with the discarded newspapers and squashed cigarette butts, since he was afraid the conductor might notice it before he had time to get away and call him back. He jumped from the step as soon as the door was open, before the trolley had completely stopped, and he walked the last few hundred yards to Declan's office in a curiously buoyant mood, rehearsing his stories and his apologies as he went.

Declan was furious, of course. He locked the office and marched Xavier across town to the lost property office at the depot, ignoring Xavier's suggestion that they should go by bus. There was the bag waiting for them. By then Xavier must have been so carried away by his own invention that for a moment he felt a sense of vindication.

"What sort of world is it we live in," he wondered, as he thrust his hand into the limp and empty leather pouch, "where a man can't leave his property unguarded for a moment without some villain thieving it away?"

Unexpectedly, Declan was prepared to give Xavier another chance – perhaps he was so surprised at finding the bag where Xavier said it would be that his judgment deserted him. Xavier declined, gracefully, of course, with the smile no doubt much in evidence. It was good of Declan, but he himself saw now that he was not the sort of man to be trusted with other people's money. He was too forgetful. It would not be right.

Declan might already have been regretting his offer, because he did not push it at all, just slapped Xavier on the shoulder and said he was a good fellow after all, and the incident was not to be mentioned again by either of them. And they parted better friends than ever, Xavier only too aware of how lucky he had been, Declan proud of his family loyalty and his magnanimity.

I put down the sock I was darning.

"Well," I said. "Am I right? Is that how it happened?"

More or less, Xavier agreed. Though there was not one word of truth in the story about the racecourse, he having left the bag on the bus as he told me in the first place, and it was full at the time. And he only had a half in the Maid of Erin, and it was not Tommy Haighey, it was Dermot O'Casey, whom he had last seen in Cape Town, the time their ship was laid up there for a week, and Casey decided he wanted to see something of the country and never made it back before it set sail for Liverpool, and even if Xavier had been at the racecourse, which he had not, it was plain to see that I had never been near one, and I did not understand the first thing about horses or betting or race meetings.

"Unlike you," I said.

*

It did not take Xavier long to join the choir again. There would have been no choir at St Patrick's without the Brennans; Pat, Mick, and Declan never missed a practice, and even Vinnie joined in now that he was at home. Declan was still the star: his tenor solos were constantly in demand for weddings and funerals. Xavier's tenor was not in Declan's league: his voice had no depth to it, but it was true enough, and he was a useful addition. I took my place with the other altos. I had no illusions about my singing: it was not up to my brothers' standard, but they were short of altos. We stood at the front, looking down into the body of the church. I could not see

Xavier or my brothers, but I could hear them and enjoy the strong young sound they made.

As Christmas drew near, practices became more frequent. A whole nativity of carols had to be learned; the organist and Father Ryan's curate, Father Daly, were unusually ambitious that year. Then there was the plainsong Mass, the Missa de Angelis, with the music that looked wrong on the page somehow. Perhaps there were not enough lines in the stave, though I was too busy to count them.

"Don't hiss!" Father Daly said when we came to the Sanctus. "Just touch those s's; don't dwell on them. Just the very tip of your tongue, and then on to the next sound. Keep it clean."

I tried. The 's' at the beginning sounded clean enough, but I could hear the last one whistling through my teeth. I tried again, bringing the tip of my tongue back almost to my soft palate. I could barely hear the 's', but my tongue felt strange and awkward in my mouth.

"You're thinking about it!" Father Daly rapped. "Don't think. Do!"

That particular afternoon I could not hear Xavier's voice. There was only Declan holding his tenor, with the warm depth of the Brennan baritones behind him. Vinnie was there, then. When I thought about it, I had not seen Xavier since lunch. He had said he would meet me at the church, after I had finished my shopping. There was no time to shop during the week when I was working. So it was a mad scramble on Saturday afternoons before this extra choir practice that Father Daly insisted was necessary.

The organist had gone back to the Gloria. Declan on his own to begin with, loud and clear: "Gloria in excelsis Deo!"

The rest of us joined him then, a great swell of sound that caught me up with it. I might not have been as musical as my brothers, but I loved the surge of our voices against the high ceiling of the church.

"Et in terra pax hominibus, bonae voluntatis …"

I heard footsteps on the stairs leading to the choir. I could tell by Father Daly's frown that he had heard them too. So who was this coming in late, when the practice was half over? I did not need to ask. I knew those footsteps as well as I knew my own. For a moment I turned my head to smile at Xavier as he slipped into his place beside Declan, but he was not there. If I turned round any further, the priest would notice my lack of attention. But what was Xavier doing?

"Thirty to one." I heard the light voice whispering somewhere to my left, beneath the rich sweep of the Gloria.

"Glorificamus te. Gratias agimus tibi propter magnam gloriam tuam."

It was hard to listen to what Xavier was saying and to follow the plainsong. My voice faltered, then faded. I could hear Vinnie now, his words indistinguishable, and then Xavier again. "Argentine Girl, in the two o'clock. Look!"

I could not resist it. I turned completely around, and there the two of them were, peering at a scrap of paper, their faces sharing a single incredulous smile.

"Et exspecto resurrectionem mortuorum……"

But the choir never made it to the expectation of the life to come. There was a sudden shout, the organ rumbled into silence, and the choir followed suit. Shocked, we strained to hear what Father Daly was bawling with such unpriestly ferocity.

"Vincent Brennan!"

"Father?" Vinnie's dark silk voice held a trace of amusement. I wanted to crawl under the pew, hide, deny I was related to him or Xavier.

"What, in the name of all that is holy, do you have in your hand?"

Vinnie looked down at the scrap of paper, turned it upside down, pretended to read the words. "I do believe it's a betting slip, Father."

Father Daly was a young man, not much older than Vinnie and Xavier, thirty at most. But he spoke with all the certainty of nearly two thousand years of moral authority as he stared up at the two of them from his place in the aisle.

"And what would Our Lord have to say about that?"

Xavier could not resist it. "I was not aware he was a betting man, Father. I don't remember a single account of a horse race in the gospel, more's the pity."

A muffled snort of laughter. Was it Pat or Mick? It was not Vinnie. I had never seen him so straight faced. The priest was red-faced, breathing hard.

"Is it not written, "My Father's house is a house of prayer, and ye have made it a den of thieves"?"

"Ah, hold on, Father," Vinnie said. "That's going a bit far. It's only an old betting slip, when all's said and done."

"Away with you!" said Xavier. "It's far more than that. Didn't Argentine Girl come in at thirty to one? It's our passport to riches."

"How much did you have on her?" Declan asked. The rest of the choir waited breathlessly for an answer, every face turned towards Vinnie and Xavier.

Vinnie was casual. "Five pounds between us."

"Holy Mother of God! That's …"

"A hundred and fifty pounds," Xavier said with some satisfaction.

The priest in the aisle had passed through all the shades of red to an ominous purple. Even from my place in the choir I could see the veins in his forehead, sense the tension in his fisted hands.

"Get out!" he roared. The yelled words shocked us all.

"Would you be talking to me, Father?" Vinnie asked, suddenly all ice, not a trace of Brennan charm in his voice.

"You and the viper at your side! Yes, you, Xavier Quinn! Out of my sight, the pair of you, and don't come back!"

"We shall never darken your choir stalls again," Vinnie said, and the hint of a smile was back as he spoke. "Come, Quinn."

The whole choir watched the two of them make their way to the stairs. It hurt me to see them go; I was infuriated and proud of them together, but it never occurred to me to follow them. Instead I turned in my plainsong book to the Agnus Dei and joined in the plea for peace.

"*Agnus dei, qui tollis peccata mundi, dona nobis pacem.*"

I tried to drown out the little voice in my head which was Xavier's voice, reminding me, as he so often did, that there was no peace for the wicked. But I could not ignore it entirely and, as the choir came to the end of the third repetition of the Agnus Dei, my mind was full of the two of them, off to collect their winnings presumably, and good luck to them, though only God knew when I would see Xavier again.

*

I had misjudged him. He was back by Monday morning, though he made no mention of the money he had won, and I did not ask. He was too full of the new project.

"Come now," Xavier said. "A little recitation, that's all I'm asking. Surely it's not beyond you to stand up and spout a few verses? It's for a good cause."

I could not deny it. Every Catholic church in Hull was weighed down with debt and St Peter's, with its new school, was one of the hardest hit. I knew it was my duty to support with any fund-raising effort, and I helped out with the best when it came to jumble sales and sales of work, but forming part of the Brennan-Quinn concert party was something else again. How could I be expected to stand up in front of hundreds of people and recite?

"You stand up in front of a class every day," said Declan, whose idea it had been. Now that he had joined Vinnie and Xavier in their exit from St Patrick's choir, he was looking for new opportunities to shine, to make use of that outstanding voice.

"It's not the same," I protested, but they were not listening to me. My name – my maiden name – went down on the programme along with theirs.

"It's your school we're doing it for," Xavier pointed out. "I'll put you down for two items, shall I?"

"What about Kit?" Declan asked Vinnie. "Does she have any talents?"

"You'd best ask her yourself. She can dance."

Indeed, she could. I noted sourly that it took very little persuasion for Kit to agree to take part. "Something expressive with veils," was what Kit offered. "Isadora Duncan brought up to date," she elaborated when I looked sceptical.

"Modern dance?"

"Exactly. What about you? 'The boy stood on the burning deck'?"

"Of course not."

"What then?"

I was still asking myself that question the day before the concert was to take place. I read a lot of poetry, but that was not the same as reciting it, or even reading it aloud.

"How about something funny?"

"Like what?"

"Hilaire Bellock? G K Chesterton? Good Catholic authors, the pair of them."

So just over twenty-four hours later, I stood waiting in the wings of the makeshift stage while Declan finished his homage to Richard Tauber with "The Holy City", and the auditorium was alive with the slither of handkerchiefs being pulled from coat pockets or extracted from sleeves to wipe away tears of pleasure. I could not remember when I had felt so nervous. The prolonged applause for Declan, the curtain calls he took and then filched, did nothing to reassure me. By the time I stood in the spotlight, hands clasped below my chin, I was trembling. I looked around frantically, but there was no way out of it. I had to make a start.

"Matilda told such dreadful lies

It made one gasp and stretch one's eyes …"

It went down well enough. The audience laughed in the right places and clapped when I had finished. But that was the least of it. What stunned me was how much I enjoyed it, the spotlight, the blurred mass of the audience, my own voice holding their interest. I could see that it was something I might want to do again, but I did not tell Xavier that.

13

(1939-1945)

"What else would you expect from the Irish?"

The words tailed away as I entered the staff room and looked at the speaker.

"Well, Edna," I said. "You tell me. What would you expect from the Irish?"

I was not the only teacher of Irish extraction on the staff; it just happened that the four women sitting in the staff room before lessons began were all English Catholics. There were no men of course, apart from the Headmaster, who was in his office. War had been declared just before the start of term, and all three men on the staff had joined up. For a time it had looked as though there would be no pupils. The whole school had been evacuated to the East Riding, though I had not gone with them, claiming I had to stay to look after Mammy. Another lie to add to the list.

At first it looked as though I was going to be out of a job. If anything, I was relieved: at least I would no longer have to pretend that I was still single. But then the children started drifting back, and within a fortnight it was clear that the school would have to reopen. Only a handful stayed in the country; all but two of my own class had returned by the end of September. School life was progressing much as usual, save for the gas masks, the air drills, and the lack of men.

"I was just remarking how few Irish immigrants are prepared to defend the country they live in," Edna said. "Though I'm sure it doesn't apply to your family, Grace."

It did apply and Edna knew it did.

"My brothers and husband-to-be are in reserved occupations," I said. "They're all helping the war effort in their way."

"How?" Edna asked.

I fought to control my anger. I was no good at expressing it; I always ended up crying. Better to remain calm. "Pat, Mick, and Declan are all at Fenner's. That's an engineering factory, in case you didn't know. My fiancé and my brother Vinnie work at Blackburn's in Brough. We do need aircraft, don't we?"

"Take no notice of Edna," someone else said. "No one thinks any the less of your family because they're in reserved occupations. Someone's got to keep the country running."

The talk passed on to other things and the awkward moment was more or less forgotten. But I did not forget. Two years earlier Pat and Mick had both been working on the docks, Declan had been in insurance and Xavier had been taking casual work wherever he could find it. By the time the war started in September 1939 all of them were fully employed in reserved occupations. I was glad none of them would be sent away to fight, not even Sean, who had volunteered but failed the medical because of a perforated eardrum and was now working in a butcher's in Holderness. Butchery was another reserved occupation.

I mentioned Edna's remark to Xavier.

"It's not that I want you to join up. But doesn't it make you feel guilty, being safe at home while all those other men are out there fighting?"

"Why should it?" Xavier replied. "I'm Irish, amn't I? It's not my war."

"It's everybody's war," I said. "Wait until they start bombing Hull in earnest. Bombs don't stop to ask your nationality. And they're bound to target Blackburn's."

"You think I'm a coward, is that it?"

"No, of course not. That's not it at all. I only –"

But I stopped short because, yes, I did think he was a coward. I could not help it though my intelligence told me that aircraft engineers like Vinnie were indispensable, and even Xavier, as a riveter, was essential to the war effort. I did not want to lose him, or any of my brothers either. I knew that what I was feeling was irrational. Perhaps it was just part of the unthinking fervour that was beginning to buoy up even this war which had never been going to happen. Or perhaps it was my own guilt. Because I too was in a reserved occupation, and one which I enjoyed.

Late November 1940. A clear moonlit night. Xavier was working the late shift at the factory ten miles outside town. In the summer he had cycled there in the early evening, coming home in the morning before anyone else was up. Now in November the blackout and the treacherous weather made the journey more difficult. So he stayed in the village, lodging with the fish man's widow, who was as tall, strong, and grim as her husband had been. Meanwhile I continued to live in Hopwood Street with Mammy, Kit, and five-year-old Julia. Vinnie and Kit had given up their rented house on Beverley Road.

Vinnie was doing something secret in Chatham; neither Kit nor I had seen him for months. Of us all, it was Julia who missed him most.

That evening the sirens sounded early. Mammy and I picked up blankets, candles, and matches, all the things we did not leave in the Anderson shelter, which always felt damp but might only have been cold. Mammy searched for the white fluffy cardigan she was knitting for Julia: precious wool saved from before the war. I picked up my books and Julia's wooden kangaroo, the one that Vinnie had made her, which "walked" down a slope. Kit sat by the fire and did nothing.

"Aren't you coming?" I said, as I always said, and Kit answered as she always answered.

"No."

The rest of the conversation, which had to do with danger, and stuffy underground holes, and the merits of the scullery table as a bomb shelter, we skipped. Both of us knew it by heart. Mammy was uneasy, more so than usual, though she did not seem to know why. She hurried me on.

"Fetch Julia. I don't think they're far off now." Experience had made us all experts.

Julia in her pink flannelette nightdress stumbled after Mammy and me, out through the back door, down the garden, past the bike shed and the small square of lawn, to the piece of ground which was once the vegetable patch and was now home to the Anderson shelter. I lifted the clumsy corrugated iron door, and Mammy pushed Julia in ahead of her. Julia had been through this so many times that she no longer bothered to wake up properly; she simply lay down on the bunk, face to the wall, kangaroo clutched in her hand. Mammy sat opposite her, and I reached up to fasten the door in position.

The blast hit me before the noise. Something swept me up,

squeezed the breath out of me and then slammed me back, sending me flat and hard against the rough concrete of the floor. I heard the explosion as I lost consciousness.

When I came round, the first thing I was aware of was Julia's crying, followed by Mammy's voice whispering the same meaningless words of comfort over and over again. I tried to move. As I did so, it felt as though I was leaving the skin of my face behind. Apart from that, it was not hurting; I was still numbed. I could feel soil and grit sticking into me, into my face and all down my chest, and in front of me I could see the tiniest sliver of moonlight, which gradually widened. Someone was trying to dig us out. I closed my eyes.

Hands caught me by the shoulders and dragged me upwards into the air. Someone else had crawled past me to lead Mammy and Julia to safety.

"A five hundred pounder," a voice said. "It just landed in front of the shelter. You're lucky to be alive."

I did not answer. I was staring at the house, which was still standing, its walls intact, but with something funny about the angle of the roof.

"Kit," I said, and broke free of the restraining arms to claw my way to the back door.

"You can't go in there, love," a man said gently. "It's not safe. Wait for the wardens. They'll be here any minute."

But I was not listening. I wrenched open the back door and stumbled through into the scullery. At first, I could see nothing, but then my eyes grew accustomed to the darkness, and in the faint glow of the moonlight from the open door I could see that things had changed. A heavy torch was passed forward into my hand, and I switched it on. I was afraid to move it around, but I did move it so, aiming the beam upwards first. There was a six-foot hole in the ceiling. I brought the torch down to the floor. The old scrubbed table lay flat and filthy beneath a mound of rubble and boards. But I could see Kit's head and shoulders, could see her eyelashes flicker and the pained circle of her mouth, its lipstick scarlet against the drained white face.

"Can you move?" I asked foolishly. My own voice sounded strange to me, coming from a throat at once raw and choked with dust.

Kit tried to wriggle out from beneath the table but made no progress. She screamed and tears wet her cheeks.

"My legs," she sobbed. "My beautiful legs."

*

"I'll take Julia with me, of course."

I found it hard to form the words. The raw skin of my face had scabbed over, and dead white crusts of skin stiffened the corners of my mouth. I could still feel the sting and prickle of gravel rash on my neck and breasts, the ache in my bones. Still, I said it again. "I'll take Julia with me."

Kit said nothing. She lay in the white centre of the hospital bed, her dark hair lank against her small neat head, her unmarked elfin face turned towards the ceiling. Her arms were stretched out on top of the starched white cover, palms down, fingers splayed as if they were spanning octaves on an imaginary piano. An unseen metal cage raised a mountain of sheet and blankets over her damaged legs. We did not know if she would walk again, and I dared not ask what the doctor had said. The hospital ward stretched away to either side. I did not look at the other visitors, all of whom seemed as engrossed as I was in the one person they had come to see. I drew my wooden chair nearer the bed. I tried again.

"They've offered me my own school, you see. Oh, I know it's only because it's war time, and the men are all away. I wouldn't have got it otherwise. It's small – just two classes – but I shall be in charge. Imagine me a headmistress, Kit!"

I did not bother Kit with the rest of the story, which still filled me with humiliation – Xavier coming home from the night shift at Blackburn's to a bombed Hopwood Street, searching for me and not finding me, running half-crazy across the city to St Peter's, bursting into the headmaster's office before school began to ask what had happened to his wife. Then, when I was discharged from the hospital, the dreadful interview with the priest who had appointed me; the faint hope that arose when I heard the East Riding education authority was so short of teachers that it was prepared to overlook the marriage bar. All this I glossed over.

"Julia will be much safer there while you are recovering," I said. "Mammy's coming too. She'll look after Julia. You won't have to worry about her."

"Why should I worry about her?" Kit said so faintly that I had to bend to catch her words. "She's a Brennan, isn't she? She can look after herself."

I held very still. Julia's name was Brennan, of course it was, but I did not really think that she was a Brennan.

"You said she wasn't Vinnie's child. That's what you said when I asked you that time in Hammond's, when you told me you were … when you told me."

"She isn't Vinnie's child."

"Then –"

"Work it out for yourself. Vinnie's not the only Brennan brother, is he? Heaven knows, there were enough to choose from. Pity I married the wrong one."

She closed her eyes.

I carefully loosened my fingers, which had knotted themselves together and were slick with sweat even though it was cold on the ward, the few small heaters doing nothing to dispel the December chill. I did not speak; I could not speak. But my mind was squirreling away, dragging out forgotten incidents, half-phrases that had seemed unimportant at the time. Pat? Mick? Those possibilities I could not believe. They were my big brothers, Knights of St Columba, both of them, regular Mass-goers, family men, so devoted to each other and to Teresa and Maureen that there was no room for anyone else in their world. Never had been and never would be. Not Pat. Not Mick. Declan then?

I thought about Declan, the most uxorious of my brothers, half of the pairing that had been for so long known to the family as Declan-and-Josie. Dark, like all the Brennan boys, handsome, like all the Brennan boys, but somehow blurred, the cleft chin softened to a dimple, the strong cheekbones rounded. Having thought about Declan, I thought about Josie, plump as the chestnuts her grandmother sold on the market, and about the chubby, laughing two-year-old whom Julia called, quite without malice, Fatty Tommy. The three of them were an indissoluble unit. Mammy and Julia and I had been living with them since the night of the bomb. We had been made welcome, but we still felt ourselves to be outsiders. I found it impossible to imagine that there had ever been a day when Declan had put Kit and the desires of the moment before his commitment to Josie. Declan liked comfort and generosity. I was the only one in the family who appreciated Kit's combination of fragility and spikiness.

I did not even think about Sean. Not then. Instead I opened my mouth to say something, I was not sure what, but suddenly there was no time. A handbell was clanging out the end of the afternoon visiting hour; brisk nurses hurried friends, relations, neighbours out and on their way. I was caught up in a crowd of raincoats and head scarves. I looked back as I was being swept out of the door, but all I could see of Kit was the angular shape of the covers stretched across the metal support at the end of her bed. I had not even said goodbye.

Walking home from the hospital, I barely noticed the trail of rubble and empty sites near the station, where German bombs, intended to cut off rail communication, had instead cut short the lives of families in crowded back-to-back houses. For once the war and its effects were far from my mind. Nor did I pay attention to the cold greyness of the day, the hunched figures I passed in the street. I was thinking about Julia, about her dark curls and full-lipped mouth, about her straight, unchildish nose, about the strength of her rounded chin. Why had I never noticed how much like me Julia looked? What had I missed? Kit had always said that I was naïve. She was right.

14

The schoolhouse was like no other house I knew. It stood on its own, in a sprawling, overgrown garden, next door to the little school. The hedges were so high that I could barely see the house from the road. I did not know what sort of hedges they were – certainly not privet but something spiky and evergreen and thick. A gap in the front hedge was half obstructed by a gate, bare wood, and rusty iron, the sneck hanging off. I lifted it up and aside, and Julia edged in after me, down the crazy paving path to the front door. The lock was stiff and the wood swollen. It was a hard task to get the door open, and when it did open, there was a stale, sweetish smell in the hallway.

Julia stood at the foot of the stairs, waiting for me to say she could go up. I put down my brown cardboard suitcases and straightened my back. I had no idea what I was going to find in any of the rooms, though I knew the place was furnished. The last headteacher had died without living relatives: the school board had decided it would be simplest to leave everything in place for the next occupant. I was glad they had; I had no furniture of my own, and Mammy's had been wrecked in the bombing. I opened the first door on my left and began a methodical exploration of the house.

It could have been worse. Too much furniture crowded every

room, all of it old-fashioned, but there were chairs and tables, and beds to sleep in. There was cold running water, but no hot; an antique bath that would have to be filled from kettles stood in the corner of the kitchen, covered by a wooden board. A straight path led from the back door to a ramshackle earth closet at the bottom of the garden. The seat was a polished wooden plank with two holes in it, one larger than the other. There was no light in the privy, though the house itself had electricity, but a small window near the roof gave some illumination, at least in daylight. Julia was fascinated by the earth closet, and particularly by the two holes and the spiders whose webs hung in the corners.

Back inside, we climbed the stairs. The sweeping banister and polished landing made this the grandest part of the house. There were four bedrooms to choose from, plenty of room for Mammy if she changed her mind yet again and decided to come and live with us after all, instead of staying with Declan and Josie. Perhaps the first headteacher of the school had had a family, though for the past thirty years only one precise, dry old man had lived in the house. It did not look as though he had decorated at all during that time. The dark walls and gloomy paintwork might have dated from well before the Great War, and the cords on all the sash windows were fraying. It was January, but I needed to let air into the house, though I was afraid to open the windows without help, in case I never got them closed again. The windows also needed cleaning, but then so did the whole house, though it was orderly enough beneath the thick layer of dust.

"When did the man die?" Julia asked, direct as always and totally unsentimental.

"Before Christmas," I said. "I'm not exactly sure when."

"Which room did he die in?"

The question was hard to answer. I was glad that I did not know, but I was reluctant to let Julia think it could have been any room in the house in case she became afraid to enter it. I was sure that any child would be afraid to enter a room where there had been a recent death. "I expect he died in hospital," I temporised, but it was obvious that Julia did not believe me. She carried on exploring.

"I'm going to have this room," she announced, and I was relieved to see that she had chosen the little single bedroom at the back of the house, which overlooked the garden and the neglected vegetable patch. We stood side by side, gazing at overgrown cabbages and frost-bitten brussels sprouts. I did not know much about the growing of vegetables, though I was willing to learn. But for now, it was the house on which I had to concentrate, though it was difficult to know where to start. In the end I decided I would scrub Julia's room and make the bed up; then at least the child would have somewhere clean to sleep.

There were brooms and mops in the cupboard under the stairs, along with other things less identifiable. I tied a headscarf round my hair, and then had to find one of Xavier's handkerchiefs for Julia, who insisted that she was going to help.

"After all, it's my room."

She was too quick, too bright. I wondered suddenly whether I was going to be able to cope with this strange, intelligent little girl, who at five read as fluently as some of the ten-year-olds I had been teaching in the city. She did not seem to be missing her mother at all, but then Kit had been in hospital for nearly two months; living at Declan and Josie's with Mammy and me, Julia had had time to get used to her mother's absence. She talked a lot about Vinnie though. He had been home for Christmas, and it was clear that Julia was missing him.

"When Daddy comes home next time, he's going to bring me a kitten."

"He is?" I said doubtfully. I had not counted on sharing my home with a cat, as well as a small niece for whom I would have sole responsibility, and a husband who came and went at weekends.

"You had a cat when you were little. Daddy told me."

I remembered the cat, a sinewy black tom who spent most of his time out of doors, only coming in for scraps. I was slightly reassured.

"What sort of kitten?" I asked.

"A stripy girl." Julia was quite definite. "Then she can have lots and lots of babies."

I had a sudden, horrified vision of a house swarming with cats and kittens but pushed it to one side.

"When is your Daddy coming home?"

"Soon," Julia said – because she did not know, I decided – and changed the subject. "I haven't got anywhere to put my books."

"I didn't know you'd brought any books with you."

"Look."

I looked. Two small books with glossy pictures: *Tales from Shakespeare* and *The Adventures of Robin Hood*.

"Can you read them?"

"Some of them. Daddy used to read them to me before I went to bed."

"Then that's what we'll do," I decided. "We'll read them before you go to bed. Put them on the windowsill for now. We'll go and make a start on the kitchen."

It had just occurred to me that we needed to eat, and the thought of preparing food in the dust-covered room filled me with despair.

"And then can we go and see the school?" Julia asked.

"No!" I cried, and then laughed when I saw my niece's startled face. "We'll go now. Bother the kitchen!"

"Bother the kitchen!" Julia echoed, and we ran out of the house, up the path and through the gate to the little school where we would be spending most of our waking lives. If the house was large, the school was tiny. It was little more than one large hall, divided into two classrooms by a folding screen. Each classroom was filled with double desks of heavy wood and solid iron, their lids sloping down towards the integral benches. To me they looked older and more worn than the desks I remembered from my own days at St Patrick's elementary school. The teachers' desks were at opposite ends of the two classrooms, each raised on a dais. I found I had to struggle to reach the seat of the chair in what, presumably, would be my room. Mr Hearnshaw must have been a big man.

"How do you know this is your room?" Julia asked.

"See how much bigger these desks are than the ones next door? These are for the older children, the ones I'll be teaching. You'll be in the other room with Miss Deakin."

"I'd rather be here with you."

"You're not old enough," I said. "But it won't be long before you move up." It sounded as though I was expecting the war to go on for a long time. Julia might be back at home long before she became old enough to join the juniors. In any case, she needed to get used to the idea of Babs Deakin and the infants as soon as possible.

"What's this?" Julia asked.

I went over to join her. A table with a few small stones, a jam jar filled with dry brown flowers and no water, a feather and a bird's nest.

"The nature table," I said knowledgeably, although there had been no nature table at St Peter's. "You'll be able to collect things for the one in your classroom." I removed the fading stalks and crumpled flowers from the jam jar and took them to the bin outside the main entrance. Julia followed me.

"I'm going to chalk on the blackboard. May I?"

"Just this once," I said, curious to see what Julia would do, but conscious that in future I should have to treat her as I treated the other children, at least while she was at school.

The blackboard on its easel was too high for Julia to reach. I moved the pegs down to the lowest holes and carefully replaced the board. Julia began to draw what were recognisably human figures, three tall and one short in a row, then another, much smaller, at the other side of the blackboard.

"Who are they?" I asked.

"That's Daddy, and that's Uncle Xavier, and that's you. And that's me."

"What about this one?" I pointed to the tiny figure on the right-hand side of the blackboard

"That's Kit in hospital," Julia said. Neatly she placed the stick of chalk in the runnel at the base of the easel and brushed the dust from her hands. "Let's go home now, Auntie Grace."

I looked at her serious face and put aside my own desire to look for exercise books, textbooks, maps, and rulers. I took Julia's hand, and we left the building. I locked the main door and for the first time felt the heft of the iron key in my pocket. It weighed me down.

*

Babs Deakin was round and smiling and conventionally pretty, all curling golden hair and wide blue eyes. I decided I disliked her even before she opened her mouth.

"I'm so pleased you're here, Mrs Quinn," she said. "I'd only been here a term when Mr Hearnshaw passed away. I was dreading having to run the school all by myself." I did not believe her.

"I'm sure we'll get along famously," I said, "provided you're happy to do things my way. After all, this is my school, and I'm responsible for everything that goes on in it."

"Yes, Mrs Quinn," Babs said. Her face was sulky. I smiled at my assistant.

"Perhaps you could show me where everything is kept. And then I'd like to see your records for last term: topics covered, progress reports, that sort of thing."

"Mr Hearnshaw never …" Babs began, and then changed the subject. "Mr Quinn. He'll be in the army, I suppose?"

"You suppose wrong," I said tartly. "Mr Quinn is working for the Ministry of Defence. He'll be here at weekends, but that shouldn't inconvenience you." I too could change the subject. "Are you a local girl, Miss Deakin? Do you live at home?" Miss Deakin was a local girl. Well, not exactly local, she explained. She lived in the next village, with Mother, who was widowed in the last war, in February 1918, two months after Miss Deakin was born.

"So I never knew my father," Babs Deakin said. "Isn't that a shame?" It was the first of many unsolicited confidences she would make to me. I had always done my best not to invite confidences from strangers. I could not understand why Miss Deakin – 'call me Babs!' – should want to relate so much of her life story on such short acquaintance. So I brought Babs back to the question of supplies – books, chalk, dusters, powdered ink. Two large locked cupboards, one in each classroom, contained all the equipment the school possessed. Mr Hearnshaw, it appeared, had been very frugal when it came to ordering supplies. For the first time I began to realise the enormity of the task before me.

Later in the day, I introduced Miss Deakin to Julia.

"My niece, Julia. She will be in your class, Miss Deakin."

Julia looked up at Miss Deakin with her Brennan eyes and my own pout, which Daddy had called my "trunkeen". It was plain that she did not approve. She did not, as I feared she might, repeat her preference for my class. Instead she made it clear to Miss Deakin just what she was taking on.

"I can read by myself. In my head. And I know my six times tables."

"Seven sixes?" I asked.

"Forty-two. Pence three and six."

I looked at Babs Deakin, and saw, with satisfaction, that she appeared almost frightened.

"How old are you, Julia?" Babs Deakin asked.

"Eight," Julia lied.

"She's five," I said. "But she has a vivid imagination."

"A green vivid imagination," Julia confirmed.

Julia's imagination and intelligence proved too much for Miss Deakin. School had been open less than a month when she came to see me, one evening after the children had gone home.

"It's your niece, Julia," she began.

"Has she been naughty? Do you want me to have a word with her?"

"No, it's not that." But Miss Deakin seemed unable to proceed any further.

"Then what exactly is the matter?"

"She makes the other children feel inferior," Miss Deakin said in a rush. "She always has her hand up before anyone else, and she's always right. It's not natural. She even corrected me the other day when I called Venus the morning star. 'My Daddy says Venus is a planet,' she said. Not trying to be cheeky, you know, just sure she knows best."

It's you, not the children, who feel inferior, I thought. Aloud I said, "I see. And what do you suggest we should do?"

"You might take her in your class."

"I already have sixteen," I said, "and you have only twelve. That is right, isn't it?"

Miss Deakin admitted that it was, but she was sure a child as advanced as Julia would do far better with me and the older children. She would not feel so out of place.

I had never known Julia feel out of place, but found I enjoyed the idea of teaching my niece. "Very well," I said. "We'll give it a trial."

It worked well enough in the classroom. Julia kept up easily with the younger members of the class. It was only at home that the problems surfaced.

"Why can't Barty Phillips read?"

"He can read, Julia. He's just not a very confident reader."

"He's ten," Julia objected. "He says knife k-nife. I heard him when he was reading aloud to you this morning."

"You shouldn't have been listening."

"I couldn't help it. He reads so loud."

It was true. Barty Phillips had a great honking voice that carried to every corner of the classroom. And Julia was quite right. He could not read. There was a slowness about some of these village children that puzzled me, used as I was to the pupils at St Peter's. I made the mistake of mentioning it to Babs Deakin.

"I suppose you think that I'm slow too," Babs said. "Just because I was brought up in a village. It doesn't mean we're all simple, you know."

Townie that I was, I was not so sure.

I have to admit that part of me did not want the war to end. I could not admit it then, not when people in Hull were living in fear of the next raid and the house I was born in had disappeared entirely. But out here in the East Riding life was calm and ordered; it seemed the war barely touched us. Even the aircraft factory by the Humber where Xavier was working as a riveter had never been bombed directly: one stray bomb had left a crater in the road half a mile away, but no one was hurt. Xavier, who had to wheel his bike around the edge of the crater on his way to work, made a great story out of it. And that was the nearest the real war came to me. As the headmistress of the local school, I felt important and accepted, and when I walked through the street with Xavier at weekends, people stopped us and spoke. I liked him to see me being treated with respect.

*

Things were better at home too. I had less to do now that Mammy had finally been persuaded to abandon Declan and Josie and come and live in the schoolhouse with me and Julia. She was even bringing Tommy with her, because Josie had no faith in the Anderson shelter in their garden, preferring to send him out to the country with his grandmother. I was pleased to have him. He was company for Julia, and another pupil for my school when he was old enough.

Mammy and Tommy had arrived late one Monday afternoon, having walked the three miles from the station with their cases on a handcart borrowed from the stationmaster. Mammy, of course, ignored the front door and came round to the back of the house, to the door that led to the outer kitchen. Tommy trailed after her, his four-year-old legs unaccustomed to walking so far, though I learned later that he had spent most of the time on the cart with the cases. Mammy did not knock, just stepped inside the door as if she had always lived there, scraping her feet on the doormat and making Tommy do the same. Her eyes went immediately to the wooden board over the tin bath, but she did not comment, just took me by the shoulders and gave me a brief, pinched hug. I kissed her cheek, and then turned to Tommy, but Julia was there before me, arms around his small shoulders.

"Fatty Tommy!"

"Fatty Julia!"

Greetings and further endearments were exchanged, and they went off together to look at the room Tommy would share with Mammy. I took Mammy through to the kitchen proper, put a kettle on the range and prepared to make tea.

"Don't forget to warm the pot," said Mammy. She could not help herself. At least she did not comment on the pile of exercise books on the table, the unpolished range, the opened letters and unpaid bills in their manilla envelopes stuffed behind the clock. She could have pointed out, quite truthfully, that my standard of housekeeping had deteriorated since the Hopwood Street days, but she did not. Instead she sat at the table and sipped her tea.

"Is there anything else I can get you, Mammy?"

"Don't fuss, child. I'm fine as I am." It was a good ten minutes, during which we were both uncharacteristically silent, before she said what must have been on her mind since she came through the door. "I can see there's plenty for me to set my hand to here."

Within two days she had taken over all the cooking, and the cleaning of the downstairs rooms. Once she began to shop, meals changed. The meat was better and there was more of it. Vegetables were fresher. It was only when I came home from the library on Saturday morning to find gifts of leeks and potatoes wrapped in newspaper on the kitchen doorstep that I asked Mammy what was going on.

"I just made a point of telling some of these shopkeepers who they were dealing with. After all, it's not everyone who has a daughter as headmistress."

"And the potatoes?" I asked, watching Mammy pare away a thin unbroken spiral of skin from a particularly fine specimen, and noticing that the old blunt vegetable knife now had a newly honed blade.

"You wouldn't say no to a gift from a grateful parent, now would you?"

I decided it was better not to point out that none of my pupils' parents had shown themselves very grateful before Mammy had arrived. With two children in the house, the extras were welcome.

"You're a wonder, Mammy," I said instead, and carried on with my marking and preparation while I waited for Xavier to come home.

Because that was the best thing about the war, really. I knew where Xavier was. I knew he was unlikely to run away again. I might not see him during the week, when he was working at Blackburn's aircraft factory in Brough, but on Saturdays he left work at one and was at the schoolhouse by three. That particular Saturday I heard the front door opening and, by the time I reached the hallway, he was bending down to remove his bicycle clips. He tugged them off impatiently, the metal humming in his hands. I hardly had time to put my arms around him before Julia and Tommy were there, hugging his legs, climbing on his back and eventually riding on his shoulders. All four of us went through to the kitchen, where I made a pot of tea and Xavier talked through his week, the children close to his side. After that. He took them out for a walk. Mammy, who had disappeared as soon as Xavier had arrived, emerged from her room, and together we set about preparing the tea. It was the one meal of the week at which I was allowed to assist. When Xavier and the children returned, we sat formally around the table, Julia and Tommy continually reminded of their manners by Mammy, who ignored all Xavier's attempts at conversation.

"Why doesn't your mother like me anymore?" Xavier asked as we were getting ready for bed.

"You noticed at last? You left me. Remember?"

"That was before the war, and, besides, I came back."

"Mammy has a long memory," I said.

It was amazing, though, how soon Mammy forgot her antagonism when Xavier set out to charm her. I watched him, saw how he deferred to Mammy, noticed the smile in his eyes whenever he talked to her. By the end of Sunday morning, when he had escorted us to Mass in the upstairs room of the Cross Keys, Mammy was laughing and joking with him as if the last few years had never happened.

"You've forgiven him, then?" I asked as we stood at the gate to see him off early on the Monday morning. His bicycle wobbled as he turned for a last wave.

"I'm too old to bear grudges," Mammy said. "And I'm living under your roof now. Away in now and get ready for school."

"Mammy," I said. "I'm not a child. You don't have to tell me what to do."

Mammy ignored me. "I'll just get started on the washing," she said.

15

The first year in the school had run its course. In July we celebrated Julia's sixth birthday with Kit, who came to stay for a few days. Her legs had finally healed, though she was left with some stiffness in her walk that she hated. At least she was past the stage of sitting with her back to the window, as she had done when she first came out of hospital and returned to her parents' house, unwilling to see people walking by on two good legs.

In September Tommy started school, settling into Babs Deakin's class with a pleasure and a determination that immediately won her approval. At home he continued to follow Julia everywhere, but at school he ignored her, preferring to spend his time with the village boys of his own age. Both children seemed happy, even though they were separated from their parents. They had me and Xavier and Mammy, after all.

At Christmas Declan, Josie, and Kit came to join us. Vinnie was there too, bringing with him a silver-grey tabby kitten, which took over the household completely.

"I knew you wouldn't mind," Vinnie said. "You were always so fond of our old cat."

"Was I?" I asked, astonished. I could barely remember the cat.

"You used to smuggle it up to bed with you and hide it under the bedclothes when Mammy came to kiss you goodnight. And you had an old wooden box with blankets in. You used to dress the cat up in doll's clothes and tuck it up tight, no matter how hard it struggled. But it never clawed you."

I'd been about to tell Julia that she could not, under any circumstances, take the cat upstairs, but I changed my mind. No need to make an issue of it.

Soon Christmas was over, and our guests were gone. Now every Friday when I ran out to the fish van, I added three penn'orth of fish scraps to my order. The stench from the boiling scraps filled the kitchen, while little Polly padded eagerly up and down the draining board. Julia hated the smell and always held her nose while the cooking was going on. All the same, she was determined to feed Polly herself. Refusing to pick up the flaky fish in her fingers, even when it had cooled, she would attempt to use a fork. That way a lot of it ended up on the floor, but Polly did not mind. She ate it anyway.

At first the kitten was impartial in her favours, moving from knee to knee and from hand to hand between scurryings and excited dashes from one end of the long hall to the other. But since I continued to encourage Julia to feed her, in spite of the mess, and since Julia took her duties very seriously, Polly soon became Julia's cat, riding on her shoulder, sharing her chair and, I suspected, her bed. I did not try too hard to find out. Polly was polite to me, no more: Julia had all her attention, except when Xavier was at home. Then Polly forsook everyone except him, following wherever he went, crying if she was separated from him. Strangely, she did not cry during the week, when he was at work. It was as if she knew when he was in the house, and then she demanded his attention every minute of the day.

Xavier, for his part, was enchanted by the little animal. He would tie cotton around a newspaper bow and trail it gently in front of her paws, only to jerk it away at the last moment when she was ready to pounce. At other times he would make small scratching noises on the side of his chair with his fingernail, while Polly sat mesmerised at his feet, only flinging herself rapturously at his hand after several minutes had passed.

"You shouldn't make such a fuss of the cat," I said one night after Julia was in bed. "After all, she is Julia's pet, but Polly takes no notice of her at all when you're around. It's not fair."

"Julia doesn't mind a bit," Xavier said, but I was not convinced. Once he had gone back to work, I asked Julia how she felt.

"It's all right, Auntie Grace. I do understand. It's like me when Daddy comes. I get so excited I can't sit still, but I'm perfectly happy here with you the rest of the time."

I noted two things: how grown up Julia sounded for a not quite seven-year-old, and the fact that, once again, she had not mentioned Kit.

When Polly was eight months old, something I was dreading happened. The little cat's body swelled with the weight of a brood of kittens, though she was hardly more than a kitten herself. Xavier was more concerned than anyone. He made her a nursery from the case of an old wireless set, lining it with blankets and ignoring my suggestion that newspapers would be more hygienic. When he was in the house, he watched Polly intently, and was thrilled when he realised the kittens would arrive one Saturday evening when he was at home. He placed Polly's nest in the cupboard under the stairs, and sat hunched up beside her, his legs poking out through the door and blocking the hallway. At half past eleven he came out to heat milk in a small pan on the range. It was not for him, he explained, but for the new mother, who had just delivered her first kitten and was in need of refreshment. He even held the saucer for her.

When he came up to bed at three in the morning, five kittens had been born, two black, one ginger, one grey and white, and one silver tabby, like its mother. He tried to tell me how it felt to be there at the births, and for once failed to find the words. After a while I realised he had tears running down his face.

"Xavier? What's wrong?"

"I'll have to drown four of them in the morning," he said.

I had no words to comfort him.

In the morning, very early, before Julia and Tommy were awake, we went downstairs to the hall. Polly purred and stretched, the five blind bundles of fur firmly attached to her side.

"You choose," Xavier said. I hesitated but eventually chose the tabby which so resembled its mother. Xavier did not disagree, though he pointed out that it was probably female. Then he asked me for one of my old lisle work stockings, and very gently eased the four wriggling bodies of the remaining kittens into it. He tied a knot in the top. I had a bucket of water waiting at the back door. Illogically, I had wanted to warm the water, but Xavier said no, the shock of the cold water would ensure that the babies would die more quickly.

"Don't look," he said, and I turned away as he held the lumpy, struggling stocking under the water with both hands. Both of us were crying. I wiped away my tears, sniffed to clear my nose, and went to fetch a spade. The hard work of digging a pit in which to bury the kittens helped me recover, but even so I was shocked by the sight of

Xavier's stricken face as he laid the stocking, limp now, in the makeshift grave and piled earth over it.

When we went back into the house it was barely six o'clock. It was seven before Julia came downstairs, yawning and sleepy, to be told that Polly had had her baby, and that she could look at it if she promised not to touch.

"Only one?" Julia asked. "I thought cats had lots of babies."

Xavier and I looked at each other.

"She's not much more than a kitten herself," Xavier said at last. "She couldn't cope with more than one."

Nothing more was said, but I watched Julia's face as she looked at the kitten and gently stroked Polly's back. I wondered whether we were right to lie to her. But I said nothing.

*

"We need an empty matchbox," Julia said. She and Tommy stood beside my desk, Tommy with his hands cupped tightly together.

"There's one on the mantelpiece that has only a few matches left in it. You can empty them out and put them in the box in the kitchen."

Julia did so. Then she stood with the matchbox in her hand, looking at me.

"Don't you want to know why we want a matchbox?"

"Not particularly," I said. "But I expect you are going to tell me."

"Polly found a money spider," Tommy said.

"We're going to put it in a matchbox and give it to Uncle Xavier when he comes home."

"You think that might improve his luck with money?" I asked, interested. "I doubt it, but I suppose it's worth a try. Your Uncle Xavier has only to look at a pound note for it to turn its back and fly away."

The money spider was placed in the drawer of the matchbox and the box was closed. Then Julia demanded a darning needle to make holes in the lid so the spider could breathe. I explained that she would need to take the drawer out first if the spider was to have any chance of surviving. While Tommy was standing with his hand cupped over the drawer and Julia was making holes in the outer cover, Xavier arrived. As usual, he had cycled back from the factory, and as he bent to remove his bicycle clips, Julia was already explaining about the spider.

"Let's have a look," Xavier said. He tipped the spider gently onto his palm and let it run across his wrist. Then he went to the window, pulled up the sash and shook it off.

"Why did you do that? We saved it for you." Julia was hurt.

"It's not natural for a spider to live in a matchbox," Xavier said. "It needs to be free." He smiled suddenly. "Did your daddy never tell you about the time he killed a tarantula, Julia?"

"Xavier!" I protested. "Don't lie to the child."

"God's own truth. We were in some island in the West Indies, Jamaica maybe, and the ship was taking on a cargo of bananas. You'll not remember bananas, Tommy: big, yellow fruit. We had them before the war. Look." He found a pencil and a scrap of paper and made a quick sketch for the children to look at. "Anyway, they come in big bunches called hands – they're like the fingers, see? Vinnie – your daddy, Julia – and I and a few friends were going ashore when a docker passes us with a hand of bananas on his back. Twice the size of him, it was. And just as he walked past us, this huge, furry spider fell out on the ground and started to move towards us, all its eight horrible legs advancing on us at once."

"A tarantula," Julia said. Like me, she enjoyed words, and this was a particularly good one.

"Yes, or it might have been a Black Widow. Well, most of us just ran like hell. I must have put fifty feet between myself and that horrible spider in under a second. But your daddy didn't run. Oh no."

"What did he do?" asked Julia. She and Tommy were both leaning forward, eager to catch every word.

"Picks up a shovel someone's left lying around and swings it down so hard he squashes the spider flat. And that was the end of it."

"What colour was the spider's blood?" Tommy asked.

"Do you know, I didn't think to look," Xavier said. "You could ask your Uncle Vinnie though. He had to scrape it off the shovel."

"Why do you fill the children's heads with such stories?" I asked him later.

"Every word of it is true," Xavier said.

"Vinnie killed a tarantula?"

"Some sort of poisonous spider. I'm no expert. Mind you, the only reason he didn't run away like the rest of us was because he had a sprained ankle at the time. The spider could move quicker than he could."

"It's a wonder he hasn't told Julia about it himself."

"Her ladyship wouldn't approve."

"No, I don't suppose she would,"

"He should never have married her," Xavier said.

"Why didn't you stop him?"

"Why didn't you stop her?"

"Have you ever tried to stop Kit when she has set her mind on something?" I laughed. "Do you think I didn't try?"

"And me. Don't you think I tried to stop Vinnie?"

We looked at each other. I reached out and took his hand. He squeezed my fingers once, briefly.

*

The war continued. Signposts disappeared from lanes around the village. Posters and magazines exhorted us to be increasingly watchful and frugal. Soon, as best we could, we were celebrating Julia's seventh birthday. At school she spent her time with nine to twelve-year-olds, something I knew would not be allowed at St Peter's, but it was for Julia's benefit, I thought. She knew as much as any of her older classmates about the progress of the war; she could point out on the map the names of places we heard on the wireless; she knew who the allies were. The books she read were as advanced as any the oldest children were reading: *The Water Babies, The Coral Island, Hereward the Wake*. It was only at the end of the day, when tiredness overtook her, that I saw in her the small child she still was. Because of Tommy, bedtime was early; even in the long summer evenings Julia did not protest. Once she was in bed, I would read to her for half an hour, or she would read by herself, and soon afterwards she would be asleep. Normally she slept through until morning.

One Friday evening in late July, just before the school closed for the summer holidays, I sat in my study marking. Xavier would not be back until the following day and Mammy was out somewhere, on church business I presumed, even though our church was nothing more than a room in the local pub where we met each Sunday to celebrate Mass. I was half aware of the tangled front garden outside the window and the path leading to the house. I was expecting to see

Babs Deakin walk along it just before eight o'clock: we were going to discuss arrangements for the end of term. It was light outside, the evening sun still high in the sky. There was no sign of sunset, no blushing streaks of cloud, no sign of colour on the western horizon: only a clear sky and a slight sickle moon. I bent over my work, no hardship since it was mathematics I was marking, and no complicated working out but just the results of that morning's mental arithmetic test. Usually I checked the answer on the spot, but I had decided it was time I took the books in.

The faint creak of the gate caught my attention and I looked up. Babs Deakin was standing at the end of the path, making no move to come towards the house. Instead she was looking up at the window above the study, which was the window of my bedroom. Her mouth was slightly open and the colour leached from her face as I watched. Babs glanced towards the house, saw me and gestured at me urgently and silently. She wanted me to go out to her, I realised, but as soon as I opened the door Babs made signs for me to be quiet, finger pressed to her lips in exaggerated warning. Curious, I moved forward. I stood beside Babs and looked up.

Above my head two short bare legs dangled from the sill. The sash was thrown up as far as it would go, and I could just see the pink of Julia's nightdress in the darkness that was the open window. I began to move forward, then realised there was nothing I could do from where I was. I dared not move quickly, in case I startled her, and she fell. Instead I turned to Babs, whispering:

"Stay here. Be ready to catch her."

My assistant's face was more doll-like than ever, her eyes unnaturally wide, but I had no time to say anything further. I went back into the house and tiptoed upstairs. It seemed to take an age. I managed to avoid the squeak on the third stair, and by the time I reached the top I was sweating. The bedroom door stood open. I could see Julia on the sill, arms braced, her body silhouetted against the evening sky. When I moved to the side, I saw that her eyes were open but unseeing. She was still asleep.

I edged my way forward. When I was less than a foot behind Julia, I stopped. My impulse was to reach for the sash, ram it down on Julia's thighs, trapping her so she could not fall. But it was too easy for me to imagine the pain, the shock of the awakening. I rejected that idea.

Very slowly I raised my arms until my hands were just below Julia's shoulders. I slipped them beneath her armpits and leaned forward until I could link my fingers together across her chest. Now that I had the small bones safe between my hands and could feel the steady beat of her heart, I allowed myself to breathe. I still had to resist the temptation to jerk Julia backwards into the room. Instead I spoke softly.

"Julia, wake up. It's all right. Auntie Grace is here."

Mammy would have said I should never wake a sleepwalker, but I did not see what else I could do. Any movement would wake Julia: it was better that she should wake to the sound of a well-known voice.

I heard a rustle behind me.

"Is she all right?" Babs Deakin had left her post in the garden and followed me upstairs.

"I thought I told you to stay down there and catch her if she fell."

"I could see you'd got her safe." Babs sounded frightened; she had never heard me so abrupt.

"Safe? She's not safe yet. Help me get her back in."

Gently we helped Julia back inside. I carried her through to her bedroom and tucked her up in bed. Then I fetched a hammer and nails and nailed down all the sash windows on the first floor, leaving a two-inch gap at the top. It would be fine while summer lasted, and in winter the blackout curtains would keep out most of the draught.

Julia watched me from her bed as I hammered in the last nail.

"Why was I sitting on the windowsill?"

I stopped my work and sat down on the side of the bed. Babs Deakin still hovered in the doorway, unsure what to do. It took no time to dismiss her.

"I think we'll leave it there for tonight, Miss Deakin. You can see yourself out, can't you?"

I waited until the sound of Babs's feet on the stair stopped. The door closed behind her. I turned to Julia.

"I don't know, Julia. Can't you remember?"

The eyes beneath the wave of dark hair were frightened.

"I had a dream."

"Yes?"

"I dreamed Daddy had gone. He has gone, I know that, but in my dream he was never coming back."

"He's in Chatham, Julia. Remember? He's working for the government. He'll be back once the war is over. Before then. When he has a holiday."

"I wanted to find him."

I did not want to think about it anymore; I did not want to imagine how Vinnie would have felt if Julia had fallen. I held her close and stroked her hair.

"It's all over. It was only a dream. Go to sleep."

It was a long time before I could sleep myself.

16

Half past three on a moonlit night in 1943. I was unaware of the moon: I was asleep and the blackout curtains admitted no trace of light. A sudden thudding at the door startled me into wakefulness. I stumbled out of bed, switched on the bedroom and landing lights, and made my way downstairs. Not yet fully awake, all I could think of was the porter in *MacBeth*, imagining himself the gatekeeper at the doors of Hell. But the comparison was ridiculous. I did not know who was knocking but I was going to find out. I nearly forgot the blackout, but Mammy had followed me onto the landing. "Turn off the light so that I can open the door," I called up to her. With my hand on the latch I shouted, "Who is it?" through the door.

"Declan."

I had scarcely begun to open the door when my brother and Josie hustled past me into the hall. Josie was crying out, "Where is he? Where's my baby?"

I had the door shut and the hall light on in time to see Declan, behind her, shrug and spread wide his hands. My sister-in-law, wide-eyed, wild-haired, repeated her demand.

"Tommy's in bed. He's asleep."

"Fetch him. Fetch him this instant."

"I'll go," Mammy said, while I put my arms around Josie to prevent her running upstairs to search for her son. I could feel her shuddering. Soon Mammy was back with Tommy heavy with sleep in her arms. His left cheek was flushed and creased where it had been pressed into the pillow. Carefully Mammy descended the stairs, but as she reached the bottom Josie darted forward and seized Tommy so violently from his grandmother's arms that he woke with a cry. Josie made for the door, but Declan and I moved in front of her.

"What are you doing?" I asked, bewildered.

"I'm taking him home."

"She had a dream," Declan began, but did not explain further. Together we steered Josie into my study and made her sit down, Tommy on her knee. She stiffened and, collapsing into herself, began to sob.

"How did you get here?" I asked Declan.

"We cycled."

I could not believe it. Eighteen miles in the middle of the night.

"What if there'd been a raid? You might have been killed!"

"I couldn't stop her."

Mammy appeared in the doorway with a tray. Tea and biscuits I did not know we had. She loosened Josie's fingers from Tommy's wrist and forced a cup of tea into Josie's hand.

"Drink this." Obediently, Josie drank. "Now, what's all this about?"

Again, Declan shrugged. "She woke up screaming. I think she dreamed that someone was hurting Tommy."

"I want him with me," Josie said. "He's my son. He should be with me."

"Josie, it's not safe." I spoke as gently as I could. "He's better off here with Julia, away from the bombing. It's what you wanted."

"I want him with me," Josie repeated.

Eventually it was decided that Tommy would go back with Declan and Josie, but not until daylight. After all, it was not long now until dawn, and it would give Tommy time to wake up properly. He would need to be fully awake if he was going to ride in the little saddle fixed to the cross-bar of Declan's bike, the only transport there was. I got up to pack his clothes, then realised that Josie could carry little more than a small bag on the carrier of her bike, though some of his favourite toys could ride in the basket. I was shaken by what had happened; it seemed so out of tune with the uneventful life we had been leading. It reminded me, yet again, of how different things were in the city, and how little I understood what my brothers and their families were going through.

"You be careful now," Mammy said as Declan and Josie wheeled their bicycles out of the schoolhouse gate. I reached out a hand to steady Tommy, who was swaying on his seat.

"Are you sure he is ready for this?" I asked. "He looks so tired."

"I have to be at work at eight," Declan said curtly. "We can't wait any longer."

Josie, who had not waited, looked back over her shoulder and said nothing, but began to pedal harder. Declan swung his leg over the saddle and leaned forward, his arms extended to the handlebars to keep Tommy safe as the bike began to move.

The whisper of wheels on the road diminished, but Mammy and I watched until Declan, Josie, and Tommy were out of sight.

Julia's disappointment at losing Tommy faded in the preparations for her First Communion.

"She's almost eight years old," I said to Kit. I was in the public telephone box outside the Cross Keys, unfamiliar territory because no one we knew, except Kit's parents, had a telephone. "It's past time she made her First Confession and Communion."

"Do what you think best," Kit said

"Let me talk to Vinnie," I suggested.

"He's still in Chatham. I don't have his number. I've told you. Do what you think best. You're her godmother, after all."

There was only one other Catholic child the right age in my school: eight-year-old Veronica Duggan, daughter of the family who ran the Cross Keys, where Sunday Mass was celebrated in an upstairs room. After consulting Father Saville, I made arrangements to keep the two girls back after school one afternoon a week to work though the catechism.

"Who made you?"

"God made me."

"Why did God make you"

"God made me to know Him, love Him, and serve Him in this world and to be happy with Him forever in the next."

Julia had no further trouble with memorising or understanding the words. Veronica was slower and more plodding, but I coached her patiently. After six weeks, the date was set. Father Saville would come to the schoolhouse on the Saturday to hear their confession, and on Sunday they would make their First Communion together.

I made another telephone call to Kit.

"What do you want me to do about a dress?"

"What do you mean, a dress?"

"Julia will need a white dress. And a veil."

"And white shoes while we're at it, I suppose. God, Grace, what a fuss. It isn't as if it's all that important."

"It is to Julia," I said indignantly. It was important to me too, though I did not say that; I still remembered how precious my own First Communion had made me feel, how I'd loved the opportunity to dress up and be holy.

"Doesn't she know there's a war on?" Kit said wearily. "Do what you like, Grace. We shan't be there anyway."

I stopped myself from commenting. Vinnie would have difficulty getting away and, as for Kit… "Right," I said. "I'll do what I think best, shall I?"

"Isn't that what I've just said?"

But it was not so easy. Where was I to find the material suitable for a First Communion dress? As the date drew nearer, I began to panic.

"You'll have to cut your wedding dress down," Mammy said pragmatically. "You'll never wear it again."

The wedding dress was one of the few articles of clothing Mammy had managed to salvage from the rubble of Hopwood Street. It was not the most practical item she could have chosen, but I'd always been grateful to Mammy for saving the most important dress of my life. And now I was going to have to sacrifice it for Julia. I straightened my shoulders, refusing to remember the feel of the heavy material on my skin.

"Of course. Why didn't I think of that?"

The veil, too, could be used, and the white floral head-dress. I thought with regret of my old treadle sewing machine, irreparably damaged when the bomb fell on Hopwood Street. But the hand machine Xavier had found for me in a second-hand shop on Spring Bank West would have to do. It was not as if there was a lot of sewing involved in a dress for Julia.

The material was stiffer than what I would have chosen for a child. I remembered my own Communion dress, the silky feel of it between my fingers. Only a simple cut would serve if Julia were not to look like some fashion doll: round neck, short straight sleeves without puffs, skirt short and full, but not too full. I made a pattern from brown paper and pinned it to the skirt of my dress.

The first cut was the most difficult. After that it was no longer my wedding dress that was being demolished beneath my hands, merely a length of material which had to be tamed and shaped. I pinned the pieces together, tacked, sewed, and hemmed. The dress once finished, I cut the veil short and attached it to the headband.

"It's very modern, isn't it?" Margaret Duggan commented, when the two girls were trying on their dresses on the Friday night before The Day. I looked from Julia to Veronica, frilled and tucked and festooned with Brussels lace.

"I hope so," I said. "What do you think of it, Julia?"

Julia turned slowly, the full skirt following her. She looked down at her feet in white socks and sandals.

"I think it's beautiful." She turned to look at Veronica. "Yours is nice too."

There was a moment's hesitation during which I expected Veronica to stamp her feet or burst into tears. Instead, she smiled.

"Mine cost more than yours. Yours is home-made."

"Veronica!" Margaret hissed, but I was not offended. Nor was Julia.

"So it is," I said. "Well, we'll see you tomorrow, Veronica. You'll have her here for ten, Margaret?"

"Indeed, I will."

Saturday morning. I had to stop myself from questioning Julia about her preparation for Confession. In some ways this was the first really private moment of her life; I had to leave her to make her own way through it. But the temptation to ask her to repeat the Act of Contrition, to rehearse her list of "sins", just so she would not forget when the time came, was immense. Julia herself was subdued and thoughtful. When first Veronica and then Father Saville arrived, I hastened to show them into the study.

"I've put this armchair here for you, Father. If the girls kneel on this rug by the arm, they'll be near enough for you to hear what they're saying. Is there anything else you need?"

The young curate, who had the responsibility for our Mass centre took out his stole and placed it carefully around his neck.

"That's fine, Grace. Now, which of you is to be first?"

"I shall," Julia said. The door closed behind her and the priest, and I sat down at the kitchen table with Mammy, Margaret Duggan, and Veronica. We could hear nothing from the study, not even the murmur of voices, until the door opened and Julia came out. Father Saville appeared in the doorway behind her.

"Did she –" I began to ask.

"She was fine. Now, Veronica, let's be having you."

"Did you remember everything?" I asked Julia anxiously.

"Yes."

"And your penance? Did you say it?"

"Yes." Suddenly Julia beamed. "Father Saville said I was a good brave girl."

I hugged her. Then it was Mammy's turn.

"There's my clever girl!" she said, and the three of us stood silent for a moment, knowing an important milestone had been reached.

Finally, I stirred and looked across at Margaret Duggan.

"Veronica's a long time," I said and then immediately regretted it. It was impossible for Margaret to knock on the door and ask what was keeping them. We continued to wait. After twenty minutes, the door opened and Father Saville came out.

"Nora, Grace, could you take Julia out for a minute?" he asked. "I need to speak to Margaret."

Mammy and I looked at each other. What was going on? But we rose and led Julia out through the scullery into the garden.

"Not long to wait now," I told Julia. "Tomorrow morning you'll be going up to the altar with the rest of us, wearing your white dress and your veil. And when Uncle Xavier gets here this afternoon, he'll maybe have a First Communion present for you. No, Mammy, don't tell me we spoil the girl. She deserves it."

A short, stilted cough alerted us to Father Saville's presence on the doorstep. His manner was awkward as he lay a hand on Julia's shoulder.

"Well, Julia. I'll see you at Mass tomorrow. Don't forget to make a good preparation now." He turned to me. "I'm afraid Julia will be making her First Communion on her own, Grace. But that'll make it more special, after all. Good day to you, Grace, Nora."

He was gone before I could question him. I followed Mammy back into the house, where a silent Margaret Duggan had Veronica by the wrist, and was about to drag her to the door.

"Is there something wrong, Margaret?" Mammy asked.

"You might say so," Margaret snapped. "Hasn't she disgraced me entirely?"

"Surely, it can't be that bad?"

"What would you know about it, Grace Quinn?" Suddenly Margaret was crying, her face growing redder and her grip on her daughter tightening by the second. "Didn't she tell the priest that she'd never committed a sin in her life? And she wouldn't budge, no matter what he said. Eight years old, and he says she's not *mature* enough to make her First Communion. What does she mean by it? I told her what to say: 'I've told lies, I've been rude to my mother, I've missed my morning prayers.' Where's the difficulty in that? But she'll not admit it – oh no, not she."

I could not help myself. There was something irresistibly funny about spoiled little Veronica's refusal to admit that any act of hers could be wrong. I turned away to hide the smile that was threatening to break even while I assured Margaret that it was only a temporary setback, that I was sure it would not be long before Veronica had her own special day, and perhaps after all it would have been easier for her in her own home rather than in the schoolhouse. Mammy took Margaret and Veronica to the door, saw them on their way and then returned with pursed lips to exchange glances with me. I looked around, noted that Julia was out of sight and hearing.

"Bless me, Father, I have not sinned," I said.

"Mary Grace!"

But Mammy was not shocked, not really, and the two of us laughed until my chest ached and I had to wipe the tears from the corners of my eyes. When Xavier came home, he had to be told, of course, and then there was more laughter; and then Julia's excitement when he produced a small parcel from his pocket, and it turned out to contain a string of pearl white rosary beads – our present – and a white leather first Missal from Vinnie and Kit. Mammy produced a handful of holy pictures, and Julia went contentedly to her bed that night.

Sunday morning was difficult and glorious. It was impossible for the Duggans to miss it: after all, it was their upstairs room that was used as the Mass centre. They sat stiff and withdrawn on the wooden chairs nearest the window, as far away as possible from Xavier, Mammy, Julia, and me in our places of honour at the front. Julia's behaviour was impeccable. She listened seriously while Father Saville addressed the sermon exclusively to her, welcoming her into the fellowship of communicants, in words that, though formal, were ones she could understand. My pride grew and kept on growing through the rest of the Mass as I watched Julia attempting to follow the Latin in her new Missal. When we reached Communion, I pushed her gently forward to be first in line on the carpet square before the altar. I had to resist the urge to watch as the host was placed on Julia's tongue, telling myself that Julia would not drop it: she would not let herself down and she would not let us down. We were like a proper family, I thought. Kit should have been here, though. And then the priest was in front of me, and I tried to drive out every thought save that of the consecrated sliver of unleavened bread on my tongue. *Corpus Christi.* Amen.

Afterwards, everyone wanted to congratulate Julia. I was praised for my clever handiwork on the dress, and Xavier was congratulated, it seemed, simply for being there. Mammy was anxious to get us home – 'that child will be famished' – for, of course, Julia had fasted from midnight like the adults. As we made our way down the twisting stairs to the back entrance of the Cross Keys, Mammy produced a package wrapped in greaseproof paper, from the pocket of her coat.

"Just a little something to put us on," she said, unwrapping her parcel. "Here you are, Julia. Get that down you. You two as well," she added. "And don't be asking where it came from. I have my sources."

Bacon sandwiches.

"You're a wonder, Mammy," I found time to say. Then, like Xavier and Julia, I succumbed. There we all stood, outside the Cross Keys at twenty past ten on a Sunday morning, savouring the unaccustomed taste of bacon.

*

Not long afterwards, a rumour reached the village that German bombers had scored a direct hit on Blackburn's aircraft factory. I did not hear of it until the afternoon, when the children came back to school after lunch.

"Miss!" One of the remaining evacuees from Hull tried to catch my attention. "Miss, they're saying …"

"Mrs Quinn," I said. "Not Miss. Mrs Quinn."

"Mrs Quinn, they've bombed Blackburn's."

"Nonsense," I said.

"It's true, Miss. The lady at the post office told my mum this morning," one of the local children confirmed.

I forbade any further discussion. I did not even allow myself to wonder if it might be true until school was over for the day and Julia and I were on our way home. Even then, I did not mention it to Mammy until Julia had gone outside to play.

"Vinnie?" Mammy said.

"Vinnie's still in Chatham. But Xavier …"

"Xavier will be fine."

"Why? Why should he be fine? The luck of the Irish, perhaps?"

Mammy gave no answer. The evening rolled on, and I tried not to think about it. Only when Julia was in bed and it was dark outside did I realise that I could not go on without knowing. I had to find out whether Xavier was safe.

"Go and ask the doctor if you can use his telephone," Mammy said.

"I don't know who to call."

"You could try the factory."

I could try the factory. The fact that I did not want to, that I had no idea whether anyone would respond, that I felt embarrassed to ask Dr Arden-Jones if I could use his telephone rather than walk the three-quarters of a mile to the public telephone box outside the Cross Keys – all that had to be discounted.

"What about the blackout?"

"It's only a hundred yards down the street. Get your coat on and go."

I hurried into my outdoor clothes. I switched off the light in the hall before I opened the front door and let myself out. At first, I could see nothing, but I could feel the path beneath my feet, and eventually the darker bulk of the hedge began to stand out a little way ahead. The night was quiet, no sign of German aeroplanes, no faintly perceptible glow on the eastern horizon. Hull was not burning, even if Blackburn's was.

The schoolhouse gate stood open as it always did. I turned left, but I had gone fewer than twenty yards when I heard footsteps approaching.

"Who's there?"

It was a stupid question to ask, the kind of mistake I was always warning the children about. It could be anyone, there in the dark: it could even be a German spy, though I did think that was unlikely. It was probably one of our neighbours, wanting the doctor or his telephone.

"Mrs Quinn, is that you?"

"Dr Arden-Jones?"

"I was coming to fetch you. There's been a telephone call. Your husband."

"Xavier? He's hurt?"

"No. Do not distress yourself. It was Mr Quinn who called. He wanted you to know he was safe. I said I'd bring you to the telephone, and he could ring back in ten minutes.

I apologised for the inconvenience I had caused him, but the doctor brushed it aside. When we reached his house, he showed me into the room just inside the front door which he used as his consulting room. The telephone stood on his broad oak desk. It rang almost immediately, and for a moment I was afraid to pick it up.

"Yes," I said eventually, my voice higher pitched than usual. Dr Arden-Jones withdrew, closing the door behind him.

"Grace? Is that you?"

"It's me. How are you?"

"Fine. Fine."

"Is it true what they're saying in the village? Was Blackburn's bombed?"

The line crackled.

"– completely destroyed one of the air-raid shelters."

"What? How many – ?"

"No one. No one at all. It was empty. No one would use it, because of its number."

"Its number?"

"Yes – air-raid shelter number 13."

I remember nothing more of the conversation. I did ask Xavier why he had not contacted me earlier, since he must have known I would be worried. The doctor was the only person in the village with a telephone, he said, and he had wanted to wait until surgery time was over. But surgery had been over hours before, I said, and it was then, conveniently, that his money ran out. I thanked the doctor and went home to tell Mammy what had happened.

"Thank God for small mercies," she said.

To me it did not seem a small mercy. But even the relief and gratitude I felt, knowing Xavier was safe, could not stop me wanting to laugh. All those lives saved by a superstition. What was it the Catechism said? We were to have no faith in 'charms, omens, dreams, and suchlike fooleries.' If they had been good Catholics, they would all have been dead. I could imagine what Daddy would have made of it.

17

(1945-1953)

The first time it happened after the war, in July 1945, the signs were obvious, or should have been if I had chosen to read them.

For three days running I had found the *Daily Herald* folded open at the racing page. On the fourth day, words and symbols were scribbled in the margin. On the fifth day, Xavier decided we must give a tenth birthday party for Julia.

"But she's only just gone home," I said. "Don't you think she'll want her party there, with Vinnie and Kit?"

"She'll want it here," Xavier said. "We'll have the whole family round. And the Morrisseys too, if need be. We'll make it a day she'll always remember."

"What about her school friends?" I asked.

"She'll not be wanting them. This is a family occasion."

Just for a moment I wondered again about Xavier's own family, whom he never mentioned, the brother who might or might not have died in the Easter Rising, the mother he must have had, though he had never said a word about her. But I could not resist the idea of having all the Brennans together in the big schoolhouse, and so I agreed.

I did not invite Sean, however. Just before the end of the war he had negotiated a peace with Uncle Martin and was now back in Withernsea running the corner shop. Brennan and Nephew were doing well, and no doubt Sean could have found the time to join us but, as I said to Xavier, he would have to catch the train into Hull, and then a further train or bus to reach the village, and he would no sooner be with us than he would have to think about getting back. The truth was, of course, that I did not want him there. Not on Julia's birthday. For, though I had not discussed it with Kit, I had finally come to realise that it must have been Sean who had fathered Julia. I had no way of knowing if he had realised this himself.

I did speak to Kit about the party. She seemed relieved to have the responsibility taken from her, which did not surprise me.

Two days before Julia's birthday, Xavier came home with his present for her, the Everyman edition of *Asgard and Norse Heroes*, small enough to hold in one hand, with a dull blue cover that was rough to the touch.

"We already have a present," I objected. I showed him the dress I had made for her: navy cotton with a white crochet trimming on the collar and the sleeves. Julia had chosen the material and the pattern herself, and I knew she would like it.

"What sort of present is a dress?" Xavier asked. "The child has to wear something anyway. Where's the joy in that?"

I thought of the love and care I had put into making the dress, but I said nothing. Instead I compromised.

"You can give her the book, then. It will mean more, coming from you."

"It will, won't it?" Xavier agreed, and he handed me the book to wrap up.

On the Saturday of the party, while I was making an orange jelly and cutting sandwiches in the kitchen, Xavier appeared in the doorway.

"I'm away to buy Julia's present," he said, showing me a tightly folded piece of white paper. "I've taken the five pound note you keep in the tea caddy."

"What?" I cried, and then, "Wait!" Had he not already bought Julia a present? And the idea of spending five pounds on any child, even Julia, horrified me. "Wait!" But I was too late: he was out of the door and away off up the drive. I had no chance of catching him, not with everything that still needed to be done, and plagued as I was with a queasiness I was trying to ignore.

At half past three the guests started to appear, but Xavier was still not back. First to arrive were Doctor and Mrs Morrissey, so punctual that they were five minutes early. Like Mammy, they were beginning to show their age, though Doctor Morrissey was still in practice, and Ethel continued her round of church bazaars and Sodality meetings. Her pale blue dress was entirely unsuitable for a child's party, I thought as I took her coat. It was far too formal and easy to stain. I smiled and offered my hand. It was Doctor Morrissey who took it: his fingers were dry and cold, and I was aware of the bones beneath.

"Do come and sit down. I'm just finishing up in the kitchen, but the others will be here in no time."

Kit's parents lowered themselves carefully into our sagging armchairs, and for a moment I saw the room through their eyes. I was so used to the heavy, crowded furniture that I no longer noticed it, but I suddenly caught sight of Xavier's fretsaw, tucked away in the corner where he'd left it last Christmas, the last Christmas of the war, when he had made a jigsaw for Julia. The windowsills were piled with exercise books that had somehow found their way in from the school next door, though I had sworn to myself that I would not bring my work home but finish it before I left the classroom. So much for my good resolutions.

I was glad when the door opened again, and Kit and Vinnie came in. They had been living apart for most of the war; I wondered how they were coping now that they were living together again, and with Julia. Julia had gone looking for Polly and her latest kitten, left temporarily with me because Kit did not want cats underfoot while she was settling into her new home on Newland Avenue. I watched Kit briefly kiss her mother on the cheek. She did not hug her, as I hugged Mammy when she arrived with Declan, Josie, and Tommy, with whom she had been living since the end of the war. Tommy was seven now and far from fat, though he was still round and rosy in the face. Then there was a whole scuffle of arrivals, with Pat, Teresa, Mick, and Maureen and their children. Teresa and Maureen were carrying the two youngest Brennans, William and Frank. These cousins were six and seven months old and very alike, with their pale skin, blue eyes, and tufts of dark hair. The babies were settled down on the couch in the study, wedged safely with piles of blackout curtains, which had been taken down but not yet put away.

Now that everyone had arrived, Julia opened her presents: the dress from me first, so that there was a pause while she rushed upstairs and put it on. Paints and a sketch pad were from Mick and Maureen, handkerchiefs from Pat and Teresa, a brush and comb set from Declan, Josie, and Mammy. It was only when Julia unwrapped the copy of *Asgard and the Norse Heroes* that I realised that Xavier had still not returned. Not today, I prayed. Dear God, let him not start his wondering today. If he must go, let it be tomorrow, or next week, but not now, not on the day we celebrate Julia's birthday with the whole family here.

"Is Xavier not with us?"

Ethel Morrissey, of course. I chose my words carefully.

"He's just gone out for a while. There's something he had to fetch. He'll be back soon."

And sure enough, before we had sat down at the table, he was there, and perhaps I was the only one to notice the flush and glitter he carried with him. He had a huge cardboard box in his hands, which he presented to Julia.

"For the birthday girl. How do you like that?"

She opened it eagerly but faltered when she drew out an enormous china doll, with golden ringlets, blue eyes that opened and closed, and a lilac dress that resembled a Victorian crinoline. Ten is too old for dolls, I thought, and for a moment I was sorry for Xavier, though the waste of it appalled me.

"It's very nice," Julia said dutifully. "I loved the book, Uncle Xavier."

If he was disappointed, he did not show it. We all sat down to tea, the children at a separate table I had set up in the kitchen, since there was not enough room for us all in the dining room. The noise began to rise, and with it the laughter, and at some stage Xavier pushed a crumpled wad of paper into my hand.

"Here. You'd better have this."

I opened it in the larder when I went to fetch more milk. Ten creased five-pound notes. I knew at once where it had come from. Xavier had the glamour of the racetrack about him, and he had obviously been lucky. I wondered how much more he had won: there was no doubt in my mind that he had kept back more than he had handed over. Well, if he lost it, at least I'd have this. I knew better than to hide the money in the tea caddy again. Instead I took it upstairs and tucked it into the hair tidy that hung on the spare bedroom wall. Xavier would not think to look there.

When I finally returned with the milk, the adults had finished eating and had cleared the table. They were playing cards, even the Morrisseys giving the game their full attention. They played Newmarket and Chase the Ace, something Xavier swore was nothing like poker. By the end of the evening he had won more games than I could count, and he shovelled the coppers into Julia's hand – the children had long since given up their own entertainments and had come to lean over their parents' shoulders, watching Xavier cheat his way, blatantly and spectacularly, to an amazing total.

"Two shillings and fourpence," Julia breathed. Childlike for once, she was more thrilled with the money than with any of her presents.

Finally, it was time for them all to go, the Morrisseys by car, Kit, Vinnie, and Julia by motorbike and sidecar, the rest by the last bus. The babies, who had slept for most of the evening, woke and began to cry. I eventually located all the coats and hats; Julia could not manage to carry all her presents and Vinnie ended up with the doll. Kit carried only her handbag. They all tried to get out of the door at the same time, waving, shouting, and issuing invitations to one another until I thought my head would burst. And at last they were gone.

It was then that I realised that Xavier had gone with them, or possibly before them; I was not sure. Too tired to think about it and too tired to care, I left the house as it was and went to bed.

In the morning I knew that it was true: Xavier had gone. This time, however, I knew he would return. There was no room in my thoughts for the raging despair I had felt the first time, before the war, when I had believed he was gone forever. He had been an occasional husband for too long, joining me at the schoolhouse only at weekends, happy to work at the aircraft factory and board in the village during the week. I had grown use to managing without him.

He no longer needed his job. The war was over; there was no reason for him to work in a reserved occupation to make up for having an Irish passport and to help him avoid the fighting. He was free to wander again.

But that morning I closed my mind, refusing to think any more of Xavier. I had the house to put to rights and the furniture to straighten. I needed to wash the plates and glasses stacked in the kitchen and to clear away the empty bottles. I could not believe how many empty bottles remained after what was supposed to be a child's party. I stacked them in rows on the kitchen table. Each one would be worth something if I returned it to the off-licence, though I did not know how much. We did occasionally have bottles to return, but it was always Xavier who took them. Now Xavier was gone, and I did not know when he would reappear. In the meantime, the bottles had to be returned. I could not walk through the streets carrying a shopping bag filled with empty bottles. I was, after all, the headmistress of the local school. I might meet one of my pupils or, even worse, one of their parents. For the first time since Xavier had gone, I felt like crying.

Eventually I fetched the old brown suitcase I had brought with me when I first arrived at the schoolhouse in 1940 and filled it with the empties. I snapped the lock and lifted the case. Glass chinked on glass rather noticeably in the quiet house. It would appear even worse to be heard carrying a case that chinked. I opened it again, rolled each bottle in newspaper, lined the case with an old towel and put the bottles back. This time, when I lifted the case, the bottles were silent, though the case was heavier than I had expected.

I put off taking the case outside, finding chairs to push back into place, spills to be wiped up. I washed the plates and glasses and put them away. Then I could delay no longer.

"Good morning, Mrs Quinn."

I was not three steps outside the front gate when the doctor's wife greeted me. Out for a walk with her new twin boys in their expensive grey pram, and ready to show them off to anyone she met.

"Good morning, Mrs Arden-Jones."

"I see you're off on holiday, Mrs Quinn. Or visiting your mother, perhaps?"

"No," I said. "I'm not going away."

"Oh, I'm sorry," said Mrs Arden-Jones. "I didn't mean to pry." Her eyes stayed on the brown case I was carrying so carefully. I searched for an acceptable lie. And I found one.

"My husband has been called away. A family emergency. He had to leave immediately. I'm taking his case to the station to put it on the train. He'll pick it up at the other end."

"Three miles? You're walking three miles with that case? You'll exhaust yourself. And the family emergency? Nothing serious, I hope?"

Was I detecting a note of excitement in her voice?

"Oh no," I said. "Just one of those things. You know how it is. Anyway, the walk will do me good."

We parted before I had to manufacture any more details. Luckily, the off-licence was on the way to the railway station, so I was able to set off in the right direction, hoping I would not meet anyone else I knew.

I had not considered how embarrassing it would be to go into the shop, open the case on the counter and unwrap the bottles. One by one. As though I had a secret to hide. I could not bring myself to explain, but Mr Wentworth, the licensee, was tactful. He did not look me in the eyes even when he handed over the money for the deposits. I did not count it but merely opened my purse and dropped in the coins. I was desperate to be out and away.

"Good day, Mrs Quinn," he said as I left, and I shuddered, conscious of the empty case in my hand. What would I say if I met the doctor's wife again? Could I pretend that I'd bundled Xavier's clothes up in a brown paper parcel? I hurried home, head down, not looking at anyone I passed in the street.

The house, when I reached it, was entirely empty. Even Polly was gone and now living with Julia, Kit, and Vinnie, because Julia had refused to be parted from her. I was thankful for her kitten, but even he was out playing somewhere in the garden. Last time Xavier had left me, we were living with Mammy; I had had my mother for company, and none of my brothers had been very far away. Now Mammy was living permanently with Declan and Josie. She, like all the rest of the family, was in Hull, eighteen miles away, and I was entirely on my own.

A sudden lurch of nausea caught me off balance. I had finally accepted that it was true: I was pregnant at last, and life was about to get much more complicated. I pushed the brown suitcase to the back of the cupboard.

*

Xavier came back just before Christmas. At thirty-three, I had just been told by Doctor Arden-Jones that I was an elderly *primigravida*. I was nearing the end of the eighth uneventful month of my pregnancy, and I had not been expecting his return. He had sent postcards, first from North Wales and then from Ireland, but the information they contained ('passing through' and 'Regards') at least made it clear that he was alive. So, on that unexpectedly mild morning in mid-December, the only thing on my mind was the difficulty I was having in pegging heavy washing on the line. Still, I was grateful for the drying properties of the day. The house, which I had rarely left since finishing work at the end of term, would not now be steamy with drying sheets.

A movement behind made me turn, ponderously. Xavier was less than a foot away from me.

"You're back," I said.

"You're pregnant." A sharp intake of breath. "V.E. Day?"

"V.E. night," I corrected him. I wondered if other women could be quite so precise.

"I called in on Vinnie at the factory on my way here," Xavier said. "I thought they might give me my old job back. Vinnie has invited us to spend Christmas with them"

"You'll be giving her another doll, then?"

"Perhaps not."

I did not ask him where he had been. I knew I would not get a proper answer. But there was one question to which I needed and answer.

"About the job …"

"No luck."

I was not really surprised.

"Will I carry that in for you?"

Silently, I handed him the now empty laundry basket. I had carried it out full with sheets, which I had already washed by hand and fed through the wringer; I had also carried out the tin bath full of grey water to empty on the vegetable patch. Still, I let him carry the basket, and was annoyed with myself because I felt his solicitude breaking down all my attempts at maintaining a distance.

"It's good to have you home," I said grudgingly.

*

In spite of the rationing that was still in force, Christmas with Vinnie and Kit was unexpectedly comfortable. The Morrissey money made its presence felt, but Vinnie, increasingly in demand for research and development work with the Ministry of Defence, was also contributing to their post-war affluence. They could afford to keep fires going in the kitchen and the two other downstairs rooms, and even the bedrooms were perceptibly warmer than those at the schoolhouse.

Kit told me she was hoping to get a post in the new National Health Service once it was in place – not as a doctor, of course: her father thought she would make a good almoner; he was sure he knew someone who knew someone useful. I thought Kit was far too self-centred to make a success of any job which required her to make decisions on behalf of other people, but I kept silent. Ethel Morrissey could not see why her daughter should want to work at all. Ethel had never worked.

"Of course, it's different for you, dear," she said to me, "with your husband being the way he is." And she nodded to Xavier, who smiled, not at all disconcerted. "But you'll not be going back to work after the baby is born."

"Indeed, I will," I said, though I did not see what business it was of Mrs Morrissey. I had arranged with one of the girls in the village to look after the baby from Easter. That way I would only have to miss one term of school, and Babs Deakin would not be able to make too many changes without my approval.

"You'll not find it easy, bringing up a baby," Ethel Morrissey said. "And you can't tell me that a child doesn't need its own mother. I'd never have left Kit to a stranger's care."

"Times have changed since we were children," I said. I regretted my words immediately, for Ethel Morrissey was now off on a string of complaints about the war and the new Labour government. I had adopted my father's political beliefs as a child and had seen no reason to change them. But I said nothing further. I had known Mrs Morrissey too long to argue with her.

Julia danced through it all happily, delighted to have her Uncle Xavier and Aunt Grace with her in the house she had not yet grown used to calling home. She was, I noticed, stiff and defensive with Kit, but her pleasure in Vinnie's company was lovely to see. Julia found time for Xavier, too; together they played with the latest batch of kittens, while Polly, middle-aged now, looked on disapprovingly. And if I found myself doing most of the cooking, I was at least sharing the kitchen with Kit, who could still make me laugh. We came back early from Mass on Christmas morning, determined to make the most of this first post-war Christmas, even though rationing was still in force and there were few luxuries to be had.

Although we had decided that the adults would not exchange

presents, I had not been able to resist buying Xavier a book, a tiny second-hand copy of *The Rubaiyat of Omar Khayyam*. He was delighted with it, reading it aloud to anyone who would listen. Julia kneeled up on the piano stool to read it over his shoulder, left hand resting on his neck for balance. Together they scanned the pages for particularly memorable lines, Julia's own presents lying neglected where she had unwrapped them. I wondered if Xavier would be as tender with his own child as he was with my niece. He was sure the baby would be a son. I hoped not. Not if he was going to grow up like his father: one charming, slippery, unreliable rogue was enough for any family. I wanted a daughter like myself, not as bright as Julia, perhaps, but intelligent and hard working.

"Not long to go now," Kit said, seeing how tired I was. I was grateful for even that much expression of sympathy, and even more grateful for the pre-war pram, which Kit would not be needing again and which she insisted we have. Ethel Morrissey, who had chosen it ten years earlier, sniffed. It was the one mannerism she had in common with Mammy, and it was equally annoying in both of them.

*

Later, I blamed Kit for the fact that I could remember very little about Bridie's birth. The closeness engendered by Christmas had loosened her tongue; she at last told me about Julia's birth, which she claimed was the worst experience of her life, worse even than being bombed, and certainly never to be repeated.

"My mother was right about that, if she was right about nothing else."

"What do you mean?" I asked. I was not following her argument.

"She said that once I was born, that was the end of it. She wasn't going through that again."

"The end of what?" I asked, feeling stupid.

"What do you think?"

"What's it like? The pain, I mean."

"Awful. Terrible."

"Mammy says –"

"Then she's lying. Believe me. I know."

I was not good with pain. A paper cut could make me cry; a bad headache, very rare in my experience because I was normally so healthy, seemed like the end of the world.

"Isn't there any way …?"

"Gas and air," Kit said. "If they offer you it, grab it with both hands. It's the only way. It was good enough for Queen Victoria, after all."

"I thought that was ether," I objected. "Or chloroform."

"Same thing," Kit said dismissively. "Anyway, make sure they give you it."

So, when I felt the first painful contraction, and Xavier telephoned from the new callbox at the corner of School Lane for a taxi to take me to Hedon Road Maternity Home, I began to panic. By the time I was in the delivery ward I was quietly hysterical. Soon the gas and air were offered, I remembered Kit's advice and grabbed at it.

I did not mind the heavy black mask over my nose and mouth; I barely noticed how the rough edges pinched at my skin; I did not even recoil from the smell of rubber. Instead I gulped in the gas and air as if my life depended on it and, by the time that Bridget Quinn made her first appearance, I was floating high above it all. I moved through hazy clouds towards a light and warmth that beckoned me away from the bed and the blood and the pain, and away from the daughter I had so much wanted to see.

Some minutes or hours later, when the baby was placed in my arms, my first reaction was one of puzzlement. Who was this small person who had so suddenly joined me? I looked at the baby and did not recognise her. This was not a Brennan baby. From where had she got that paleness, the red-gold fuzz of hair and long legs? I looked down at my daughter and felt the beginnings of pride, but it was a faint emotion compared to what I had felt when holding Julia for the first time. This was my own child: where was the tenderness I was supposed to feel?

The midwife, who had met and been charmed by Xavier when we first arrived, smiled at me.

"She's the image of her father," she said.

When my visitors arrived, they thought so too.

"Well," Mammy said. "You can see she's her father's daughter right enough. Not a Brennan bone in her body."

"She doesn't look much like you," Kit said doubtfully. "I suppose she is yours? They haven't mixed her up with someone else's baby?"

"Don't be daft," Vinnie said "She's the spit of Xavier. Well done, Grace."

I was too exhausted to respond. My fears had been justified, after all. And though I could not remember much about the birth, I was told that it had been unusually difficult. It was something to do with the angle of the birth canal, the midwife had explained.

"Don't tell me," Kit said. "I don't want to hear about it."

Somewhere amidst the tiredness and pale memory of the pain, I conjured up that Kit who had once wanted to be a doctor and I was saddened. What had happened to that girl? I lifted my head and looked towards the foot of the bed, where Xavier stood gazing at his daughter, his likeness. If loving a child was enough to make someone a good father, I thought, there was hope for Bridie yet.

*

I found it hard to acknowledge, even to myself, what I soon knew to be true: I cared more for Julia than for my own daughter. Not that there was anything wrong with Bridie. She was bright and lovely, already showing signs that she would be early to walk and talk. And she was the image of her father, as everyone said.

And that was it, I thought, when you came down to it. I looked at my baby's fine red-gold hair and saw Xavier, at her eyes that were his eyes, at her long limbs, fingers, and feet. Did this outer resemblance echo an inner one? Would Bridie grow up charming and as irresponsible and unreliable as her father, or was there a rudimentary touch of Brennan in her, just one touch of gravitas to balance Xavier's quicksilver? I watched my daughter anxiously, while Xavier watched her indulgently, and Julia watched her with love.

It was Julia who made sure that our two families met frequently. I had dutifully asked Kit to stand as Bridie's godmother, and was both relieved and hurt when she refused. Now, though I was less inclined to work at friendship than formerly, I dreaded losing contact with my brother and my niece. Julia would not let that happen.

Every Friday evening Kit, Vinnie, and Julia arrived at the schoolhouse for the weekend. They would travel by train as far as the station in the next village and, when it pulled in at six, Thompson's taxi would be waiting to carry them the last three miles. The taxi was squat and black, like a truncated hearse; it had slippery leather tip-up seats fixed to the partition between the driver and passengers. On one of these tip-up seats, precarious though it was, Julia always perched. That way she could be the first out of the taxi when it arrived.

I was not sure how it came about that Xavier and I always played host though, of course, as Kit frequently reminded me, it was more difficult travelling with a baby. Perhaps it was because Mammy was once again staying in the schoolhouse, taking what I considered an unnatural pride in her youngest granddaughter. After all, she had plenty of other grandchildren. Still, she delighted in Bridie. I suspected that Mammy's initial infatuation with Xavier, temporarily soured by his absences, had been transferred to his daughter. You had only to hear the comment she made one evening as she was changing Bridie's nappy: "This baby's bottom is prettier than some people's faces," and she smiled as she held her granddaughter's ankles, bending the babies legs towards her head as she cleaned her.

Xavier would not let this pass.

"The woman's mad," he said. "That child has a bum like an ancient British arrowhead."

"All babies are boring," Kit said, looking at Mammy, Julia, and the now smiling Bridie. "At least that one doesn't cry as much as some of them." She placed a card on top of the pile in the centre of the table, a card I identified as the Queen of Diamonds by the crease in the corner, even before Kit turned it upwards. "My trick, I think."

We were playing Whist, as we did most weekends. I had finally grasped the rules, though I tended to forget them between one session and the next and had to be reminded by Xavier or Vinnie. When it came down to it, I was not that interested in cards: I would rather read a novel or take a walk with the pram.

The other three were addicted, and no Saturday was complete without at least one hand of Whist. We tended to sit down in the evening, after tea and the football results on the wireless: we never started playing until Xavier had checked his eight draws and four all ways, filling in all the results in the column at the back of the Saturday edition of the *Hull Daily Mail*. I was not in the least interested in football either and did not care whether Hull City was beating Grimsby Town in the Third Division North, but I did like the results, or at least the sound of them being recited; I particularly enjoyed being able to guess the number of goals scored from the intonation of the announcer's voice.

"I'm putting the child to bed," Mammy said, and I rose to my feet.

"No, Mammy. You take my hand. I'll put her to bed." I lifted my sleeping daughter from Mammy's arms and went upstairs, followed by Julia.

"Can I lay her down?" Julia asked.

Carefully I handed Bridie to my niece, who tucked the baby into her cot with a tenderness that brought me close to weeping. I wanted to stay there with the two children in the quiet semi-darkness of the bedroom, but instead I went back downstairs. Julia followed me and, together, we did the washing up.

18

The third-class carriage smelled of dirt and coal and smoke, of countless greasy heads which had stained the seatbacks below the holiday posters of Skegness and Mablethorpe. Wedging Bridie into a corner seat, I pulled the door shut. The window was open. I hauled it up with the cracked leather strap. The leather was also greasy, and I wiped my hand on my coat. There was no one else in the carriage to see.

Bridie was trying to look out at the platform we had just left, but the window was mottled with dust and smuts from the engine. There was a sort of yellowish light in the compartment, a light that exaggerated the pewter tones of the sky. I shivered and pulled Bridie onto my lap. It was going to snow. I could taste and smell it in the air.

By the time the train pulled into the first station down the line, the dusk was alive with the whiteness of the snow and the platform was an inch deep in it. Dark figures appeared and disappeared as the wind buffeted them with horizontal flakes, though flake was too gentle a word to describe that onslaught. I could tell that there was a danger of serious drifting across the fields soon. A mile further and the lights in the compartment flickered and went out, and the train shuddered to a halt. It was not completely dark outside, but I could see little through the whirling snow. The carriage grew colder and Bridie began to whimper. I unbuttoned my coat and wrapped her inside it, against my heart. It warmed both of us a little.

Some twenty minutes later the train lurched into motion once more. Perhaps the guard has been digging us out, I thought wildly. I began to wish there were someone else in the carriage, for the lights had not come back on and I felt very alone. But eventually the train drew up at our station and, with numb fingers, I released the leather strap, with Bridie, now asleep, clutched to my side. It was difficult leaning out of the window to turn the door handle with my daughter in one arm, but I managed it. The guard was already lifting the old Silver Cross pram out onto the platform, where the bottom third of the wheels immediately disappeared in the snow. My feet, in the new shoes I had worn for our trip to Hull, were already covered. I could feel the melting snow between my toes, but I was so cold that I hardly cared. Xavier was not there. I wondered why I had ever thought he would be. And it was still snowing. There was no taxi waiting and the taxi office was closed and dark. I was going to have to walk the whole three miles while pushing the pram, just Bridie and I on our own.

Usually I enjoyed snow, but that was in the daylight and when I was fully prepared for it, with boots, socks, and woolly hat. I had never known anything like this slow plod through a wall of whiteness, the pram growing heavier and more difficult to push every minute. At least Bridie was sleeping through it all, hidden beneath the hood and the oilcloth apron of the pram.

I was wearing gloves, but they were silly fabric gloves, and I could no longer feel my fingers, which were locked around the pram handle. I was thinking of nothing, not even of what I would say to Xavier when I saw him. Instead I hummed tunes inside my head, counted telegraph poles, and tried to keep to the road. At one point the pram slid suddenly away from me and buried itself in a ditch filled with snow. I tugged at the handle, rocked the pram, pulled again. Nothing. I had no way of knowing how far I had come or how far I had to go. I tried again. Still nothing.

I could not leave Bridie in her pram while I fetched help. I could not stay where I was. I peeled back the pram's apron. Bridie, with her thumb in her mouth, was lying on her back, snug in the cot blanket. She stirred but did not wake as I lifted her up out of the pram and hugged the warm weight of her in my arms. Once again, I opened my coat and folded it over her, even managing to button it. It was as well that I had lost weight since she was born. I wrapped my arms around her, stuffed my fingers in my armpits and set off, one dogged step after another, along the road in the direction of home.

I was singing aloud now and thinking how foolish I would sound. But there was no one to see me, no one to hear me, and singing aloud was one way of reassuring Bridie, one way of stopping myself from thinking. All the same, every now and then, I found my mind wandering. I will kill Xavier for this, I thought at one point, and then again there was only the awareness of the child in my arms, and of the cold that had driven all feeling from my hands and feet and face.

Eventually I found myself at the entrance to the lane that led up to the school and the schoolhouse. There were only another hundred yards to go. Bridie was awake and grizzling; she too must have been cold. Another ten steps. The front door was locked. No Xavier here either. The flowerpot under which I kept the key was buried in snow. I bent down, left arm still clutching Bridie, and scrabbled on the ground. At last I managed to open the door. It was freezing inside too. Xavier must have been gone some time. I put Bridie in the armchair and heaped blankets on top of her, then attempted to make up the fire.

Finally, after struggling with newspaper to create a draught, I managed to get it going, with flames roaring up the chimney.

Xavier did not appear that evening. At first, I decided that I would not care if I never saw him again. But I did see him again, sooner than I expected, and I had just got used to his presence when he was gone again. It was a pattern that was to continue for the next five years and there was never any explanation or apology. Bridie did not seem to suffer from his absences: they were just a normal part of her life from the beginning, but she was always happy to see him back. That was no longer true for me. I had lived too long with uncertainty.

*

I disliked the honeyed, fretted wood of the confessional booths almost as much as I liked the clean lines of the new church. Though they were attractive in themselves, the booths seemed to lack the necessary seriousness, the sense of age and repentance created in city churches by the weight of past sins accumulating in the incense-smelling air.

I pulled the door towards me and slid into the small cell which still did not smell like a confessional but did not smell like anything else either. I knelt, shifting uncomfortably as I tried to find a point of balance on the uncarpeted kneeler. The priest pushed back the shutter that separated us.

"Bless me, Father, for I have sinned. It is six weeks since my last confession, and these are my sins. I have missed my morning prayers, been inattentive at Mass, told lies …"

The catalogue went on. It crossed my mind that it never changed; I was always reciting the same petty inadequacies. I had listed the same ones at every confession since that first confession so many years before. This day I had something else to say, something I had been considering for days.

"Yes, my child?"

I realised that I had stopped. This was it, then. I had to fight for a moment to hide my resentment at being called a child by Father Coogan, who was only five years out of Stoneyhurst. I was thirty-six years old, after all, and he must still have been in his twenties. What experience did he have of the world?

"There is something else, Father."

"Yes?"

"Lately, I have caught myself wishing that my marriage was over. I don't know how to live with my husband anymore. If it wasn't for the child …"

It was a mistake to have said anything, I realised, as I heard a strange sound from the other side of the grille, a sound I eventually identified as Father Coogan simultaneously taking in a breath and sucking his teeth. Marriage was a sacred institution given to us by God. That was not an exact representation of the wording, but no doubt I would be told what it was. Young celibate priests were always great experts on marriage.

"Is there any particular reason why you are feeling this way?"

"I can no longer stand the uncertainty, Father. Not knowing whether I'll wake up in the morning and find him gone. Not knowing where he's going when he does go. Not knowing whether he'll ever come back."

"But he always has come back, hasn't he, Grace?"

I hated that. Priests were not supposed to know whose confession they were hearing. I had travelled five miles to have my confession heard in a proper church and I had not expected to be so easily recognised. It just showed how widespread the knowledge of Xavier's absences had become.

"I've tried, Father. I have really tried. I just don't understand what makes him do it."

"Tell me, Grace," the priest said. "Is your head covered?"

"Why, yes, Father. I'm wearing my mantilla."

"So you've taken St Paul's words to heart?"

I knew then what was coming next. If there was one saint I could not stand, it was St Paul, that jumped up little Roman functionary, who thought that women were inherently evil and needed to be covered up and subjugated. I did not need to listen to Father Coogan to hear the saint's words: "Let the wife be subject to her husband …"

I was wasting my time. My skirt had rucked up underneath me; I could feel the thick fabric digging into my knees. I shifted my weight and closed my ears to the rest of what Father Coogan was saying to me. Suddenly he was allocating my penance, and I could not believe it.

Three decades of the rosary! It was ten times what he or any other priest usually gave me, and it was not for any sin committed by me. I was the one who stayed at home and kept things going; it was Xavier who routinely abandoned Bridie and me. And I had not even mentioned my suspicions about where he might have been when he went away.

"Yes, Father. Thank you, Father. O, my God, because Thou art so good, I am very sorry that I have sinned against Thee, and with the help of Thy grace, I will not sin again."

I stumbled out into the aisle and set myself down in a pew. Three decades of the rosary were going to take far longer than I had anticipated. It was useless to hope that Kit might have done anything about tea, and Mammy, who was staying for the weekend, had followed me into the confessional. What if I were still praying when Mammy came out? What heinous sins would she think I had committed to be given so harsh a penance? I pulled out my rosary beads, began to gabble a Hail Mary, and promised that I would finish my penance at home, if time ran out. I hoped God would understand, even if St Paul and Father Coogan had not.

As it turned out, I had no need to worry about tea. Xavier and Vinnie, jubilant after the Tigers' home win, had cycled back from Hull via the local chip shop and had brought back fish and chips for everyone. Xavier, Vinnie, Kit, and Julia ate theirs from the newspaper but, since I had to provide a plate for Mammy, I used one myself.

"You were late back," Kit said as we washed up. Because there were so few dishes, she had agreed to help me for once. Besides, she was curious. She wanted to know what had been going on.

"Young Father Coogan gave me a really long penance. Mammy had to wait so long for me, she must have thought I'd been up to something awful."

"Had you?"

"No."

"I haven't been to confession for years," Kit said. "I don't hold with it."

I was profoundly shocked. "What do you mean, you don't hold with it? You're a Catholic. You have to go to confession."

"At least once a year, and that at Easter or thereabouts," Kit quoted from the catechism. "No, I don't. You don't have to go along with all of it, Grace. Just the worthwhile bits – Midnight Mass, incense, the Easter Vigil. The other stuff, confession and churching and all the other nonsense, well, just forget it. That's what I do. You don't have to go along with everything the church says."

But you did. That was the point of the Catholic Church. It was a whole faith; you had to accept it all. You couldn't pick and choose. You could reject it all, as my father, Red Jack Brennan, had done, or you could say, "Lord, I believe. Help Thou my unbelief." There was no third way. Not even for Kit.

*

"I know what you are thinking," Kit said. She applied a broad stroke of crimson polish to a thumb nail. Looking at my own nails, which were short and bitten, I found myself veering momentarily between envy and disgust. Then I turned my attention once more to the window. Xavier, Julia, and Bridie were halfway down the path, setting off for a walk. Bridie was already on Xavier's shoulders: for her, at three, a walk still meant a carry. All three of them turned at the gate and waved. I was struck once again by Julia's strong resemblance to the Brennans, by Bridie's exact echoing of Xavier's colouring and features. Strange to think I had once wondered whether Xavier could have been Julia's father.

I turned to Kit. "What did you say?"

"I said I know what you are thinking. It's what you've been thinking every time you've looked at me for the last twelve years. You're wondering which of your precious brothers is Julia's father."

"No, I'm not," I said. "I don't need to wonder. I know. It's Sean."

There was a tiny clatter as the bottle of nail polish was overturned. I watched the red pool spread over my chair arm, but I said nothing.

"How long have you known?"

"I don't know. Years. It had to be Sean. He's the only one who had the desperate need to avenge himself on Vinnie and me. I can see how it would have appealed to him."

Kit stared at me. "You've got it all wrong. That's not how it was. Sean loved me."

I wished she had not told me that.

"Did he?" I am being cruel, I thought, but I did not stop. "Then why didn't he ask you to have your marriage annulled and marry him? You have grounds for an annulment; we both know that. But perhaps Sean did not know. Or perhaps I have it wrong. Perhaps he did ask you, and you turned him down because you couldn't bear the idea of being a shopkeeper's wife. That could be it."

"I love Vinnie," Kit said. "You know that. I've always loved him, even if he doesn't love me. I do! And of course Sean didn't know how things were between us. You're the only one I've ever told. I thought you were supposed to be my friend."

Her lower lip was trembling. In all the years I had known her, I had never seen that happen before.

"I am your friend," I said briskly. "Your best friend. It doesn't mean I have to like you or go along with your make-believe. Now, clear up that nail polish before it wrecks the chair arm."

"It's your chair," Kit said.

"It's your polish. You'll find a cloth in the kitchen."

It was too late to save the chair arm, but I did not offer to help Kit as she scrubbed ineffectually at the stain. The brown moquette had absorbed most of the colour: it was the texture of the material that had been affected. In truth, I was not particularly worried by it. I was too interested in how things had changed between Kit and me.

For once I felt that I was the stronger, and it was a good feeling.

"Are you going to tell Vinnie?" Kit asked when she had finished her attempts at cleaning.

"I imagine Vinnie already knows. If I can work it out, so can he."

"He's never said anything."

"He wouldn't." I knew my brother, and I spoke with complete authority.

"Will it make any difference?" Kit asked.

"Any difference to whom? Me? Vinnie? Julia?"

"You wouldn't tell Julia?"

"No, but one day you will."

"Never!"

I wondered why she was making such a fuss. Kit did not love Julia; she never had done. But perhaps she felt that Julia needed to look up to her. There was little else in her life.

"You should get a job," I said abruptly.

"I've tried," Kit said. "You know I've tried."

"Daddy's string-pulling didn't do much good, did it?" I was horrified that I had spoken the thought aloud, but I could not stop myself. I was grateful for the slam of the door, which meant that Julia and Xavier were back from their walk. I ran to take Bridie from him.

"Do we have to go home tonight?" Julia asked. "I love it here."

"You have school tomorrow," Kit reminded her. Her voice was cold and contained; she would show no sign of distress in front of her daughter or Xavier. "We've put on Grace's hospitality long enough."

"Bring Vinnie next time," I said before I could stop myself. "Xavier always enjoys his company."

"He's very busy at work." It was a perfunctory reply, the least Kit could acceptably give. I really hurt her this time, I thought, and then I wondered if 'hurt' was the right word. 'Disturbed' might be more accurate.

"You could invite Declan, Josie, and Tommy," Xavier said. "The four of us could get some fishing in"

"Drown yourselves, more like," I said cheerfully. The idea was an attractive one. Josie's presence would ease things between Kit and me, and the three cousins would enjoy one another's company.

"Next month," Xavier said. "We'll do it next month. Do we have an agreement, Julia?"

"We do, Uncle Xavier," Julia said. And then, belatedly, "Don't we, Kit?"

*

Saturday 16th February 1952. The day after the old king's funeral, and six months after Xavier had last gone missing. He had not yet returned. He had never been absent for so long before, and I was worried. I was standing in the kitchen, putting away my shopping, while Bridie sat at the scrubbed table with a pair of blunt-ended scissors, scanning the week's papers with their record of mourning and loss. Miss Barbara Deakin's Mixed Infants had abandoned their scrapbook on the royal tour of Africa in favour of a collage of royal grief. Privately I thought that, at just turned six, Bridie was too young to be involved in the project but, like her cousin Julia, she was ahead of her peers and working with the seven-year-olds in Top Infants. I no longer interfered much with Babs Deakin's teaching style. She got the job done, and it was not her fault that I was my father's daughter, with his ingrained distrust of kings and queens and English pomp.

I looked over Bridie's shoulder at the heap of grainy photographs cut from the front pages of the local and national press, and was struck by one of the three queens together, faces veiled, stiffly upright in their dark winter mourning. Old Queen Mary held the centre, a reminder of another age in a long coat that swept the floor, her black peaked head-dress making a stark white heart of her face. To her right, and slightly behind her, stood the young queen, slender and diffident, her legs in their sheer stockings oddly vulnerable, touching even. But it was the third queen, the king's widow, who moved me most, standing with head held high, plump chest in profile, gloved hands clutching her solid black bag. I knew that stance. It was one I had seen in recent photographs of myself, along with the lowered eyelids and the firm mouth that announced one was in control of one's feelings, thank you very much.

"What's a coffin?" Bridie asked. She had put down her scissors and was tracing with her finger the words beneath the picture of the funeral cortege leaving Westminster Hall. I peered more closely at the cutting to see what she was reading.

"A simple oak coffin," I said aloud. "Well, it's a sort of box, I suppose. It's what you put people in when they die."

It seemed bleak to me, now that I had explained it to my daughter, who had no experience of death. I wondered what she would ask next and prepared myself to answer truthfully. But Bridie had lost interest; she turned back to her heap of pictures and began to sort them. After all, the headmistress's daughter had to keep abreast of the work, even if it was work whose value the headmistress doubted.

The familiar sound of a motorcycle pulling up at the gate alerted me to Vinnie's arrival. I wondered if he had come alone, or if he had brought Kit and Julia. The motorcycle had a sidecar; on rare occasions, rather than coming by train, Kit would perch inside it while Julia rode pillion. I hurried to the front door and looked out, in time to see Vinnie dismount. He went around to the far side of the bike and lifted the roof of the sidecar to help someone out. Not Kit, surely. She would not have come without Julia.

The passenger stepped out shakily, and for a moment I did not recognise him. Then I was running down the path as fast as I could, dignity forgotten, because it was Xavier come home at last, and all I wanted to do was to hold him in my arms and tell him I loved him. Questions and recriminations could come later; there was no time for harsh words now.

I was running so fast that, when I reached him and pulled him to me, he stumbled, and would have fallen, had it not been for Vinnie's supporting arm. Even before I looked at Xavier, I could feel the difference in him, nothing much between me and his bony frame but the thickness of his coat. I had a sudden vision of his shoulders as I had once seen them, rounded and muscled, water standing out in drops on his skin as he sprang up laughing from the cold waters of the North Sea. But when my hands reached up to grasp him, it was like holding the shoulder blades of a skeleton. Fearfully, I raised my eyes to see his face.

His hair was white beneath his cap. Blue white, with not a trace of the red-gold curl. The stubble on his chin and neck was white too. Beneath his eyes the bruised circles were touched with indigo. He was forty-three, and he looked like an old man.

"Better get him inside," Vinnie said, and together we helped him along the path. He coughed once or twice, and when he did there was a bluish tinge to his face and lips, but it was not until he put his handkerchief to his mouth and it came away bloodied that I realised what was happening.

"Oh, my dear," I said. "You're dying."

Vinnie told me not to be so daft. Once we were inside the house, he settled Xavier in the old leather armchair by the fire in the living room, and sent me to fetch blankets to wrap him in. Then he rang the doctor on the new telephone, which I had recently had installed, but which I rarely used. I did not need a doctor to tell me what was wrong with Xavier. I might not have seen tuberculosis at first hand before, but I knew about it. What I did not know was what to do.

Bridie came out from the kitchen.

"Is it my daddy?" she asked doubtfully.

"Yes, sweetheart," Xavier said. "It's your daddy, come home at last." It was the first time he had spoken, and I could see it was an effort, but I did not stop him. It was bad enough for Bridie to see him like this. But when he reached out his arms to his daughter, I shook my head.

"Better we wait until we know what it is."

"It's just an old cough," Xavier said, but he made no further move to touch Bridie, who stood in the doorway, frowning.

"What happened to your hair, Daddy?"

"Didn't I wash it too often?"

Bridie did not believe him: she was too old for such fancies, but she laughed anyway.

"Have you finished your work for Miss Deakin?" I asked. "If so, can you clear the table for us like a good girl. Your daddy will be wanting his lunch."

Bridie shook her head. She had not finished the work.

"Away with you then," Vinnie said. "Or would you like me to help you? You'll be all right here, Grace, till the doctor comes?"

I nodded and smiled at him. Hand in hand, uncle and niece went through into the kitchen, and soon I could hear their voices as Bridie explained what she was doing, and Vinnie asked her the sort of questions that would keep her mind off her father, slumped in his own armchair, before his own fire, and so changed from the Daddy she remembered.

I kneeled beside Xavier and rested my hand on his knee. It was as if I had to keep reminding myself how thin he had become, thinner than I had ever thought possible, though he had never been a heavy man. He took my hand in his, but there was no strength in his grasp, and his skin was burning up.

"Why didn't you come home before?"

"How could I come home like this?"

"Well, you're here now."

"I'm here," he agreed.

Doctor Arden-Jones arrived ten minutes later, and I let him in the front door. I had never felt entirely comfortable with this man – for a start, I could never forget the day when his wife had stopped me on the way to the off-licence with a suitcase of empty bottles. There was more to it than that. He was the sort of man you expected to see wearing tails and pin-striped trousers, with a grey top hat in his hand. He did not wear tails, of course; what he habitually wore was the hand-tailored suit he was wearing that afternoon, but there was an expensive elegance about him, an assumption of his own importance that I found hard to deal with.

Doctor Arden-Jones put his medical bag down and offered me the tips of his fingers. They were cool and slightly damp; when I drew back my hand, I had to will myself not to wipe it on my skirt.

"And where is the patient?" he asked, though Xavier was clearly visible not five feet away from him.

"It's my husband," I said. "Xavier, the doctor's here."

He tried to rise, but I would not let him. The touch of one hand on his shoulder was enough to retrain him, and he sank back into the chair, seeming to grow smaller before my eyes. Doctor Arden-Jones opened his black leather bag.

"How long has he been ill?"

I had to admit that I did not know. The doctor made no comment, but the end of his right eyebrow moved just enough to make his thoughts obvious.

"Have you been ill long, Mr Quinn?"

"A week or two, perhaps," Xavier said. The doctor and I both knew that he was lying, and a fit of coughing left us in no doubt. Xavier tried to swallow the mix of phlegm and blood he had brought up, but the effort made him retch, and a shower of red drops coated his hand and handkerchief. Mutely, I took the handkerchief from him and cleaned away the blood.

"Your husband is extremely ill," Doctor Arden-Jones said, as if I had not worked it out for myself. "I shall make arrangements for him to be admitted to the sanatorium directly."

Xavier's lips moved, but I could not hear what he was saying. I bent over him.

"What is it?"

"Don't let me die in there," he said.

19

"What are you doing?" Bridie asked. She was holding onto the door frame at the entrance to the study, leaning so far forward that most of her weight was on her hands and she stood on tiptoe. I tucked in the sheet along the side of the single bed and then looked up.

"Making up a bed for your Daddy."

"Is he coming home? Is he better?"

I straightened my back and brushed the lock of hair which had fallen over my face.

"He may never get better," I said carefully.

Bridie stopped swinging on her arms and looked at me.

"Do you mean he is going to die?"

"Possibly." I wished once again that I had not promised myself always to be honest with Bridie. It was going to be hard for both of us over the next few months, for me to tell the truth and for Bridie to accept it. I would not go back on my decision: there was a habit of honesty between us.

"Will my Daddy go to Heaven?"

"I hope so."

"But he's coming home today?"

"This afternoon. Your Uncle Vinnie and I shall go to fetch him. Julia's coming over to keep you company while I'm away."

"And Auntie Kit?"

"No," I said shortly. "Kit isn't coming."

Kit had not visited the schoolhouse since Xavier had come home ill. We had spoken on the telephone once or twice, but I had not had time to see her, and Kit would not visit me. I wondered if our friendship was finally over. I had not asked her for help, but surely a friend would have offered it.

Someone knocked at the door and Bridie ran off to open it. Julia, of course. She came in glowing, and the fresh autumn smell of the September wind came in with her. It was one of those clear days when the whole world ought to seem golden, but here in the house it was dark and airless.

"Daddy's gone to the garage at the corner to fill up with petrol. I've put some blankets in the sidecar, Auntie Grace. You'll be able to make Uncle Xavier comfortable."

I hugged Julia.

"You could pick some flowers and put them in a vase," I said to Bridie. "Julia will help, won't you, Julia?"

"Of course I shall," Julia said, as I knew she would, and she steered Bridie out into the garden, one hand behind her cousin's shoulders.

Left alone, I sat on the newly made bed and tried not to think. It had been difficult enough with Xavier in the sanatorium, trying to combine my day in school with evening visits, which I had to make by bus or train when neither Vinnie nor Declan could take me. I still had to find time for preparation and marking. I knew the children's work was not being read as thoroughly as it used to be and, once, in the middle of a lesson on Marco Polo and the Silk Road, I had found myself stopping to wonder what road had brought Xavier to where he was now. I knew there was no hope left, really. I knew he was coming home to die, though I did not know when that would be, but I did know that Bridie would have to watch his decline. Sending her away would have been even more cruel.

Vinnie came in without knocking, as he always did, carrying a leather helmet for me. It was the first time I had ever ridden pillion, but the sidecar had to be reserved for Xavier.

Julia and Bridie came out to wave good-bye. At least it was not raining, I thought, as the bike took off towards the city. The September wind was cold, though; I huddled against Vinnie's back and gripped the tank firmly with my knees. That way my skirt did not fly up, and at least the tops of my legs stayed warm.

We reached the sanatorium at half past two. Xavier was out on the balcony waiting for us, sitting in a wheelchair, wearing an old camel dressing gown over his hospital pyjamas, his legs wrapped in a plaid blanket. They had not bothered to get him dressed.

He lifted his face to be kissed. I bent over immediately, and after a few seconds Vinnie did the same. I watched my brother's lips touch my husband's forehead. It was an unexpected, strangely precious moment. I wanted to leave the hospital immediately, carrying the memory of that moment with me, but the arrangement for our exit was not so simple. A nurse insisted I must sign a variety of forms, then check Xavier's possessions and sign for them too. It was like being let out of prison.

Getting him into the sidecar was problematic too. Vinnie helped him to rise to his feet, but he had no strength to climb in. Eventually, I held the top open while Vinnie picked him up like a child and lowered him gently onto the seat. Together we wrapped him in the blankets Julia had provided.

"Knock on the window, if you need me," I said. Xavier smiled, but did not answer. When, after a few miles, I turned my head to look at him, I saw that he was asleep.

We travelled more slowly on the return journey, with Vinnie careful to avoid any bumps or hollows in the road. I had time to look around and see how suddenly autumn was upon us. As we drove the last few miles through the countryside, leaves whirled above our heads and flew beneath the wheels. The sky was beginning to darken.

When we pulled up outside the schoolhouse, Vinnie did not hesitate. Opening the top of the sidecar, he motioned for me to hold it in place. Then he lifted Xavier up, carried him into the house and sat him down on the bed to remove the dressing-gown. He then held him in one arm, while with the other he drew back the covers and gently manoeuvred him into the bed. He wasted no time on chat; in any case, Xavier looked too exhausted to listen. He allowed himself to be lowered to the pillow before trying to speak.

"A very neat operation, Mr Brennan, Mrs Quinn."

Now I had him at home, I was not really sure about what to do next. But Julia and Bridie came in from the garden, and I was able to stand back and watch. Bridie had not seen Xavier since his admission to the sanatorium; very few hospitals allowed children to visit, and this was not one of them.

Bridie stood silent for a moment, looking at her father.

"Did you come home on Uncle Vinnie's motorbike?"

"In the sidecar," Xavier said. "It was very comfortable."

"He slept most of the way," I said.

"Can you walk, Daddy?"

"I don't know. I'll have to see."

"Now?"

"Tomorrow, maybe."

"We're getting a television."

"Are we?"

I intervened. "I thought we'd get one for the coronation, but there doesn't seem much point in waiting. If we get it now, you and Bridie can watch it together."

As soon as I said it, I realised. It sounded as though I thought he was not going to last until the following June. And, honestly, that was what I had been thinking. More, I hoped he would not last that long, for his sake and for ours.

"Have you ever seen a television, Daddy?"

"No," said Xavier. "I don't believe I have."

"I have. Ronnie Duggan let me watch hers once."

"Who's Ronnie Duggan?"

"A girl. A big girl."

"You remember the Duggans," I said. "They own the Cross Keys. Veronica's the same age as Julia,"

"Ah, yes," Xavier said. "A publican and a sinner, though it wasn't that sort of publican the gospels had in mind. And what did you see on the Duggans' television, Bridie?"

"Muffin, the Mule. It's a puppet."

"Muffin," Xavier said. "That's a strange sort of name for a mule." But he was asleep almost before he finished the sentence. Taking Bridie by the hand, I led her out of the study, into the kitchen. Vinnie and Julia followed.

"Will you be all right now?" Vinnie asked. "Only we have to get back."

"As right as we'll ever be. Thank you for everything, Vinnie. And you too, Julia."

"We'll come over next weekend," Julia promised.

"Yes," Vinnie agreed. "Mind you help your mammy now, Bridie."

Bridie promised that she would, indeed she would. The four of us made our way to the front door and, inevitably, Vinnie said the words that we Brennans had always used when we said good-bye to each other, words which I now dreaded, and so I simply smiled and waved. He said they would see us on Saturday, "all being well." What if all was not well, what then?

*

"Promise me you'll never visit my grave," Xavier said.

I had run home during the pupils' afternoon playtime to make sure he had a hot drink, but now I stopped, kettle in my hand.

"What made you think of that?" I asked lightly, though I already knew.

"I don't want you and Bridie making a pilgrimage every Sunday afternoon to stare at a patch of earth," he said. "When I'm gone, I'm gone. If you love me, you'll let me be."

"Am I not to remember you then? No Masses, no prayers?"

"I wouldn't mind. I won't mind. Masses, if you must, but no

headstone. No In Memoriam notices in the paper. No trips to the churchyard, not ever."

I was about to tell him that he would be around to plague me for years yet, but I did not. I knew it was not true, and that he would know it too. Instead I put the kettle on the stove and went to sit beside him. I took his cold fingers in my own two hands.

"If that's what you want," I said.

"It'll be for the best. You'll see. And Bridie will be able to get on with her life without me. It's no way for a child to spend her youth, traipsing back and forth to a grave."

"We'll not even remember where you are," I assured him, as I wondered if that was how his own childhood had been spent. Not that he would have told me.

"You promise then?"

"Haven't I told you so already?"

"That's my good girl," and he closed his eyes. "I'll sleep for a while now, I think."

"You haven't had your tea."

"No, I haven't, have I?" he agreed, but before I could make a move for the kettle, he was indeed asleep. I stood looking at him for a moment. Then I drew the covers up under his chin and tucked them around his shoulders.

*

His death, when it came, was an anti-climax.

The evening before it happened, the study was crowded. So many people had come to make their farewells. Vinnie and Declan sat either side of the bed, Xavier's head between them on the single pillow that was all he could bear by then. Julia stood next to Vinnie. Bridie, who should have been in bed, clung to Julia's arm with one hand, while the other curled around her father's fingers. Opposite them, and next to Declan, were Doctor Arden-Jones and the curate from Our Lady of Lourdes, Father Peter Saville, who had been a constant visitor over the last month. At the foot of the bed lay the huge black tom cat who had no name other than Polly's Baby. Since Xavier had returned from the Sanatorium, Polly's Baby had rarely moved from his bed. At night he slept on Xavier's shoulder, broad head butted up against Xavier's ear. Sometimes I moved him, but he always came back, and Xavier liked to have him there, liked to feel his warmth and strength.

And then, at the foot of the bed, there was me.

Xavier had been growing weaker all day, which was why we were there, waiting for his death. None of us, Doctor Arden-Jones perhaps excepted, could bear to leave him to face it alone. But it went on, and it was difficult not to look at the clock, difficult not to wonder when, exactly, it would be over. Xavier too seemed embarrassed; he muttered something about being an "unconscionable long time a-dying", which was obviously a quotation and one I felt I should know. Then he turned his eyes towards Vinnie, and his head moved a little on the pillow.

"I'm going fast," he whispered. I was horrified, even more so when Vinnie laughed.

"How fast do you think you're going, old chap?" he asked, and both of them smiled. I was not the only one who did not understand what was going on. Xavier struggled to explain.

"A joke. It's in a story. Stephen Leacock. A, B and C."

"I took him the book in hospital," Vinnie said. "I think they burnt it."

Since no one knew what they were talking about, another silence followed. Finally, I broke it.

"Past your bedtime, Bridie. Kiss Daddy good night. Julia, would you take her upstairs and see she gets into bed? She can read for a little if you don't mind staying with her."

Julia had not learned how to disguise her feelings. I could read her thoughts: relief at not having to be present until her uncle died was warring with the conviction that she should be there, that it was her duty. She hesitated.

"Go along now, Julia," Vinnie said gently, as if she were much younger. "It's the most useful thing you can do."

Bridie and Julia kissed Xavier's cheek. He smiled at them, and I caught Declan rubbing his eyes. For myself, I had no desire to weep, only a terrible longing for this all to be over, and for everyone to go away.

Five minutes later, Doctor Arden-Jones announced that he was leaving.

"It doesn't look as though there's likely to be any change in the next hour or so, Mrs Quinn. If there is, you can always call me."

Father Saville stayed to say a decade of the rosary with Xavier, and then he too departed.

"You know where I am, Grace," he said. "I'll come the moment I'm needed."

Now only Vinnie, Declan, and Polly's Baby remained. When Julia came downstairs to say that Bridie was asleep, I sent her and the two men away.

"Come back tomorrow. There's nothing happening here. You'll sleep better in your own beds. No, I'll be fine."

I could sense their relief. The three of them drove away on Vinnie's motorbike and sidecar, Declan riding pillion this time. I went back into the study, and saw that Xavier was asleep, Polly's Baby curled up near his neck. I took the opportunity to make my way down the garden to the earth closet. The weak light of my torch showed up a faint covering of frost on the grass: it was going to be cold. Even so, I sat longer than usual on the wooden seat, letting my mind drift, glad to be away from the sick-room and the waiting.

When I came back, Polly's Baby met me in the doorway and slid past me, out into the night. I felt the darkness of his fur against my legs as I turned to close the door, and when I went back into the study, I was not surprised to find that Xavier was dead.

Initially I felt nothing. Then I began to wonder how I knew for sure that he was dead. I had not checked his breathing, and his skin when I touched it was still warm. But something had gone, and I had not been there to see it go. None of us had.

Still, there were practical things I could deal with now. No point in recalling Doctor Arden-Jones and Father Saville; there was nothing they could do that could not be better done in the morning. There was no point in waking Bridie; she would know soon enough. But I did telephone Kit, so that Vinnie could be told when they reached home.

"I'm very sorry," Kit said formally.

"Thank you," I replied, equally formally, and then found myself saying what I must have been thinking. "It was time."

"Yes," said Kit. "I suppose it was."

It seemed there was nothing else to say. I replaced the telephone receiver in its cradle, and straightened the cord, which had twisted, as it always did. I closed the door of the study and went into the kitchen to make myself a pot of tea. As I sat at the scrubbed old table, a cup between my hands, the easy tears came at last.

*

At some point during the night I must have made my way upstairs, for I woke in the morning in my own bed, conscious only of the soft weight of Polly's Baby on my cheek, the rolling judder of his purr in my ear and the buzz of it on my jawbone. For a moment I lay still, blocking out the day, my eyes closed against the light that came through undrawn curtains. Somewhere inside me, however, I knew what was waiting when I finally woke: the beginning of a day in which everything in my life had irrevocably changed.

The first thing I had to do was to tell Bridie. That much was clear. But I delayed, going downstairs to check that the study door was closed, deliberately not going in but making my way to the back of the house, where the door to the garden already stood open.

"Mam's here," said Vinnie, tall and solid on the step. "Shall I fetch her in?"

It was still early; not yet seven. What time had they left the city? In my slippers and nightgown, I ran round the side of the house, out into the lane. Mammy, black hat jammed squarely on hair that still retained a little of its copper glow, sat upright and grave in the sidecar, waiting to be helped out.

"Mammy," I said. "You came."

"I came."

Together we went into the house, through the back door and into the kitchen. Mammy put her handbag down on the table, next to the blue and white cup which still held the remains of my late-night tea. She picked up the cup and sniffed, perhaps because there was no saucer with it. She poured away the dregs, swilled the cup out in the sink and stood it upside-down on the draining board, something she would not normally have done in my house. These were exceptional times.

"Where is he?" she asked and, when I had indicated the study, "Have you laid him out yet?"

"No," I said, startled and at a loss, because I did not know what laying-out involved. "No, I haven't."

"I'll see to it," Mammy said. "You go and deal with the child. Vinnie, make yourself useful. You can telephone the priest and the doctor – and the undertaker. Grace, I thought I told you to get yourself upstairs."

I did as I was told. I was grateful for the lack of fuss, the absence of tears. Mammy knew how to get through things better than any of us. She had had more practice.

Bridie was awake and sitting up, Polly's ubiquitous Baby on her knee. The red-gold curls on the right side of her face were damp with sweat, her cheek creased where it had been pressed into the pillow. I sat down on the end of the bed but said nothing. We looked at each other.

"My daddy's dead," Bridie said at last.

"Yes."

"I knew he was dead when I woke up this morning."

"How? How did you know?"

"I forgot my prayers." Bridie rubbed sleep and tears from her eyes. "When Julia put me to bed, I forgot to say 'God, keep my daddy safe this night'."

"No," I said gently. "No, Bridie, you mustn't think that. It has nothing to do with whether you said your prayers. God knows you were tired and worried. He wouldn't let your daddy die because you forgot your prayers this once."

"Then why did He let him die?"

"It was time." I had no other answer.

"Were you with him?"

I hesitated, remembering the promise I had made always to be honest with my daughter, then lied. "Yes," I said. "He died in my arms." I could not bear for Bridie to think that he had died alone, even if, as I suspected, he had died in his sleep. The lie built up, escaped in easy clichés. "He just slipped away. Between one breath and the next."

"Is he in heaven?"

"Yes. Yes, I'm sure he is. Wasn't the priest with him just before he died?"

Bridie climbed out of bed, dislodging Polly's Baby, who stalked off to the landing, tail held high.

"Can I see him?"

"If you want to. When you're dressed."

"What shall I wear? Am I going to school?"

I had not thought about school.

"What do you want to do? Do you want to go to school or do you want to stay here with me and Granny Nora?"

Bridie considered. "I think I'll go to school. Aren't you coming?"

"How can I?"

I found it hard to believe that I was having this conversation with my daughter. Why were we not crying into each other's arms, stretched out on the bed, with our heads pounding and our hearts broken? When had we become so stoical? I remembered the times I had cried over Xavier, the times when he had left me, the times when he had returned. Now he had left me forever. Why did I feel nothing? I helped Bridie into the blouse and skirt she wore for school, pulled the navy-blue jumper over her head, brushed her hair.

"Shall I tell Miss Deakin my daddy is dead?"

I shook my head. I would need to go to school myself to tell my assistant that I would not be in. Babs would just have to take the two classes together. Both of us had done it before. It was perfectly feasible, if she pulled back the folding partition that separated the two rooms.

"I'll tell her."

"Are you going to get dressed first?"

I looked down at my nightdress and at my feet in their woolly slippers. I began to laugh, and then suddenly I was crying, and Bridie was clinging to me, and Mammy's feet were heavy on the stairs as she came to put her arms around us both, and the three of us stood there, shoulders heaving and faces ugly with sudden sobs.

*

After breakfast, which Mammy made us all eat, though it was dry and tasteless in our mouths, Bridie and I walked over to the little school. We waited in the infants' classroom for Babs Deakin to arrive. She was there at half past eight precisely, a little surprised to see us waiting for her, but smiling and ready to listen.

"I have to tell you," I said, hating myself for my formality but unable to deal with what I had to say in any other way, "that Mr Quinn died last night." I rushed on, not giving Babs time to respond.

"I shall not be in school today, though you may expect me back tomorrow. Bridie would like to stay with you if that is convenient. I'm hoping you can combine the two classes just for today. If you need work for the older children, I'll send it over later."

Babs hurried to reassure me that there was no need, she could provide work for them all and she would be more than happy to keep an eye on Bridie. She would tell the other children, and then they could let their parents know. She was pink with the importance of it all, and perhaps there was excitement there too. I was suddenly too tired to care. Leaving Bridie with Babs Deakin, I went back to the schoolhouse, where Mammy, Vinnie, and Father Peter Saville were waiting to discuss the details of Xavier's funeral.

It could not be held in the village. There was no doubt about that. The upstairs room of the Cross Keys might be fine for a Mass centre, but it was no place for a funeral service with full Requiem Mass. We would have to take Xavier's body to Our Lady of Lourdes, five miles away in the next small town, and no doubt there would be more than one priest at the altar, though I wanted Father Saville to officiate. After all, he and Xavier had been friends.

"I shall count it a privilege," Father Saville said. He was a relatively young man, raw-boned still, with black hairs thatching the flesh between the joints of his big hands. He had heard Xavier's last confession and brought him the sacrament and, like everyone else who knew Xavier during the last months of his life, he had been impressed by my husband's quiet acceptance and patience, and his faith in the goodness of God. I did not say that to me it had looked as if my husband, once more, had been playing a part, this time the part of a dying man. There was no point in showing my anger. When we were alone, later, Mammy assured me that it was natural to feel angry; I must not worry if I veered between rage and numbness.

"Is this how you felt when Daddy died?" I asked.

"You don't know the half of it," Mammy said.

Kit arrived at about four, in a taxi. She was looking sophisticated in a black suit that was obviously new. It was obviously the first chance she had had to wear mourning. People should die more often, I found myself thinking, and then was appalled at the thought. I hugged Kit, trying to hide my face. Vinnie looked on, detached.

Mammy and Bridie returned from the school, having come by way of the village shop. The news of Xavier's death had travelled through the neighbourhood; Mammy had with her a handful of notes of condolence and a small posy of wildflowers. I was thankful that no one had yet knocked on the front door to sympathise in person. It was one thing to discuss his death with the family and the curate from Our Lady of Lourdes; it was another thing entirely to talk to neighbours and the parents of children at the school. The telephone had rung once: Mrs Duggan at the Cross Keys. She was a fellow Catholic, after all, and of Irish extraction. I could cope with her.

I could not cope with the letters from my pupils which Babs Deakin brought round after tea. Every child in the school had written something, even the babies, and I felt that I had to read them all. "Dear Mrs Quinn, I am so sorry ..." "Dear Mrs Quinn, Miss Deakin said to write to you because ..." "Dear Mrs Quinn, we did not know your husband was so ill." I read every one, smoothing out the paper, making a neat pile, knowing I would have to reply to them all. "Dear Jennifer ..." "Dear Richard ..." "Dear Janet ..." How was I ever going to find the strength?

20

Time had blurred my memory of my father's funeral: there were gaps and moments I did not remember at all. Perhaps I had never remembered them. Xavier's funeral was different: I registered every detail, from the instant when the undertaker lowered himself onto the settee in the front room, trouser legs straining over his fat thighs, to the ever-present feeling that it was all a mistake, that Xavier was not dead, that he had only disappeared one more time. If I turned around quickly, I might even see him sidling in at the door, red-gold hair gleaming as it had when I first knew him, his eyes narrow and smiling. But I was never quite quick enough.

Eventually, it was all arranged. His body was taken to Our Lady of Lourdes, where it would lie overnight. The day before the funeral, the schoolhouse was full of Brennans, talking, organising, never letting me have a moment on my own. Mammy and Julia were there, taking it in turns to sit with Bridie, who would rather have been with me. Kit, who had come and gone briefly earlier in the day, arrived once more in her father's car.

"You need something decent to wear," she said, and drove me into Hull, where she parked the car outside the Station Hotel in Paragon Square.

"Not Hammond's," I protested, but Kit ignored me. She marched me into the store, where she picked out a black two-piece costume similar to the one she had bought as soon as she had heard of Xavier's death, a close-fitting black hat with a tiny veil, a black handbag, and black court shoes. "It's too much," I wanted to say, but when I saw myself in the mirror I was silenced. A stranger looked back at me, taller, more poised than my everyday self.

"There," said Kit. "Now you'll be able to cope."

*

The church was packed. I saw people I did not recognise, some of them crying, as I walked up the aisle with Mammy and my five brothers. The front pews were packed with my sisters-in-law and the oldest nephews and nieces. There was no Julia, however. She was at home looking after Bridie. I was not sure who had decided Bridie was too young to attend her father's funeral. I had had no views on it. It seemed to me that I had no views on anything.

Unlike my father, Xavier was being sent off with the full rites of the church: it was a sung Requiem Mass, and it seemed that every priest we had ever known was in attendance at the altar. Declan was leading the choir; it was where he belonged, and it was better that Pat, Mick, Vinnie, and Sean, who were all much of a height, should act as coffin-bearers. Xavier's brothers-in-law would not let him down; they would not stumble under his weight.

The coffin, which had been standing in front of the altar overnight, was light oak. Light wood for a light man. My mind did not just wander: it jumped. One minute I was looking at the altar, the next I was straining to make out an individual voice in the swell of responses. I could not keep my attention on anything; at the same time, I felt nothing, which was why I was not crying. It was not a matter of being brave, though that was how my friends and family would see it.

One of Pat's boys was serving on the altar. For a moment I could not remember which one.

The *"Dies Irae"*. Usually it made me cry, but not today. I found myself listening critically to Declan's voice. It was as true as ever, but there was a new note in it, one I did not recognise. Perhaps it was grief.

Although my mind was fitful, my body knew when it was time to stand and time to kneel. It took me up to the communion rail, and for a moment I was shocked into awareness. "He that eateth and drinketh unworthily eateth and drinketh judgment unto himself." I made a conscious act of will, opened my mouth, received the Host on my tongue. Mammy took my elbow to lead me back to my place.

Outside, on the church steps, I suddenly felt alone. I looked around for Xavier, whose coffin had just been loaded into the hearse, ready to be taken back to the cemetery in the village. People crowded me, offering me their condolences. All of them in pairs. Uncle Martin and Auntie Eileen, Pat and Teresa, Mick and Maureen, Declan and Josie, even Vinnie and Kit. Mammy with Sean. Pairs of priests, a pair of nuns. For a moment I imagined they were the nuns I had seen at my father's funeral, nearly thirty years before, but then they spoke to me and I recognised them for who they really were, women of my own age, my contemporaries at Endsleigh Training College.

"So good of you to come," I repeated, grateful when Vinnie at last steered me into the back of the car and climbed in beside me. Just the two of us. Vinnie and Grace. The way it should be.

"You'll get through this," Vinnie promised.

"Yes. I know."

Incense, music, the ritual of the church — all these things had cocooned me against my anger. But as the cars wound their way across the gentle dales of the East Riding, I could feel it rising in my throat. Thirty years of life we might have shared, all of it squandered, like my pre-war housekeeping money, on horses and lost causes, on being all things to all men. I would be glad to see the earth close over him, I told myself. But when I stood beside Vinnie, preparing to throw the first clods onto the shining coffin lid, my hand cramped, and I could not move. Vinnie's fingers closed over mine, the soil rattled down, and it was done. I would never visit this place again. That was what he had wanted. That was what he had begged me for. Let the couch grass and bindweed grow over his grave, let there be no marker for it save a small metal number. What did I care? Did he not deserve to be forgotten?

*

It was months later when I opened the brown cardboard attaché case Xavier had kept beneath the bed all the years of our marriage. It had always been locked; I had never known him open it though, whenever I cleaned under the bed, I had pulled it out and studied the faded labels it bore: South Africa, Argentina, Uruguay. I searched in vain for the key, but the locks were flimsy enough. The handle of a spoon inserted beneath them gave me enough leverage to prise them open.

I do not know what I had expected to find. Perhaps I wanted some clue as to where he had been during his absences from me. A gun perhaps? But there was little enough inside the case, apart from the torn paper lining with its mock tartan pattern of cream and maroon checks. I picked up the first object, a small battered missal bound in black leather, its pages edged first with red dye, and then with gilt. The cover was slightly greasy to the touch; it had been well used once. Carefully I opened it, the whisper thin pages separating at my touch. A Mass card slipped between my fingers. "Of your charity, pray for the repose of the soul of Lawrence Patrick Quinn, 1895-1916." Larry, who died in the Easter Rising? It was at least possible. I thumbed back the to the flyleaf with its copperplate inscription: *"To dear Francis, on the occasion of his Confirmation. V.M."* The initials meant nothing to me, but there was no reason why they should. I knew as little now of Xavier's life before he met me as I had done when we were first married. And if I wanted to know more, where could I begin to look?

The second item I pulled out of the case was a small fragile roll of paper. A birth certificate. My fingers trembled when I opened it, and I found it hard to breathe, though I did not know what I expected to find. I was sure that there would be something.

Certificate of Registry of Birth. I, the undersigned, do hereby certify that the birth of John Francis Quinn, born of the fourth day of August, one thousand, nine hundred and eight, has been duly registered by me at entry no. 97 of my Register Book No. 293. Witness my hand this twenty third day of August, one thousand, nine hundred and eight. A Bateman, Registrar of Births and Deaths in the district of Toxteth.

Toxteth. That was in Liverpool, I knew. I guessed who John Francis was. He had never been Xavier Quinn except in his own imagination. And mine. But why had he always claimed to have been born in Ireland? He had always been evasive about his precise birthplace; sometimes it was Dublin, sometimes Cork, and once, improbably, just south of the Devil's Causeway during a thunderstorm. And all this time he was as British born as I was. I counted the days between his birth and its registration: twenty days were just long enough for his mother to have come across from Ireland after he was born. It was unlikely, though, that his mother would lie to the registrar about his place of birth. I could make nothing of it.

I was disappointed that the birth certificate told me so little. I had never seen my own, but Bridie's birth certificate, three times the size of Xavier's and issued in 1946, had my name and Xavier's on it, my maiden name, Xavier's occupation at the time of the birth, and our address. I now knew his real name and possibly where he was born, but nothing of his parents and nothing of his background.

His passport, when I found it, caused me no surprise. It gave his place of birth as Liverpool. No distinguishing features. I flicked through the pages, all stamped with foreign names in different colours of ink, pausing only to look at the serious young face in the photograph. I put the passport down.

The last thing in the box was a photograph, one I knew: Xavier and Vinnie in a rowing boat, Xavier smiling, Vinnie scowling, the whole a little off-centre. I had a copy of it in the album Vinnie had given me, years ago, when he first went to sea. There was no photograph of me – just the two young men marooned in a place I could not identify. In a sudden fit of anger, I tore it in two, and crumpled the half that held Xavier into a tight little ball. Then, instead of throwing it across the room, I relented and smoothed it out and laid the two parts together again, Vinnie intact, Xavier's laughing face and strong arms now marked and scarred by white cracks from the crumpling.

I picked up everything, missal, Mass card, birth certificate, passport, and torn photograph, and threw them back into the attaché case. The locks I had forced would not close again, so I carried the case downstairs under one arm and made for the kitchen range. The bang of the poker I wielded against the sides of the grate pleased me, as did the noise the coals made as they fell, leaving a great red cave into which I thrust Xavier's petty secrets. Slow flames ate away at the cardboard, and then a sudden burst of sparks rose above the case, which collapsed.

"I'm done with you at last, Frank Quinn," I shouted, and then, immediately afterwards, "God rest your wandering soul."

*

But I was not done with him. Sometimes I thought I would never be done with him. When I took the old metal colander down the garden to strip the fruit from the overcrowded raspberry canes, I remembered the day he brought those same canes home, their whippy length wrapped in newspaper. A present from your man, he said. "Your man" had turned out to be the most miserly and territorial of allotment holders down by the railway cutting, a man who never gave "owt for nowt". Even now, I could not walk down the street without someone coming over to say how much he was missed. I could not look at my daughter without seeing him in every turn of her head. Bridie had inherited more than his red-gold hair and tilt of the chin. Already at seven she promised to be tall – and a good deal thinner than me.

Then there was Julia, who was always eager to hear how I was coping without her Uncle Xavier; she made it her business to call on me at least twice a week. It was easy enough to catch a train, and she did not mind the three-mile walk from the station, young, strong, and healthy, as she was.

"Kit wants me to go to medical school when I'm eighteen," she reported on one of these visits. "But I've told her I won't. Just because it's what she wanted to do and couldn't, it doesn't mean it's right for me. And Daddy says I must do what's right for me."

"Have you decided what that is?" I asked curiously, looking up from the pastry I was rolling out on the kitchen table.

"Oh yes. I'm going to be a teacher, like you. I'm putting my name down for training college this autumn. Here, let me do that for you."

My pastry always seemed to take on a greyish tinge in the rolling out, no matter how thoroughly I washed my hands before I began. I passed the rolling pin to Julia and watched my niece's quick fingers dust the dough with flour, then shape it. Somehow, she had become a young woman with a deft and practical hand. She had been such a clever little girl, reading early, racing through her schoolwork but showing no sign of any aptitude for craft. Now, though, Julia was as skilful at sewing and cooking as Mammy herself had always been.

"Did Granny Nora teach you how to bake?"

"No." Julia sounded puzzled. "I just picked it up as I went along. I like cooking and baking, but I like sewing better. That's what I'm going to teach, you know: needlework."

It seemed to me a limited ambition. Still, it was a useful skill, if not one I had really expected of Kit's daughter, and perhaps that was why Julia had chosen it.

"Do you remember that navy-blue dress you made me with the white edging?" Julia asked. "I'd never had anything made specially for me before – Kit always bought my clothes, though Granny Nora knitted my cardigans and jumpers. But she always chose the patterns and the wool. I was so excited about going with you to choose the material, to that little shop at the back of St Charles's, and telling you exactly how I wanted the dress to look. And it was just how I wanted it. Well, I think that was when I decided I would learn to sew, and one day I would make my own clothes. I can do that now. I want to teach other people how to do it too. Perhaps it's not as grand as being a doctor, but I'm no good with blood and sick and broken bones. I'm good with my hands and I'm good with people – children especially – and I know it's what I want to do."

"What does Vinnie – what does your father say?"

"He's happy for me if that's what I want. But he says I'm still to use my brain!"

"Oh, you'll use your brain at training college," I promised. "And you'll make friends with people like yourself. And nowadays it's a job you can keep on after you're married."

"I don't think I'll get married. Not if it means being like Kit and Daddy, all cold and distant and polite." Suddenly Julia stopped what she was doing and advanced on me, circling my waist with her floury hands and leaning her head into my shoulder. "But if I thought I could have a marriage like you and Uncle Xavier had, all laughter and excitement, every day different, then I don't know. Maybe."

"And what about the absences?" I asked unsteadily.

"What?"

"What about the times when he went away and I didn't know when I'd see him again? What about the gambling and lying and the friends who came round and stayed half the night, talking and eating and drinking us out of house and home?"

"But you always knew he'd come back," Julia said. "And as for the rest – well, it's only money, isn't it? And money's not important."

I was silent. I would not allow myself to spoil Julia's memories of her warm, doting, lying rogue of an uncle, and so I tightened my lips and took the rolling pin from her hands.

"Go and find Bridie, will you? Tell her it's time to come in."

*

We sat drinking coffee on the first floor of Ferens' Art Gallery, in front of a black and gold Chinese lacquer cabinet. Two middle-aged, middle-class women who had finally outgrown tea at Tripett's. I wore the black suit I had bought at Kit's insistence for Xavier's funeral; ironically, it suited me better than anything I had ever owned. I wore it with a blue silk blouse and a blue feathered hat. I was eating a slice of lemon meringue pie with a cake fork, gratified to see that not a crumb flaked away from the pastry base as I brought each fragment to my mouth. I could concentrate on my pastry, and at the same time watch Julia and Bridie, who had stopped in front of the bronze Epstein head of a girl, that was Bridie's favourite thing of all in the Ferens. Isobel was the name on the plaque. Bridie reached up to touch with careful fingers the stiff bronze corkscrew curls, so like, yet unlike, her own living copper-gold curls. Then she and Julia waved, before disappearing through the gallery doors. I waited until they were out of sight before I turned to look at Kit.

"Well?"

"I know we're not as close as we used to be," Kit began. (And whose fault is that? I thought but did not say.) "But I wanted to try and clear things up."

"What things?"

"Julia. Sean. Vinnie, if you like."

I closed my face. I could feel the muscles tightening, my nose sharpening.

"I don't want to know. Eighteen years ago, I might have been interested. It's all part of the past now. There's no point in dragging it up, just because you want to justify yourself."

"I don't want to justify myself! Grace, you're the only real friend I've ever had. I need you to understand." Kit was not looking at me, but I could hear the strain in her voice. I did not need to see her eyes.

"But I don't understand," I said. "I never have understood. I do not understand why you chose me for a friend in the first place, or why you married Vinnie. I certainly do not understand what led you to become involved with Sean. Two more coffees, please. No, thank you: nothing further to eat."

Kit waited patiently until the waitress had returned with the coffee but, even then, I would not let her start talking immediately. I offered her cream and sugar, watched the swirl of my own cream as it followed the spoon, lifted the cup with both hands to taste, and put it back at the first sip, explaining unnecessarily that it was too hot to drink.

"Grace, listen to me," Kit said. "You know why I wanted you as a friend. Because you were like me. Different. Because we were Mother Bernard's "cleverest girls", and you weren't impressed by my family's money like the rest of them."

"Oh, yes I was," I said. "I may not have shown it, but I was. The clothes, the house in Pearson Park, the doctor father –"

"Don't talk about my father!"

Heads turned. Kit reddened as she realised how loudly she had spoken.

Strangely unembarrassed, I answered her. "Sometimes I think your whole life has been dictated by your father. Why didn't you just stand up to him, all those years ago? Why didn't you make your own way in medicine if that was what you wanted? Or something else, something worthwhile, instead of marrying my brother because you wanted an easy way out, and you knew how much your father would hate it, if you married Jack Brennan's son? You have always taken the easy way out, Kit. That's your trouble."

"I'm not listening." Kit rose, gathered up her gloves and bag, turned to go.

"Suit yourself." I leaned back in my chair.

"Don't imagine I'm leaving without you."

"Then you'd better pay the bill while I get my things together."

Kit did as she was told. We did not stop for breath until we reached the Wilberforce memorial. I caught Kit by the elbow and pulled her to a stop.

"We told Julia and Bridie we'd meet them at the entrance to the gallery. We can't go walking halfway across the city."

We agreed to sit on one of the benches in Queen's Gardens, the former Queen's Dock. Already the tons of waste used to fill the basin before the war had begun to compact under the weight of top soil; the pavement that encircled the central fountain had dipped and cracked, making it a hazardous place for small children attracted to the flower beds or the jet of water or, in the case of one small boy, who ended up with scrubbed knees, Massarelli's ice-cream barrow.

"We could have an ice cream while we're waiting," I suggested. I expected Kit to refuse and was surprised when she rose to her feet and went across to buy two large cones. "Are you sure? Convent girls —"

"Don't eat in the street. Yes, I know. But the convent is a long time ago. Here. Take one."

I leaned back against the slats of the bench, swirling my tongue round the rim of the cornet to catch the drips. No sense in spoiling my smart black jacket, even for Massarelli's ice cream. In front of me the fountain shimmered in the sunlight; through the mist it created I could see the corner of the Yorkshire Penny Bank and the statue of

Queen Victoria over the public lavatories. I closed my eyes against the sunlight, hoping that Kit would not reopen the conversation. Better to sit there quietly and wait for our daughters to return, and to let the past take care of itself.

"I don't know why I married Vinnie," Kit said. "I thought I was in love with him. I suppose I thought I could make him love me. But he's only ever loved two women in his life: you and your mother. And Julia of course."

I did not comment. I did not want to talk to Kit about Vinnie.

"What time did you tell Julia to be back?" I said instead.

"Don't change the subject. At least marrying Vinnie made me a Brennan. I so much more wanted that."

"Why?" I sat up, suddenly interested. "Why should you want to be a Brennan? What had we that you didn't have?"

"Everything. Closeness. Energy. The feeling that the whole family was rising up, bettering itself. Who'd have thought a simple docker's children would turn out to be so successful? A teacher, an engineer, and now the next generation is on its way to university. You've no idea how exciting it seemed. Whereas we Morrisseys were settled and stodgy and boring. There were no new worlds to conquer for me."

"Whatever Daddy was," I said, "he wasn't simple. Not in any sense of the word. He was the one who made the family what it is."

"Did I say he wasn't? Though I think you underestimate Nora's part in it. There's more of your mother in you than you like to admit."

"I thought we were talking about you," I said. If I did not want to discuss Vinnie, I did not want to discuss my mother either. Not with Kit.

"I felt sorry for Sean," Kit said, and if it was a *non sequitur*, I managed to follow it. "He always seemed to be the odd one out. Not quite as good looking, not quite as bright, nowhere near as successful as the rest of you. You and Vinnie always behaved as if he didn't exist, and yet there he was, solidly between you, waiting to be noticed."

"You're not telling me it was pity?" I said.

"Not pity, exactly. Fellow-feeling, perhaps."

"Nonsense," I said. "Look, there's Julia and Bridie. Shall we go and meet them."

"I haven't said everything I wanted to say," Kit began, but she rose to her feet, checking the seat of her skirt for creases.

"Then it'll have to stay unsaid. Oh, come on, Kit. You know it's better this way."

We crossed the road, avoiding a stream of cars. It began to rain.

*

Late July 1953. Out of breath with reaching up to clean the picture rail, a duster still in my hand, I came to the front door of the schoolhouse when I heard them giggling.

"What are you three up to now?" I asked.

They came round the corner, Vinnie with Bridie on his shoulders and a mop like a lance in his hand, Julia at his side carrying the mop bucket. Greyish water slopped over and spilled onto the path as she swung it too vigorously. Bridie squealed with delight, beating her fists on Vinnie's shoulders.

"She's too heavy for you," I objected. "Bridie, come down. A great girl like you sitting on your uncle's shoulders. Get down this minute."

"She's fine," Vinnie said. "She's helping me aim this mop. It's way past time those stickers came down."

I looked up. The golden cut-out crowns Bridie had insisted we fix above the windows in honour of the coronation had been there for weeks. I no longer noticed them. But Vinnie was right. It was time they came down.

"Couldn't you get a step ladder to them?"

Brother, niece, and daughter looked at me pityingly.

"And where's the fun in that?" Vinnie asked. I glanced at him. Forty-five years old, and he still seemed a young man to me. The dark hair was as thick and springy as ever, the face barely lined.

"You've worn well," I said. "Considering."

"So have you. Considering."

It was not true, but I did not mind. I was only forty-one, after all, despite the greying hair and the crow's feet. I had a whole life ahead of me. I held out my arms to Bridie, who wriggled into them without further argument. I hugged my daughter to me, burying my face in the red-gold hair with its familiar smell, noticing how long her legs and arms were as she dangled unresisting in my arms. Oh yes; she was Xavier's daughter all right. The same thing must have struck Vinnie, for he smiled almost shyly, and touched his niece's hand.

"She's more like her father every day."

"I hope not," I lied. "I really hope not."

"Why not?" said Bridie, intrigued. "Why shouldn't I be like Daddy?"

Vinnie looked at me and I looked at Vinnie, and suddenly we were laughing, laughing uproariously, laughing so much that I had to let Bridie slip to the ground and Vinnie was wiping away the tears from his eyes. Julia and Bridie looked on amazed.

"Why not?" I said. "Why not indeed?"

ABOUT THE AUTHOR

Like her eponymous heroine, Helen Flanagan grew up in the Hull area and at the heart of a Roman Catholic family with strong Irish antecedents. Academically gifted, she won a State Scholarship and went to study at the University of Liverpool in 1962, when she was only just seventeen. She graduated with an honours degree in Russian in 1966, having taken her final examinations only weeks after the death of her father. After a brief experience as a trainee librarian with Hull City Libraries, she found her vocation in teaching. In her first posts, she taught Russian, French, and English; she later went on to become a Head of English before her appointment as a Deputy Head at Alderman Peel High School in Wells-next-the-Sea, Norfolk.

Helen's later life was dogged by ill health and she took early retirement after undergoing heart surgery in 1995. She died in 2006. An active presence in the local community, she had helped to set up a Poetry Festival in Wells-next-the-Sea, and a poetry prize for children was set up in her memory. She was also instrumental in saving a community theatre and running it for 12 years until her death.

She is survived by her two half-sisters, Anne and Eileen, and by her dearest friend, Pat.

Printed in Great Britain
by Amazon